THE LONER

Kate Moore

A CANYON CLUB Novel

———

"Simply put, The Loner is wonderful. In the spirit of Jane Austen's Persuasion, Kate Moore offers a beautiful love story with vivid characters that steal your heart. Written with intelligence, warmth, and a delightfully sneaky wit, you will root for Will Sloan and Annie James and their second chance at love."

—Laura Moore, National bestselling author of Once Tempted.

www.BOROUGHSPUBLISHINGGROUP.com

THE LONER
Copyright © 2015 Kate Moore

ISBN 978-1-942886-61-7

To my sisters in romance, readers and writers alike, who insist on happy endings. And to my husband, who always supplies the hero's best lines.

CONTENTS

THE LONER

"Thus much he was obliged to acknowledge—
that he had been constant unconsciously, nay unintentionally;
that he had meant to forget her, and believed it to be done.
He had imagined himself indifferent, when he had only been
angry."
—Jane Austen, *Persuasion*

Chapter One

Will Sloan's visitor looked and smelled like money. From his red silk pocket square and the designer cut of his lapels to the rimless glasses that pinched his narrow, high-bridged nose, Elliot Dunsmore III, director of development for the Canyon Preparatory School for Boys, reeked of dough.

Will knew that particular stench well. He'd spent four years at Canyon with the most privileged young men of L.A. The odor of money had been more overpowering than an adolescent's first application of aftershave.

He had to laugh. Dunsmore in his office asking for money! The man's suit cost more than almost everything in the room, except the Tibetan rug and the rolling desk with its buffed nickel surface. The nickel content in the desktop so outweighed the chromium that Will could line his new platinum credit cards from end to end across the thing and not demagnetize them.

Of course, Dunsmore didn't ask for money. He handed Will a fancy envelope with the Canyon logo, inviting Will to open it.

Will broke the seal, pulled out the thick piece of paper, and knew he'd been clipped, tackled from behind on a clear field, brought down with a bone-jarring thud. They had nominated him to the Hall of Canyon Men. He waited for the referee to throw the yellow flag.

Dunsmore's voice rolled on, smooth, unhurried, confident, the voice of a man who always got his donor. He spoke of the honor to Will and of Canyon's needs. But Will stopped hearing Dunsmore. The last time he'd stood in the Hall of Canyon Men he'd asked a woman to marry him, and she'd said no. He shook his head to clear it. He had put Canyon behind him, and Annie James was history.

Dunsmore pulled a single sheet of paper from the slim leather banker's envelope on the table beside him and uncapped a thick black Waterman pen. "What may I put you down for?"

"Nothing." The usual afternoon breeze off the Pacific fluttered the tear-off pages of Will's cartoon desk calendar. He liked tearing off those pages. A hundred days, more or less, and he'd be out of L.A.

Dunsmore flicked a contemptuous glance at the tacky blue plastic calendar and cleared his throat. "I'm sorry. I didn't hear you."

Will stood. "Thanks, Dunsmore, but four years at Canyon was enough for me. I'll pass on a permanent place in the Hall." He crossed to his office door, stepped out into the open walkway around the mezzanine of Z-Text Technology Partners, and sent his vice president a text. In some companies the head guy had an assistant in an outer office at a big desk, at Z-Text, Will had Beau Lassiter, half bouncer, half arbiter of taste. Reliable as ever, Beau came charging up the stairs from the atrium below with the speed that had made him one of the Pac-10's most formidable linebackers. Behind Will, Dunsmore emerged from the office.

Beau strode forward, sticking out his right hand. "Beau Lassiter, vice president of ambience and irreverence. Can I help you?"

Cornered, Dunsmore turned to Will and offered him the paper with the Canyon logo embossed across the top and a single figure written in the middle. "If you'll give that some thought before our next meeting, I'm sure..." Beau caught Will's glance and shifted Dunsmore toward the stairs.

Will turned away. Asking for money was not that easy. Asking for money laid one bare, exposed one's dreams and lacks, closed one's throat, burned one's cheeks, and bowed one's head. He had a perfect memory of the pattern of rich reds and blues of the carpet in Headmaster Chambers's office. He had let Dunsmore off easy.

Beau's voice, deep and sure as he maneuvered Dunsmore toward the top of the stairs, brought Will back to the present. The paper with Dunsmore's figure on it was still in his hand. Will flattened the creamy paper on the mezzanine railing, made a few quick folds, and sent it riding down a hidden air current into the atrium below where a group of twenty-something partners huddled around a whiteboard. Dunsmore's startled glance followed the paper briefly. He looked back at Will.

"Dunsmore, you can kiss my ass every day for a year. Headmaster Chambers can kiss my ass if he remembers who I am, but I'll never be a Canyon Man, and Canyon never gets an effing dime from me."

The little group below applauded. They liked it when he made speeches. Dunsmore took in the audience and flushed a dull red that clashed with his pocket square. Rage and dignity skirmished briefly for control of his narrow face, before he tucked the banker's envelope under his arm and stalked out.

Beau leaned against the railing next to Will. "That must have been therapeutic."

"Very." He watched Dunsmore stop to attach a pair of wafer-thin tinted lenses over his glasses before he strode from the building.

"How much did he want?"

"Three million."

Beau shook his buzz-cut blond head sympathetically. "It's tough being a High Net Worth Individual, listening to folks grovel for money."

"Success sucks." Will grinned. But revenge was sweet.

* * *

The choked lanes of the 405 Freeway squeezed traffic along at the pace of a sluggish lava flow, and the air-conditioning of Annie James's truck simply quit. Her truck, Ryan's truck, was wearing out after eleven years. Maybe her fresh start was wearing out. She was thirty-three years old. She had been a widow for eleven years.

She inched down the exit ramp and headed west toward the beach on a wide artery lined with tacky commercial establishments, a jumble of competing signs, and miles of fluttering plastic flags. Above the pale stucco buildings, the power lines, and the telephone wires, was a golden sky was on its way to a fine sunset, and she just might get home in time to watch it. Sunsets were her favorite extravagance. For a few minutes each day nature clothed the smog-filled air in bright bands of color with no concern for billable inches or deadlines or backup files.

In her tiny cell in corporate cubicle land where she handled obits and odd bits of reporting for a group of local newspapers, Annie could feel as if she'd given up on the dream of starting over that brought her to L.A. But a good sunset reminded her that if L.A. hadn't worked out quite as well as she'd hoped, if she'd given up on a few of her intrepid-reporter dreams, at the end of the day she was still Annie James, Enemy of the Passive Voice, Slayer of Buzzwords, the Comma Queen. And outside of her day job, she'd found a good use for her journalistic talent, as editor and publisher of the South

Bay Neighborhood Center newsletter and blog. Tomorrow was one of her center days.

In her driveway, she set the emergency brake, shoved her door open, and gently unpeeled the backs of her knees from the hot vinyl seat. Before her feet hit the pavement, her neighbor, Irene, lifted the lace curtain in her living room. Irene took the concept of Neighborhood Watch to a whole new level. Annie waved from her mailbox.

Sand Dollar Lane ran north and south along one of the upper dunes that defined the South Bay's beach towns. Annie and Irene had matching brown-shingle cottages on the uphill side of the street, a perfect location for watching the sunset or the neighborhood. Their front doors faced each other across adjoining brick paths and a low boxwood hedge. Irene waited on her porch in a smart, aqua warm-up suit.

She pressed one thin, beringed hand to her heart, clutching a cell phone in the other. "Annie, goodness. I was sure something dreadful had happened to you on the freeway."

"Just traffic, Irene." Annie unlocked her door.

"I'm amazed that truck of yours holds up."

"Frankly, I am, too." She shoved her door open. Out of the corner of her eye, she could see Dan Biddle crossing the street with a bottle of wine and two glasses. "Irene, did you want to tell me something?"

"Your neighborhood yard sale shift is ten to eleven this Saturday."

"Thanks, I've got it on my calendar." She stepped inside and started to shut her door.

"Annie!" Dan lifted the bottle and glasses. "Great timing! I've got the perfect sunset-watching refreshments."

"Hi, Dan. Do you and Tess need a bottle opener?"

He grinned. "Tess is at her kickboxing class." He stepped past Annie, set the glasses on her entry table, and uncorked the wine. "All ready to go here."

Annie shut the door on Irene's stare. "What about the kids?" She dumped her mail on the table and set down her bag.

"They're in front of the box." He handed her a glass of Paso Robles Pinot noir. "Cheers."

"Dan, did you feed them?"

He rolled his eyes at her, ambled down into her living room, and settled on the couch facing the big front window. Annie glanced at her watch. Okay, he was her friend's husband. He had fixed her truck a dozen times. She could be polite for half an hour. She followed him down into the living room and stood looking out the west-facing window.

He stretched his arms along the back of her sofa, his knees wide, offering her a clear view of tan, hairy thighs, and a manly crotch. With the back of his hand he brushed the wave of brown hair off his wide brow. "It must be tough to come home alone every day. I feel for you, Annie."

"I manage." Annie wondered for the umpteenth time why she didn't find him appealing. He was over six feet tall, a perfect specimen of the ageless beach boy in his board shorts, surf T-shirt, and sandals. True, he was sleazy as a massage ad in *LA Weekly.*

"How's the truck running?"

"The air-conditioning quit today."

He sat up. "You'll have to let me take a look. I can probably fix it."

"Thanks, Dan, but I'm thinking of buying a new car."

"Whoa, Annie James, a new car? That's not like you."

"Maybe it's time for a change." She rolled her shoulders. Dan stood and moved in on her. She knew his timing from dozens of neighborhood gatherings.

"You know, Annie, I give a great neck and shoulder massage." His voice was low and husky.

"No thanks, Dan. I really shouldn't keep you any longer."

"Hey, no problem." He put his hands on her shoulders. Annie was going to have to get rude, fast.

Her landline rang. "Excuse me." She slipped out from under Dan's grasp and dashed for the kitchen. She picked up and got a breathless greeting from Louisa Ruiz, the director at the neighborhood center.

"Annie, I've got some great news. Do you know Ulysses, the boy with dark glasses, the one they call 'Bookman'?"

Annie could hear the chaos of the center's main study room in the background. "Sure." Annie knew Ulysses. He was one of the regulars at the center.

"Could you take him to a private school interview?"

"Of course. When?"

"Well, the thing is, right now. I've got the address and phone number right here." Annie could picture Louisa sorting through the clutter on her desk. "The Canyon Preparatory School for Boys. They're offering a scholarship, and Ulysses has a chance for it."

"Canyon Prep?" It was everything the local high school was not. It was manicured lawns, high tech classrooms, acres of playing fields, and a student parking lot full of luxury cars. It was safety, opportunity, escape. Annie had been at the center when Ulysses's cousin had been shot two years earlier in his first week of high school.

Dan wandered into the kitchen and began to knead her shoulders, and she stiffened. On the line Louisa was explaining where Canyon was, but Annie didn't need MapQuest. She knew right where Canyon was, right where her life had taken a big detour.

Dan shifted his position, and whispered, "Hey, you're really tight here." His big thumbs dug into her knotted muscles, and she could feel his breath on her neck.

Louisa paused. "Annie, are you okay?"

She wasn't, but it was nothing she could explain to Louisa with Dan Biddle breathing wine in her ear. The rosy glow of the lowering sun lit the dining room wall opposite her. She could do this. She could go back to Canyon. The old wounds were just old wounds, faint scars, really. She could drive her truck up that long, palm-lined drive without a twinge of grief. Even if old Headmaster Chambers was still there, their paths would not cross, and the boys she had once known had all graduated. She would focus on the present, on Ulysses, not the past.

"I'll take him, Louisa. No problem."

"Oh, Annie, you're a saint!"

Annie hung up. *Saint* was a stretch, but she was helpful and she could help Ulysses. Or maybe Ulysses could help her face the past and let it go. She took a deep breath and stepped out of Dan's hold. "Excuse me, Dan. I've got to run an unexpected errand."

"Hey, slow down. Let's just finish here."

"Sorry, gotta go." She slipped around him. "Thanks for the wine. Just what I needed."

She scooped up the two glasses and the bottle, handed them to him, and headed straight for the entry. Dan trailed after her. She grabbed her purse, fished for her keys, and opened her door. Irene was watering the hanging pots on her porch.

Annie's phone rang again.

"Don't you want to get it?" Dan asked, lingering on her threshold.

"The machine will pick up." She nudged him through the door as the machine clicked on. Her sister Megan's confident voice filled the house.

It's me, Megan. Listen, Annie, we've decided on a date for Daddy's retirement party. Put the first Sunday of February on your calendar. By the way, Melanie and I think you should freeze your eggs. Don't think about it; just do it. She's sending you a pamphlet.

Annie slammed her door and bolted for the truck. *Note to self— Who needs a landline!*

* * *

Josh Huntington stared out the window of Malcolm Chambers's office, waiting for Dunsmore's rage to subside. Dunsmore paced the deep red and blue swirls of the carpet, while the sun inched its way down a golden sky. Its rays slanted under the familiar Spanish arches of the terrace outside the headmaster's office. The usual afternoon breeze quit.

Chambers leaned back, dead center on a brown leather couch, letting his underling rant. He hadn't changed much in the ten years since the class of '05 had graduated. Josh had to hand it to the guy, he had headmastering down to a fine art, like some throwback to the old English boys' school days with an L.A. twist. He had the blazer and the crisp-white-shirt-wingtip thing going, plus his signature gold and blue tie, Canyon colors in Italian silk. The sporty short-cropped gray hair and the tan gave him a youthful athletic look good for marketing in L.A. The horn-rimmed glasses and academic robes added a scholarly touch. An intimidating crimson robe with three black velvet stripes on the sleeves and a velvet-lined hood hung on the back of his door. But probably the thing that helped Chambers the most was the voice. He had a deep bell-like voice that could make pure bull sound like some toffee-accented English prime minister and James Earl Jones rolled into one.

Josh shifted his buns on the cushionless black college chair. He wanted to get back to the discussion of his plan to get the alumni fired up to give.

Dunsmore was shaking his head. "These tech types with their apps and their hot IPOs don't have any experience giving. Are we sure we want to pursue Sloan?"

Josh cleared his throat. "Sloan isn't one of them. His company does data analysis." Actually it wasn't strictly Sloan's company anymore. He'd sold it, and his share of the sale had been a cool two billion.

Dunsmore stopped pacing and threw up his hands. "Frankly, Malcolm, I'm at a loss. We offered him a spot in the Hall of Canyon Men. What more can we do?"

Jeez. Chambers was a bigger idiot than Josh remembered. At least Chambers had never figured out what Josh had been up to as a student or he would not now have the job of assistant development director. But to send Dunsmore, in that getup no less, to kiss ass for money from Will Sloan… *Jeez.* They could have asked him. He knew Sloan, knew the guy's pride, his toughness. Canyon had done its worst to Will Sloan, and the guy had never cracked. Sloan had only one weakness.

Chambers turned to Josh. "Huntington, what was that plan of yours?"

Josh pulled three copies of his proposal from the file folder on the floor under his chair. Something was going on or Chambers would never have sent Dunsmore after Sloan. Now the old farts would have to listen to him. He took a deep breath and handed the copies to Chambers and Dunsmore.

He had ten lean months ahead until he could meet his father's conditions for regaining his trust fund. The first condition wouldn't be hard—stay employed for a year. No way were they going to let him go from Canyon, not when their big campaign was going nowhere. They had yet to find a few needed seed donors for the silent phase of the campaign. Clearly, Sloan wasn't going to be one of them. The second condition was going to be harder to meet. In his father's words, Josh had to "contribute significantly to a cause larger than his own pleasure."

Josh didn't like the word "significantly." It sounded as if he was going to have to stop world hunger or wipe out some major disease.

His father wasn't likely to regard planning a gala party for Canyon's hundredth birthday as significant. But if Josh could get his class, the class of '05, to beat the Canyon ten-year reunion giving record, his father would have to agree that Josh had kept his end of the deal. If not, he'd have to give up the house in Malibu, and he wouldn't be going back to Bali any time soon.

He launched into his explanation of the series of gatherings and committees he'd dreamed up to get the alumni in the mood to give. As he spoke, a battered white four-wheel drive pickup with a hard shell top came up the long, palm-lined drive and pulled into a visitor parking spot in front of the Admissions Office. Josh knew that truck. The driver's side door opened. The woman who emerged from the truck wore a gray business suit and had deep red hair, like brandies and ports and rich single malts.

Josh felt a shiver go through him, just as it had the day he'd been tapped as the youngest prefect in Canyon history. Destiny reached down and touched his shoulder again. The redhead came up the walk and directed the young Latino with her toward the Admissions Office, and Josh had a vision, an honest-to-God vision, without the aid of any hallucinogenic substance. Will Sloan was rich, Annie James was back, and he, Josh Huntington, would bring them together.

He cleared his throat with just the tone of deference that said he knew he was merely the humble *assistant* development director but maybe he could help. "What we need to get this centennial campaign going is—foreplay."

Chapter Two

The annual Sand Dollar Lane end-of-summer yard sale was in full swing in the Biddles' front yard when Annie began her shift. Petite blonde Tess Biddle slapped a calculator into Annie's palm and yelled for her three boys to get in the car. *Now.*

Annie smiled at the earnest young couple in front of her. They were plainly on the verge of parenthood themselves and had piled fifteen baby items on the picnic table checkout counter. The husband tucked his list back into his shirt pocket. Annie figured their total as Tess herded her three boys into the family SUV. The young wife cradled her round belly with one arm and glanced from Annie to the soccer-clad Biddle boys. She was clearly rethinking the whole parenting idea when a green Range Rover pulled to a halt at the end of the Biddle driveway. The driver's side door opened, and a blond god stepped out of an Abercrombie ad into the Biddle yard in front of God, Irene Gale, and half of Annie's neighbors.

"Annie James." The god gave her a hug and an air-kiss, and handed her a heavy, cream-colored envelope with the brown Canyon palms embossed in the upper left-hand corner. "I saw you on campus yesterday, and wanted to make sure you got this invite."

Tess killed her car engine. Dan stopped touting the merits of his old surfboards. Irene had her lace curtain over one shoulder. The young couple stared openly.

Annie found her voice. She had unlocked the box of the past, and all the secrets were going to escape. "Josh Huntington, how did you find me?"

Of course, she knew the answer to that. Impossible to hide. Even she had Facebook friends.

Behind his dark glasses Josh was probably eating up the attention. He shoved his hands in the pockets of his khakis, lifting the cuffs, exposing tan, sockless ankles and three hundred dollar loafers. "It's great luck, isn't it? I saw you on campus yesterday. I work in the Canyon Development Office now, planning for the centennial."

He worked? Josh, the boy with a bottomless trust fund, the student who had mostly conned his way through Canyon with that smile.

"You're still a journalist, right? I remember when you advised the school newspaper."

Annie was conscious of her neighbors hanging onto every word of the conversation. Josh had been checking up on her. "'Journalist' is a stretch, but I do work for the local news group."

"So, have you heard from any of the guys in our class?"

"I haven't had any connection with Canyon for ten years." That had been part of the deal she'd made with Chambers when she left.

"Well," he tapped the envelope she still held in her hand, "a lot of guys would like to see you. We're getting together to plan our first reunion. It would be great to have you there."

"Thanks, Josh." *What do you want from me?*

He pulled his car key out of his pocket. "Oh, by the way. I stopped by the neighborhood center. They're big fans of that kid Ulysses you brought for an interview."

Uh oh. No question that Josh Huntington wanted something. "Canyon would be a great opportunity for him."

Josh nodded. "The admissions director told me he's got the brains to raise the class SAT average all by himself, but you know it never hurts to help a candidate along, especially a scholarship candidate. We could work together on it." He glanced around as if he'd only just noticed the garage sale in progress. "Catch you later, Annie. And don't miss this party. Everyone's going to be there."

Annie nodded. Message received. Ulysses's admission to Canyon depended on her willingness to attend this event, whatever it was. Well, she could do that. Her evenings were not exactly taken since she'd ended her latest dating experiment.

Josh gave her another quick squeeze, sauntered back to his Rover, and drove off. Irene's curtain fell back into place. Tess and Dan got into a tense discussion. Annie helped the young parents-to-be to carry their purchases to their tiny compact. When she came back to the yard, Dan was pulling out in the SUV and Tess was headed her way.

"Who's the hottie?" she demanded.

"He was a student at a school where I worked a long time ago."

"You were a teacher?"

"No, I was the admission director's assistant briefly. It was a temp job when I first came to L.A." The crowd had thinned, and Annie looked at the unsold stuff they would have to sort. Stuff that had looked perfectly decent when they started had a way of looking so sad at the end of the sale.

"So this guy had a crush on you?"

"Josh? Never. He was way too cool. At eighteen he had more experience than I did." *At sixteen probably.*

"That guy was born experienced." Tess smiled slyly. "But now, he's interested, right?"

"He's in charge of some reunion event."

"Don't kid yourself. A hand-delivered invite? Did you open it?"

Annie shook her head. She'd tucked the heavy envelope in the pile of children's books she'd culled for the center.

"Well!" Tess leaned back, her hands on her hips.

"It's somewhere in that pile."

Tess rummaged through the stack until she found it. "The Canyon Preparatory School for Boys?" She gaped at Annie. "You worked at an all boys school? You were what, twenty-something? The hormones must have been intense." She read on. "The Dunes Club. Looks like all the classes from '05 back to forever. How many men is that?"

"Married men, Tess, with their wives."

Tess shrugged. "I bet they are all rich, and some of them are bound to be divorced. It's your big chance to be a trophy wife, and you won't have to freeze your eggs."

As soon as she said it, Tess clapped a hand over her mouth. She apologized for the next fifteen minutes in spite of Annie's assurances that one apology was sufficient. Finally, she insisted on taking Annie shopping. "You've got to have a new dress for this thing if you're going to catch anybody's eye."

And that's when Annie realized how Josh had trapped her. He had dazzled her neighbors into asking questions and making it impossible for her to ignore his invitation. It was dirty, underhanded, manipulative, and so Josh, but one thing she could be sure of—Will Sloan would not be there. Some parts of the past would stay in the past.

* * *

A high cinder-block wall capped with loose bricks enclosed the modest rectangle that was Mae Sloan's new backyard. Will had tried to persuade her to live in a bigger house in a better neighborhood on the Palos Verdes hill, but Mae had insisted on this three-bedroom fixer-upper on a cul-de-sac in North Redondo Beach. He bought her a pristine set of open-weave patio chairs and an umbrella-shaded, glass-topped table, which sat on a slab of cracked, buckled cement once painted green. The concrete ended in a patch of drying, knee-high weeds, which extended to a mass of dusty ivy. Along the back wall a hedge of nondescript bushes shed inedible purple berries over the whole scene.

"Mom, hire somebody to clear out this mess."

Mae tied a faded red bandanna over her thick black hair threaded with strands of silver. "Oh, we can do it in no time."

She had tucked a Minnie Mouse T-shirt into a pair of cut-off, paint-spattered jeans. It figured. Mae faced everything with the same grin Minnie wore under her pink-polka-dotted hair bow. Mae squinted her coal dark eyes up at the late August sun. "I'm going to get some sun block. You want some?"

Will shook his head. He pulled on heavy gloves and waded into the encroaching ivy, clippers in hand. Once he'd lopped off the lower branches and cleared the ivy from the trunks, he'd use the chain saw Mae borrowed from a neighbor to take out the ugly bushes.

He was sweating by the time Mae came back out of the house, whistling for the dog she had rescued from the Humane Society. She hadn't decided on a name for him, so she was just calling him "Dog." As far as Will was concerned, Dog didn't deserve a name, he was the Mr. Potato Head of dogs with random dog parts stuck on a compact black body—short legs, bushy tail, narrow muzzle, pointed ears, and boundless energy. While Mae dragged a green plastic trash can up to the edge of the ivy, Dog raced around the patio in circles, stopped to sniff the row of new gardening tools learning against the back of the house, and plunged into the ivy. Mae laughed.

Will muttered—*stupid dog*—and turned to the ivy. It was pretty much ivy from hell, dusty, tangled layers of it. "Why does anyone plant this parasitic stuff?" Will ripped a long runner from the bush in front of him.

"It's green year round, honey." She had his phone in her hand.

"I brought your phone out. It just about vibrated right off the entry table. Are you expecting an important call?"

No, he was just dealing with one particularly persistent unwanted caller. How had the guy gotten his number?

As they clipped and tore at the ivy, Mae kept finding things and showing them to him with an archeologist's relish—a rusty toy truck, a plastic plate crusted with dirt, and a tennis ball, which she tossed at Dog, who caught it midair.

"You don't have any Agent Orange, do you?" Something in the ivy scurried off, rustling dead leaves. "Jeez Mom, you probably have rats in here."

"Or possums." Mae tossed her clippings in the plastic trash barrel beside her. "They'll have to find a new home when we finish."

"A crew of four could finish in one day."

Mae smiled mildly. "No hurry. We'll put in as much time as we like. It'll get done when it gets done." She straightened when she thought he wasn't looking and pressed her hands to the small of her back.

"You should have a gardening service."

"Me? Don't be silly."

"Why not? I give you enough money each month."

"I like working in my garden."

"You could have picked a hotter day for it." A branch Will was wrestling with snapped unexpectedly, tearing his T-shirt and scratching him across the chest, drawing tiny beads of blood. He stopped to wipe the wound clean.

His phone vibrated against the glass tabletop. Ever since Dunsmore had tried to hustle three mil out of him for a spot in the Hall of Canyon Men, Josh Huntington had been leaving the same message on Will's phone. *"I know where Annie James is. Call me."*

Huntington didn't even identify himself. He knew Will would know the voice. Of all the rich kids sucking their way through exclusive Canyon Prep, Josh Huntington had had it the easiest. Every privilege, every advantage that Canyon had to offer belonged to Josh.

The repeated messages made Will restless and edgy. He had snapped at Beau and left the office early. He didn't get it. Hating Annie James had replaced desiring her, so why should Huntington's

message campaign annoy him? He should never have returned to
L.A. where the past was waiting for him.

When the phone buzzed again, he pulled off his gloves, picked it
up, and headed around the corner of the house. "You bastard. I
should have killed you at Big Bear senior year."

"Just doing you a favor, Sloan, then and now," said the smooth
voice.

"Screw your favors, Huntington."

"She's not married, Sloan."

Will couldn't answer. He just held the phone and looked at the
cinder block wall, unseeing, sweat trickling down his neck.

"She looks good, subdued maybe, but good."

Will swallowed. He knew what she looked like. He had a stupid
Canyon yearbook. His mom had returned a box of his things to him
when she'd moved into her house, and the pathetic thing was that he
had opened that box of the past and looked at that yearbook. His first
stupid idea had been to try to find Annie. Instead he'd put himself in
Beau's hands and let Beau drag him from pool parties at the Viceroy
to private clubs in Santa Monica. So far he had clicked with no one,
and he hadn't had a decent idea since he'd returned to L.A. It made
no sense to let the past distract him. That was high school; this was
real life. He should be over Annie James.

"Listen, she's coming to a Canyon reunion event."

"Screw Canyon."

"It's not at Canyon actually. It's down your way, at the Dunes
Club."

"Screw the Dunes Club."

"I've sent you an invitation. See you there, Sloan. It'll be just
like old times."

He ended the call and returned to the patio, dropping his phone
on the table.

Mae stopped clipping and studied him. "Will Rogers Sloan,
what's eating you? You act like somebody's riding you with a burr
under your saddle."

He avoided her gaze by wiping his arm across his sweaty brow.
"Nothing." Annie James was nothing to him, right? He hadn't
thought about her in...years, not much anyway. He'd been too busy
making a fortune. Until he'd come back to L.A. Once he'd sold Z-
Text and signed that non-competition clause, he'd had nothing to do;

and as if they'd just been waiting for him to pay attention, the memories had starting banging on his door like a S.W.A.T. team.

Memory was a dog. Some people had a squirming puppy of a memory like Mae's Dog. At a touch the puppy piddled out warm images of the past. Some had a slow, faithful friend, willing to amble through the past. Will had a Rottweiler of a memory, barely chained, snarling, like the dog their neighbor, old man Gower, had kept near the fence that separated the trailer park from his property. Will had hated that dog, but he had always walked as close as he dared to the fence so that the dog strained against the chain, his teeth snapping air.

Listening to Huntington's message about Annie James was like walking just beyond the dog's reach, letting him snap and snarl and foam. From his side of the fence, he could look back and spit at the dog's feet. If he picked up the phone, down came the fence just when he'd promised himself he'd let go of the past.

"I guess I'm ready for that chain saw."

It was just like the ones he'd used as a kid working in Christmas tree lots. After a couple of tries it started up. The angry noise and foul-smelling smoke agreed with his mood. He waded through the ivy and attacked the first bush at the base. At least he could curse and swear and Mae wouldn't hear him.

His mind was on Annie James. Dunsmore's stupid ploy brought it all back. He had every right to hate her, hate Canyon. His classmates had made his days hell for four years with plenty of help from Chambers. And in his senior year Annie James had been there each time Chambers summoned him for a bit more humiliation. She sat at a desk in the open reception area that joined the admissions office with the head of school's office. Will had long stretches of time to watch her work or smile or help another student while Chambers made him wait for their meetings, often just long enough so that he missed his bus. That was one of Chambers's favorite tactics.

In his office Chambers would read the teachers' reports aloud; then he would ask Will about his bill. *"Now this is just between us,"* Chambers would say, *"your mother has done her part already, but you still need a thousand dollars."* Or two thousand—Will could never anticipate the sum. Then Chambers would ask what did he want to do to earn his tuition or his books or whatever he needed? Did he want to bus tables in the cafeteria, or did he prefer grounds work? Maybe he'd like to clean the classrooms in the evening when no one else was around?

Will had hated having to choose his own humiliation. No way was he going to forget that. And the pathetic thing was that once he'd fallen in love with Annie James, he had gone willingly to Chambers's office just to see her.

"Will!" Mae's voice penetrated the buzz of the chain saw. He disengaged the motor, and the whine settled down to a dull idle. Oily gray smoke and gas fumes drifted up around him. He stood a minute separating the anger in his mind from the destruction around him. The bushes were gone, and he needed to get a grip on himself. He turned the saw off, set it on the edge of the cracked patio, and dragged the felled shrubs down from the weedy middle of the yard, stacking them in a tall mound at the edge of the patio.

"The yard looks much better already." Mae was watching him closely, and he kept moving.

"Got to go after the root balls next." He grabbed a pick and swung it at the baked ground, satisfied when it chopped through dirt and roots with a heavy thump that sent the dust flying and left a white gash in the brown skin of a thick root. He repeated the motion, setting a savage rhythm. Mae whistled, and he rested the pick on the ground.

"What?"

"It's not an execution. Go get something cold to drink. I'll get the hose and wet this soil down."

He continued to swing the pick, putting his full weight into each stroke, cursing the vegetation, the dust, his memories. He heard Mae cross the patio, heard the surge of water in the hose and the splash on the cement. Then he was bathed in cool spray.

He spun toward Mae, tossing down the pick. She backed away, but continued to play the water over him. "Mom, what are you doing?"

"Honey, you need to cool off." Dog danced and barked at her heels.

Will stopped at the edge of the patio and put his hands up, turning his face away from the spray. "Okay, okay. I give."

She flicked the stream of water away from him and moved to the spigot. She stared at him a full minute. When he pulled his shirt over his head and began to wring it out, she turned off the water. "I'll get you a towel and some lunch."

"Sure." He tossed his wet T-shirt over the back of one of the new patio chairs. Then he sank into another chair, took off his soaked work shoes, and turned his face up to the sun. When he opened his eyes, Mae was sitting opposite him, watching him closely. She had set a lunch tray on the table with two glasses of iced tea, thick sandwiches on flowered plates, and a pair of big soft oatmeal cookies.

"You want to tell me what all the anger is about?"

He put down his sandwich and took a drink of the iced tea. "Josh Huntington wants me to go to a Canyon event."

Mae's black brows rose a fraction.

"All the same jerks will be there." *And Annie James.*

"Do you want to see those people?"

He snorted. "They want to see me. Now that I have some money."

Mae grinned. "I bet they do." She fed Dog a bite of her sandwich under the table.

He realized she could still be pretty, all cheekbones and deep-set eyes and freckles. The black bands on the sleeves and neck of her T-shirt were loose around her slim arms and throat. She could marry again.

"Aren't you ever angry about Canyon? About how hard you had to work? About how long you had to stay in that trailer just to keep me there?"

"No." Mae took a long sip of iced tea. "Look at you. Look at where you are and what you've done? I'm likely to burst with pride, not anger. So some people there tried to hold you back. They couldn't. Let it go."

"You could at least spend the money I give you."

Mae stood up. "Are you dry enough to enter my house?"

Putting his hands on his thighs, Will tested the dampness of his jeans. "Yeah."

"Let me show you something." She told Dog to stay, and slid the sliding glass door open.

Barefoot, he followed her into the house. Room by room she was making changes. She'd divided the bedroom next to hers into two rooms, making a huge walk-in closet and enlarging her bath. It was the closet she showed him now. She opened the double doors and turned on the lights. Not too many clothes hung on the rods, but two long shoe racks were full. "You know what being rich is?"

"Being a prick and having other people suck up to you?"

Mae shook her head. "Being rich is just having more than you need, more sky, more time, more love. Or more shoes!" She nudged him with her elbow.

She reached down and picked up a pair of black velvet pumps. "Versace." She picked up another. "Prada." One after another she showed him her shoes, reciting the designer names reverently. She handed him a pair of lime green, open toe sandals with three-inch heels. "You don't want to know how much these cost."

Will swallowed a painful lump in his throat. All his life before Z-Text she had gone to work in black, sneaker-like shoes, ugly rubber-soled shoes. These shoes were thin-soled, sleek, gleamingly beautiful. He couldn't imagine what engineering principle made them support a woman's weight. He leaned down and picked up a pair of silver heels with delicate straps. "And these?"

Mae laughed. "Payless." She punched him on the arm. "Come on, let's finish lunch."

When they had resettled themselves on the patio, Mae told him about her plans for the yard. "I'm going to put in olive trees and lavender and some potted lemon trees. I'd like to use your truck for hauling."

Will nodded. "Seriously, Mom, you're not bitter about the past?"

Mae shook her head. "I'm forty-six. I'm not wasting any time, and you shouldn't either. Let Canyon go. If you had a bad time there let the past stay in the past. You don't have to go back."

"I do, Mom. I have one piece of unfinished business there."

* * *

Josh left the Dunes Club after meeting with the manager of the catering department. The party was on, and he was pretty sure he'd hooked Sloan. For a smart guy, Sloan was not rational where Annie James was concerned. Josh would bet big bucks that Sloan could not resist seeing her again, and once the guy saw her, Josh would move in to get some of that Z-Text money headed Canyon's way.

He turned and headed west downhill toward the duplex he owned just four blocks from the Strand. His one investment in ten years was not striking evidence of financial genius, as his father had been quick to point out. His remaining tenants had moved out of the south unit. They hadn't exactly trashed it, but an abandoned sofa in the driveway with a missing leg and the stuffing emerging from a torn orange cushion summed up the state of the place. The thought of living there was so depressing that he headed for his favorite South Bay hangout, the Power Plant microbrewery. As he made his way past the tall aluminum tanks along the back wall, waitresses in tight black Power Plant T-shirts, cutoff overalls, and yellow hard hats greeted him. He knew them all, but he kept a lookout for Melissa, his favorite.

He spotted her, and she jerked her head toward his usual table that had a clear view of the big-screen TV where the guys waited for him. The Power Plant, a microbrewery started by his classmates Shields and Lynch while they were still undergrads had at first catered to the frat crowd, but had now become a Canyon alumni hangout in the South Bay. He realized he'd be coming even more often if his plans for the Canyon campaign didn't work out.

He passed through the crowd, mostly people in their twenties and thirties, dressed for maximum exposure of tan, fit body parts, discreet and not so discreet tattoos, and random piercings. He tossed his keys on the table and slid onto the bench beside Trevor Lynch, and opposite Greg Shields and Nate Fletcher. "What's up?"

"You've got your nerve, Huntington, dragging us to this Dunes event so Chambers can squeeze us for money." Nate wore one of his L.A. County Guards T-shirts, his dark glasses perched on his blond curls.

Melissa came and leaned her hip against Josh's shoulder, ruffling his hair. He ordered his usual pale ale, and turned his attention to Nate.

Nate's father was even tougher than Josh's. Nate would not have a penny of trust until he'd worked a full ten years. That Nate had five years as a lifeguard under his belt was a unique record for their class, but with county budget cuts, he could lose his spot.

"Don't get bent out of shape, Nate. You knew it was coming. It's Canyon tradition to give big at the ten-year mark for the first class reunion."

Nate drew circles in the condensation on his glass. "Yeah, but we're not ready. The economy sucks."

"Yeah," Trevor agreed. "For Nate. He's still scraping to buy that Burger King franchise he wants."

Nate said something nasty and Trevor grinned. Trevor had snack-food orange hair. They had called him "Cheeto Head" in grammar school until he got big enough to pound anyone who said it. He was e-trading with his trust and moaning a lot about market volatility.

"We can do this." Josh had known they'd be sore about being tapped for cash and depressed about being ten years older, but he could get them over it.

"We suck at *making* money." Nate tossed a handful of pretzels into his mouth.

"Speak for yourself, bozo. Shields and I are doing okay. I've got a Porsche." Trevor jiggled a set of keys.

"You should ask other guys in our class, not just us. There were some real geeks in our class. I bet one of them has made a bundle."

Melissa brought Josh his IPA, and the four friends drank in silence for a while watching the baseball game on the screen above them.

A commercial broke the spell of the TV, and Shields spoke again. "So, you've got a plan, right, Huntington? The class of '05 won't look like losers at the ten-year mark?"

Josh took a long swig of his ale, the golden, well-hopped brew he favored. It was painful to remember how they'd left Canyon. They'd been the class that disappointed everyone. Chambers had fired the college counselor, and rumor had it that he had taken the whole faculty on a retreat in the wine country to recover. Chambers was like that, always pulling money out of the hat for something that wasn't strictly in the school budget. He'd built an addition to his office, a wood-paneled library with a private bath, when they'd been sophomores. It had taken Josh exactly three months to discover how Chambers used that private space.

"Well, guys, the good news is there is one member of our class who's made the big bucks."

"Who?" He got them all to look.

"Sloan."

"The cowboy!" Nate snorted. "What'd he do, hock his silver belt buckle? Win the rodeo? That guy was never Canyon material. Why'd they take him anyway?"

"He could catch footballs, moron."

"Why didn't Chambers kick him out our senior year when he burned down the Canyon sign?"

Josh was surprised they didn't remember, but he wasn't going to remind them. "Actually, he didn't burn the sign."

"How do you know?"

"Not important. What matters is that he's got money."

Trevor fiddled with his phone. "He's not the Sloan of Z-Text, is he?"

Josh nodded. "Yeah, that's our Sloan."

Lynch showed the phone to the others. Josh sipped his brew, ignoring the groans and obscenities as they calculated how much Sloan had. He watched Melissa fend off a beefy customer who'd slipped an arm around her waist. Josh thought of Annie James and wondered if Melissa would be available to help him take the edge off later.

When the reaction to his news subsided, he turned back to his friends. "We don't have to be a loser class anymore. We can set the record for the biggest ten-year donation ever."

Once again he drew their stares.

Then Lynch laughed. "Yeah, but Huntington, Sloan hated Canyon."

Shields started laughing, too. "Sloan hated you. Remember our senior overnight to Big Bear? Sloan was ready to tear your guts out and strangle you with them."

"What did you do to piss him off so much?" Fletcher asked.

Lynch put down his drink. "Ms. James was on that trip, in her cabin, taking a shower. Josh suggested Sloan help her."

That was not the way he remembered it, but Josh did not correct them.

"Sloan was hot for her."

"Sloan was obsessed."

"So that's what this Dunes thing is all about. Huntington, you sly dog, you're going to get them back together. She was hot, I'll give you that."

"We made her an honorary member of our class, remember?"

Shields set his glass on the table. "It doesn't matter. Sloan won't give Canyon a dime."

Josh made sure the grin he could feel rising stayed firmly inside. "Wanna bet?"

"You're crazy." Fletcher turned back to the TV.

But Shields studied him carefully. "How much? A hundred?"

Josh shook his head. "Think big, guys, or I'm not interested."

"A thousand then," said Lynch.

Josh kept his expression relaxed. "If I get a donation out of Sloan, you give Canyon ten percent of whatever Sloan gives."

"Fair enough." Lynch extended his hand across the table. "Ten percent of nada is nada."

Josh watched Melissa hang her hard hat on a hook by the back door and head for her break. He stood. "Well, prepare yourselves, men. I say Sloan will give a million bucks as his part of the class gift."

The whooping and hollering and table banging behavior of his friends drew stares from the other patrons. Josh just waited for the din to subside. His friends exchanged glances.

"What do we get when Sloan laughs in your face?"

Josh tossed a twenty on the table. "I donate a thousand for each of us if I lose." He left them gaping and headed after Melissa.

"You're on, buddy," Lynch called after him.

Chapter Three

Josh Huntington met Annie at a white-linen-draped table spread with name tags, thick, creamy squares of paper, each with a satin loop of brown ribbon and a tiny gold safety pin at the top. No sticky-backed tags for Canyon. Josh pinned her tag to her dress and led her out onto the Dunes Club patio where huge terra-cotta pots spilled bright trails of purple and white flowers.

Beyond them a dipping expanse of lawn ended in an indigo pool where a few disciplined swimmers did laps. On either side of the long lawn, raised walkways led past green mesh walls screening tennis courts from view. From them came the sounds of serious tennis—a flurry of shots and the squeak of shoes against the court surface, a pause, and then another flurry. It was a far cry from Sand Dollar Lane.

A tall, forty-something man whose name tag read class of '89 brought Annie a wine and engaged her in light conversation. She caught snatches of the talk around them. The superiority of raw buying power made the voices sound alike.

"I've always wanted to buy an island."

"Have you been back to Madagascar lately?"

"Not the Pinot, the Viognier."

She realized she was hardly being fair to her companion and excused herself, looking for Josh. His golden good looks made him easy to spot. "Why am I here?" she asked. "This is a select crowd."

He patted her shoulder. "You are the key to a rather substantial donation."

"I don't understand."

"Will Sloan."

She tried not to show any reaction. Of course, Josh would know about Annie and Sloan. "I haven't seen him in ten years. I thought this was about Ulysses."

"It is. I just need you to be nice to Sloan. For Canyon. For Ulysses."

Annie stared at the smiling madman next to her. Had he said what she thought he said? "Josh, Will Sloan doesn't know I'm alive. And he would never come to an event like this after his experience at

Canyon. I hope he's forgotten Canyon." The wattage in Josh's smile did not dim one bit. "You're not telling me that Ulysses's admission depends on this, are you?"

"Don't worry. You're perfect for the job. Besides, you're an honorary member of our class. We've got to have you here." He gave her shoulder another pat. "Shall I send Moreland over to talk with you?"

"Mike Moreland is here?" He had been a favorite of Annie's, a sweet young man, completely unsure of himself, who had blossomed as he worked on the school newspaper. As Annie turned, Josh slipped away, and there was Mike with his short, springy brown hair, looking all grown up. He broke free from a knot of twenty-something men gathered at the patio entry, and came striding up, his blazer jacket open, striped school tie flapping, a beer in one hand.

"Gosh, Ms. James, you look fine." He immediately blushed.

"Mike Moreland, what are you doing these days?"

"Large animal veterinary medicine." He passed a hand through his curls, causing them to stand on end.

"I'm impressed." Advising the newspaper had been one part of the job at Canyon that she had genuinely enjoyed, and Mike had been one of the responsible boys on the paper's very laid-back staff

"I owe it all to you for listening to me at Canyon. You remember, you told me I could do it."

Annie shook her head. "I doubt you owe me a thing. Tell me about your work."

As he talked, Annie relaxed. She was sure she would not have to do Josh the favor he wanted. The one person who wouldn't come to such an event was Will Sloan. Later, Annie would catch up with Josh and set him straight about having anything to do with Will. Nothing, not saving the polar ice caps, disarming terrorist organizations, or colonizing Mars, was less likely than Annie James influencing Will Sloan to donate money to Canyon. Besides, Will probably had thousands of dollars of student loans to pay off. He had not had a trust fund to support him, not even two parents, only his mother. She relaxed and gave her full attention to Mike Moreland. Twenty minutes later he stopped himself. "I've probably bored you, haven't I?"

"Not at all."

He took a swallow of the forgotten beer in his hand and gave her a more serious look. "Josh says you're working for a newspaper for real now."

"Yes, I am, in a small way. It's a far cry from big time journalism, but it pays the mortgage." The young men around the entry were laughing at something. She thought she recognized two of them.

Mike picked at the label on his beer bottle. "You ever see Will Sloan?"

"No." Annie looked away, an instant flutter in her stomach.

"That's weird, because..." Mike worked another corner of the label free of the bottle. "I have this theory about Will." He swallowed and went on in a rush. "Something we learned about in one of our first animal behavior classes. Imprinting? Ever hear of it?"

Annie nodded. "It's about ducklings."

Mike nodded. "Yes. Baby birds imprint on their mothers, usually, but if the mother isn't there, they'll imprint on a human being, and it's almost impossible to get them to separate from someone they imprint on." Mike's face had turned pink. The beer label came off in his hand. He glanced around, and failing to find a trash can on the pristine Dunes Club patio, stuck the torn label in his pocket. "I always thought Will Sloan was like those ducklings in a way. I mean we didn't have any girls at Canyon, and so he imprinted on you."

Annie felt the knot in her stomach tighten. She tried to meet Mike's embarrassed gaze with a reassuring one of her own. "A crush on an older person is perfectly normal and temporary. We all recover. And I'm sure Will has met lots of women since high school."

Mike shook his head. "Yeah, well, Ms. James... Annie. We didn't think of you as...older, really. I mean—you were part of our class." He blushed. "I've got to get to a patient, a rescued horse, actually. I just wanted to see you, to thank you."

* * *

Nate Fletcher, Trevor Lynch, and Greg Shields, three guys from Will's Canyon class, were greeting latecomers when he arrived at the Dunes Club. He glanced at the name tag table. Only his tag remained. He left it to languish on the table, and when Huntington's buddies hesitated, he avoided the Canyon handshake as well. Just like old times, but he hadn't come for the conversation or the dinner. He had come to see Annie James. Once he told her she'd missed her big chance when she'd turned down his marriage proposal, he'd be the one in control, the one to walk out. He'd had a revenge appetizer when he'd turned down Dunsmore. Walking out on Annie James would be dessert. He would put the past behind him for good and get on with his next big idea.

He didn't see her in the crowd, and he wouldn't ask where she was, so he had to stand there listening to his old enemies while his revenge speech got tangled up in his brain.

They were drinking colored martinis, and Fletcher, his dark glasses perched on his blond, buzzed head, took a swallow and began. "Hey, Sloan, you the next Bill Gates or what?"

So they knew about his money. "I'm not as charitable."

"Josh says you've got a sweet place on the hill." Lynch's attempt at conversation. At Canyon, with his snack-food orange hair he had not been able to escape the grammar school nickname "Cheeto Head."

Will nodded.

"What kind of wheels you driving?" Shields, the genius of the trio, asked.

"Truck."

Will still didn't see any sign of Annie James, and he didn't have a drink in his hand. He started to move when Fletcher said, "So, are you going to be part of this reunion plan Huntington has going?"

"What plan?"

"To get our class to give big bucks to Canyon."

Will simply stared at them. They were smirking. Huntington thought Will was going to give Canyon money? Of course. Dunsmore had failed, but Huntington was going to serve up Annie James and expect Will to write the big check. Will was still registering that thought when Huntington strolled up.

"Sloan, there you are. Just in time. They're about to seat everyone for dinner."

Will spun toward Huntington and stopped dead. Moreland was coming toward them, and behind him, alone, was Annie James, in a lavender dress that looked as pale as the evening sky and as thin as tissue paper. The jolt to his system stopped movement, speech, and brain function. Will managed to shake Moreland's hand as the guy left. He was aware of Huntington clapping him on the shoulder, steering him through the crowd. He was vaguely surprised that his feet moved. He didn't feel them. Huntington's lips formed words, but Will couldn't hear what the guy was saying.

He tried to clear his throat, to rediscover the mechanism for making sound, but a powerful realization held him speechless. It was one thing to forget about Annie James for weeks at a time, to practice hating her as a ritual, to congratulate himself on the progress he had made. It was another thing to be in a room with her and to know that in less than a minute he would take her hand in his.

Huntington brought him to a halt in front of her, and from the blind look in her eyes, he could see that memory hadn't spared her either. He could crush her. On that savage thought, he found his voice.

"Annie James."

She stuck out her hand, and when he took it in his, a second wave of sensation passed through him, a feeling he hadn't had in years, a piercing sweetness that caught him in the throat and made him swallow hard. He worked to hold back the old questions. *Why did you leave Canyon? Why didn't you answer my letter?*

A microphone screeched at the head table, and Dunsmore spoke into it, inviting them all to sit.

Huntington grabbed a photographer. "Annie, can we get one more shot before dinner?" Will's jaw tightened at Huntington's free use of her name.

He nudged Annie and Will into position side by side and drew a sandy-haired man up on her right. She nodded to the other man, who smiled familiarly at her. The thought that the sandy-haired fellow might be her date momentarily checked Will. He would not get to make his speech if he couldn't get her alone.

From behind the camera, the photographer motioned them to close in. Will slipped his arm around her waist and pulled her against his side. He heard her gasp, and put his mouth to her ear. "Smile."

There was a click and a flash, too rapid to cause a blink, too rapid to savor the feel of her against him. Then Huntington took over. "Annie, Sloan, you're at table six. Let's get you settled."

Chapter Four

Will shook hands with the others at their table, telling himself he shouldn't mind the contact that erased the first touch of her waist under his palm. Then they were seated. The man on her right was talking to her, so Will took a moment to test his speaking voice on his own partner. Libby her name was. By the time Libby had explained the difficulties of remodeling her kitchen after those she'd seen on a recent trip to Tuscany, Will thought he'd recovered his normal speaking voice. Their waiter brought salads. Will picked up his fork with perfect self-control and fixed the careful opening of his speech in mind.

"I didn't think you'd be here." She spoke without looking at him, her attention on the greens in front of her.

"I'm sure you didn't." He made the mistake of looking at her. Her face was softly rounded, her deep brown eyes wary and full of submerged feeling. Her mouth was lush. A strand of that fiery hair was caught in the thin beaded gold chain she wore around her neck. Her ring finger was empty.

"I did not pick this table. Josh probably thought it would make us comfortable in this crowd to sit together."

Will shook his head. She knew better than that.

She swallowed, and he thought things about her throat that he had no business thinking. He realized that he was resting his left foot on the ball, jiggling his leg, an old strategy he had for avoiding an erection when he talked with her. He stopped. He was nearly thirty. He had plenty of experience, plus a tablecloth, a napkin, a sports jacket, and a great deal of animosity between himself and that particular adolescent humiliation.

Annie looked at the pale green baby lettuce on her fork and didn't think she could swallow. It was a shock to see him again, six feet of hard male presence, green eyes flashing disdain in that aloof, self-sufficient face. Next to her he radiated a restless energy just short of road rage. Around them rose the chatter of friendly ordinary talk. She suspected that what he had to say would be as sweet and friendly as taking a sledgehammer to the windshield of her truck.

She abandoned her salad, took a fortifying sip of wine, and faced him. "It's been a long time since we talked."

"June 9th, 2005."

She put her wine down and steadied her hand on the table. "No doubt you've had a great deal of life experience since then. Things must look different to you now."

"Some things."

His green gaze was so full of malice that she gave up all pretense of eating and clenched her hands in her lap. "You have something to say to me."

"I do."

The waiter chose that moment to ask for Annie's salad plate, and the woman on Will's left claimed his attention. He had come to say some devastating angry thing to pay Annie back for disappearing from his life, but she wasn't going to help him. She had done the right thing then, and he was obviously thriving now. His subtly expensive charcoal jacket and gray silk shirt said he had a right to be part of this crowd.

The waiter put dinner plates in front of them. "How's your mother?" she asked.

"She's good." His eyes showed that she'd scored a hit. "Thanks for asking."

She dropped her gaze to the grilled salmon the waiter put in front of her. "And have you found a girl, settled down?" It was inevitable. Years separated the boy he had been from this man he'd become, but her voice came out faint and thin.

He leaned toward her and whispered fiercely, "I haven't made a second marriage proposal if you're wondering, after the first one went so spectacularly well."

His elbow brushed her bare arm. She expected the arc of electricity between them to send the waiter scrambling for a fire extinguisher.

Will pulled back. "Where are you working these days?"

"At a newspaper group in Westwood."

Two taps on the microphone interrupted them. Annie turned her chair toward the head table where Headmaster Chambers was thanking the guests for coming. Around them waiters cleared dinner plates and brought dessert and coffee. Chambers's speech went on.

Annie felt a painful grip on her right arm. Will's voice at her ear whispered, "When did you leave Canyon?"

She tried to free her arm, but he wouldn't release her. She turned to confront him, and his mouth brushed her ear. Heat ran through her in molten rivers. "June 10th, 2005."

He froze, and his grip on her arm slackened.

Chambers's talk continued. Wine was his metaphor. Canyon was an old vineyard on the side of a hill that had produced many fine and rare vintages. Now the vineyard needed their care if was going to continue the traditions of the last hundred years. Behind her Will Sloan make a rude noise. "We'd like the leadership for the centennial campaign to come from this group." He held up a clipboard. "I encourage everyone to sign up for one of the New Directions for Canyon committees."

Conversation began to buzz as soon as Chambers stopped speaking. The man Annie had talked to earlier invited her to stay for a drink, her first invitation in a long time. He was just the sort of man Tess had imagined Annie would meet—good-looking, affluent, and available. She could imagine Tess's delight. She politely declined. She needed to get away, to free herself from Will Sloan's presence.

* * *

Will watched Annie talk to the man from the photo. She'd quit Canyon the day he'd graduated, a day after he'd proposed. It stunned him. He wanted to know why.

Huntington sidled up to him. "How about it, Sloan, can I put you down for a New Directions committee?"

"Huntington, you can suck up to me for three lifetimes, but Canyon doesn't get a dime." He kept his gaze on Annie James. She reached up to tuck a wisp of hair back into the coil at her nape, and the movement revealed the smooth white underside of her arm. The softness of it made him think of how soft other parts of her would be and started a sliding dip in his belly and groin.

Next to him Huntington shook his head. "She looks good, huh? We all wanted to see that hair down, but you were obsessed."

Will swore a brief, violent expletive.

"An unforgiving attitude, Sloan. Look what I did for you tonight. You had what, two hours here? Did you get her number? Make plans to see her again?"

"I don't think so, Huntington." It sounded stupid and juvenile, even to Will. Who was he kidding? If he hadn't gotten over her in ten years, one evening wasn't going to do the trick.

Huntington shook his blond head. "She's talking to Rothwell, probably joining his committee. She could be finishing the evening talking to you."

"Huntington, I'm trying to keep the homicidal maniac side of my personality in check here."

"I can get her away from him. A word brings her over here." Huntington held out a clipboard with a list of signatures on a sheet labeled, "Canyon New Directions Committee on Admissions." Annie's name was not on the list.

"I won't be on any committee that meets at Canyon."

"Fine."

"Whatever committee I'm on. She has to be on it."

"It can be arranged."

"Arrange it." Will turned and walked away before he did anything else stupid. He headed for the short hallway off the main patio. He hadn't made his revenge speech yet.

He leaned against the wall opposite the door marked "Women," tipped his head back against the stucco surface, and drew a steadying breath. He could count the number of times he'd seen her without a jacket. The lavender dress she wore offered revealing views of her person. From thin straps the neckline dipped in a simple lace-edged V. While Chambers spoke, Will's eyes kept wandering back to that dipping V. He imagined hooking his fingers in those straps and pushing them down over her shoulders. And then telling her how over her he was. That was the plan, right?

When the door opened, he shifted, flattening a palm against each wall, blocking her way. She halted in front of him and squared her shoulders.

"Nice lace."

She blushed instantly, and her response sent a hot flash to his groin.

She recovered quicker than he did. "Do you know why Josh Huntington threw us together tonight?"

"His deep devotion to Canyon."

A look of disgust crossed her face. "Josh doesn't do anything that isn't purely in his own self-interest."

He was glad to hear her say it. At least she wasn't taken in by the guy. His own questions were pressing on him again. "Why did you leave Canyon?"

"Why did you come here tonight?"

He kept his palms flat against each wall. "Are you kidding? New Directions for Canyon? I'm the only guy who doesn't see the place as a holy shrine. You want to hear my idea for Canyon? Sell it to developers, bring in the wrecking ball and the backhoes, and give hundreds of poor kids a full college ride."

"An excellent plan. Hostile, but practical." She tried to slip by him, and he leaned forward, bringing his face within inches of hers.

"Make me less hostile." He reached out a hand and tucked a strand of her hair behind her ear. Her whole body shivered at the touch, and he felt gut-punched. He forced himself to press for the answers he wanted. "Why didn't you answer that letter?"

He caught a puzzled look in her eyes, but the men's room door opened.

"This is not the time or the place for this conversation."

"Come with me. You can explain it."

Voices intruded. Two men stepped into the hallway and halted. Will took his hands from the walls. Deep brown eyes pleaded with him. He took her arm, leading her down the hall.

"You were eighteen," she said in a low voice.

"I knew my mind. You pretended not to know yours."

"You had an amazing college opportunity ahead of you."

"You didn't believe in me. You believed in guys like Moreland, but not in me. You thought I wouldn't make it."

"You had not even begun to live. I was a widow. My husband had been dead barely a year. A year."

"You saw where I lived," he said quietly. "You were afraid to take a chance on a nobody like me."

"I did what I had to do, what I thought was *right*. And look at you. You've done well. Without me. You can't deny it." She slipped out of his hold and headed across the patio.

A smart man would let her go. He decided to be smart.

Chapter Five

At midnight the Santa Ana winds came up, stirring the leaves of the coral trees in the garden of the house Will had bought on top of the Palos Verdes hill. It was about as far from Canyon as one could get and still be on the coast. He had told the real estate agent that he wanted a house you could get lost in, and a view. She had found him a hacienda built in 1929, enlarged over time to its present expansive square footage, descending down the hill through dozens of rooms to lush gardens and a pool-studded lawn. Pure L.A. He had bought it for his mother, but she preferred her Redondo Beach bungalow with the cracked cement patio and cinder block fence.

He opened the French doors off the living room to the warm night, loosened his tie, and dropped into a big leather chair, propping his feet on the matching ottoman. It had been a mistake to go to the Canyon dinner. The comforting aura of his new wealth evaporated. He might as well be eighteen and lying on his mother's sagging, orange-flowered sofa, staring at the stained ceiling liner above his head, and listening to his neighbors quarrel in the next trailer.

Each night after his mom went to work, Will would finish his homework, retrieve his bedding and pillow from the back room, and collapse on the old sofa, its sagging middle supported by a cinder block. Those minutes before exhaustion took him were his time to think about Annie James.

It had not taken long for most of the senior class to know that the new administrative assistant in the admissions office was young and pretty. Her crisp collared shirts, her red hair coiled in a knot at her nape, her tailored jackets, her professional demeanor, didn't stop his classmates from wondering about her. While a half dozen seniors, including Huntington, instantly volunteered to help with campus tours for prospective families, Will had been determined neither to show nor feel any interest in her. His job was just to get through Canyon and get out, and that was hard enough.

Unlike his classmates, he hadn't needed an excuse to linger near her desk. Chambers summoned him so often, for one humiliation or another, that he could see Annie James almost daily if he wanted.

Her desk in the open reception area was next to the bench where boys sat waiting to be summoned by the headmaster.

It took longer for Will's classmates to learn that Annie James was a widow. Huntington was the first one to get hold of that information and share it. The knowledge of it had awakened an unwilling sympathy in Will. His mom had been a widow before she was twenty. His father, little more than a kid himself, had tried to last eight seconds on a bull and failed. The brute's horn had nicked an artery, and his father had bled out in twenty-five seconds. There was a silver rodeo belt buckle on his mom's dresser. She never talked about it, but he had seen her sit and hold it with her eyes closed and then get up and put it back and carry on.

In his mind, Annie James's widowhood separated her from everyone else at Canyon. He dropped his usual surly manner with her, which, he could see now, had been a mistake. As soon as he dropped that barrier between them, he had liked her far too much. And liking her had led to laughing with her, and laughing with her before those meetings with Chambers had somehow reduced Chambers's power over him.

He swore and shoved himself out of the chair. He tried to put himself back in that moment in the Hall of Canyon Men, to see it from her point of view. She denied now that she had lacked faith in him then, but he knew how everyone at Canyon saw him. He was just a boy who could catch footballs, a boy with nothing but himself to rely on, an unpolished nobody, depending on scholarships and unrealized dreams.

He had more experience with women now. He could look back and understand what had happened between them, but the rules hadn't changed. Women cared more about a man's bank account and connections than his character.

Maybe the thing that most fueled his anger was that he had still wanted her after she turned him down.

After his disastrous proposal, he had written to tell her he was prepared to wait for her. If she left Canyon when she claimed, then she had never even seen that letter. He should feel good about that. She had not seen him make a fool of himself, but her leaving Canyon when she did puzzled him. It was a little mystery he could not solve. Her leaving the day of graduation did not suggest the indifference to him that she claimed to feel. What he wanted was an explanation.

Now.

Once he had it, he would say what he needed to say and get his stalled brain working again. He would unlock the past and get on with the future. Beau knew all the hot places to meet women in L.A.—young professionals, would-be movie stars, and even idealistic world-changing activists. When Huntington's committee met, Will would find out why Annie James had left Canyon and why she wasn't married with three kids. That last detail shouldn't matter at all, but somehow it seemed more important than the rest.

* * *

The heat came with the dry desert wind. That was the meteorological explanation, but it seemed to Annie as if it came from her. Some radioactive substance inside her had reached critical mass and set off a chain reaction to heat the whole L.A. basin. Their hands had met, he had put his arm around her waist, his lips had brushed her ear. Three touches so slight ought not to have awakened such desire, but her body hummed with it. Her hair crackled with it.

She moved around her garden, fending off the withering heat with her watering can. The leaves of drooping plants hung lifeless and blackened, curled in on themselves, exposing spindly yellow-green stalks. Her shirt clung to her, chafing the tips of her breasts.

The memory that took hold of her sleepless hours had been of a hot afternoon in late fall when she began to recognize Chambers's pattern of summoning certain boys for talks, the boys on financial aid. Will Sloan's presence in the visitor's chair outside of Chambers's inner sanctum charged the atmosphere of the small space. He was not like the other boys, who made her want to offer them cookies or reminders to tuck in their shirts. Will Sloan seemed more like a combat veteran with PTSD. He jiggled his foot in a tense, angry way that bounced the papers he held in a fisted grip on his knee. She should never have involved herself with him, but he had seemed so alone.

"You need friends," she'd told him when he looked up.

"I scrape their plates in the cafeteria."

"Plates have to be scraped. You don't choose that. Being angry about it you choose."

He had reached over to her desk, picking up a pencil and turning it over in his hand. "And who do you think could be my friend?"

"Mike Moreland. He needs a friend, too."

The name seemed to startle him. He looked up from the pencil. Their gazes held for a moment, and his foot stilled. Then he shrugged and started up again.

"You could come to the newspaper staff meetings."

"I notice you're not offering to be my friend."

"I'm an adult. I work here. It's not the same."

"You're what, twenty-three?"

"Exactly, not someone you can hang out with. Boring, really."

"Ancient, are you? But you and I are not so different."

"Come to the newspaper meetings."

"I'd rather join you to watch the sunset."

The comment had startled her. A week earlier she'd found a spot on campus on top of an old shed that leaned against the hillside. Someone had dragged a bench seat from an old truck on top of that roof, and from that hidden spot she could watch the sunset at the end of the day.

"That's a bad idea," she'd told him.

"It was my spot first."

The memory should make her feel good. She had behaved sensibly and rationally all those years ago. She should not have to defend her actions now. She had meant only to be kind to an outsider, to help him connect with his classmates. The trouble was it had not ended there in that sensible way.

* * *

By Monday afternoon Annie had more control over her memories. Whatever feelings Will Sloan had stirred, she did not have to worry about them because one thing was clear—he still resented the past, hated her even. She was unlikely to see him again.

There was plenty to do at the center. A dozen volunteers had come in to prepare for the annual Labor Day back-to-school festival, and meanwhile, the center had failed to win a grant that was needed to fund their youth program director for the year. Annie worked on flyers and the newsletter, leaving the latter unfinished with a space for a piece on whether they would still have the program director.

When Louisa showed up, she was frustrated from a fruitless attempt to pry Ulysses's records out of the school bureaucracy, and from a futile attempt to find the boy himself. He'd gone missing. She asked Annie to call her contact at Canyon. Josh Huntington was understanding and willing to help. For a price. He'd noticed that Annie had not signed up for any of the committees to help Canyon. Could she serve on the New Directions admissions committee? Annie protested that she really had no connection with Canyon, but Josh reminded her that she was an honorary member of their class and that Ulysses counted as a connection. Annie got the quid pro quo at once, and dutifully took down the time and place of the committee's first meeting. Josh assured her that he would stop by the center's festivities on Saturday and help Ulysses with his application.

Annie turned back to her newsletter to find that Louisa had left her a draft of a letter to potential corporate sponsors. Louisa's note read: *Can you fix it?* The letter reminded Annie of the dozens of phone solicitations she got each month—callers with genuine causes, whose pattern of false cheer, cut-to-the-chase attempts to establish intimacy, pleas for cash, and swift close always left her feeling used. Wasn't there some way to ask for money that did not demean both the asker and the giver?

The problem kept her occupied through the work of the evening until the center officially closed. Annie stayed to putter. She had learned the fine art of puttering from her dad on construction sites. After everyone else had knocked off and headed for supper, her dad would linger, sweeping up a little more, positioning stacks of wood for use the next day, straightening his tools.

Annie liked to think that a little bit of puttering kept a person focused, made her sharper the next day. Great putterers like Marie Curie and Julia Child had changed the world. Maybe Annie would, too. In any case, item one on her to-do list was a great solicitation letter. She sipped a sweet, cinnamon rice-milk drink from a nearby taqueria and began to make notes about the kids and their families. In half an hour she had two pages about Lan, a squirrelly seventh grader, Arianna, a budding artist, and of course, Ulysses. Somehow she would have to make the case that these kids deserved funding.

The noise around her had faded so a small rustling sound from the darkened computer room drew her attention.

She stood in the doorway, wondering if she had imagined the sound. Then it came again. She flicked on the lights and found Ulysses by himself in the corner, his arms around his drawn up knees, his head resting on top of them.

She knelt beside him and put a hand on his shoulder. "What's going on?"

He tilted his head from side to side, mumbling. "Nothing. I'm thinking."

There was a raw scrape on the side of his face. "Louisa missed you today at school."

"I'll tell her I'm sorry." A shudder went through him, and Annie realized he wasn't wearing his glasses. She had never seen him without them.

"Can I stay here tonight?" He didn't lift his head.

Annie held back the answer she was supposed to give. She thought about what she knew of him. He had been coming to the center as long as she had. Usually, he was the one giving help, especially with math. Annie knew he was years ahead of the school curriculum, and he liked helping the younger kids. She had taught him the Dewey decimal system, and at eleven he had taken over reshelving the books in the center's small library. The work had earned him the nickname, "Bookman." The nickname and his dark glasses were his badge. Tall for his age, and rail thin, he always wore the designer dark glasses, rounded triangles of reserve and cool.

In the time she had known him, Ulysses had not asked for help for himself. He lived with his mother in one room of an apartment rented by her brother and his family. His missing father was a Greek merchant marine. Two years earlier his older cousin had been shot on the way home from school.

"What happened to your glasses?"

"I lost them." He pushed himself to his feet, the wall at his back. He wouldn't look at her, but Annie sneaked a peek at his face. His lip was split and a tiny half-moon of dried blood crusted one nostril.

Annie rose slowly. "Lost them, huh?"

Ulysses nodded vigorously, but another shudder ran through him, and his stomach growled. He flicked a glance at her and looked down again.

"Your mom will worry. Want to get something to eat while we figure out what to do?"

He shook his head. "No thanks, Ms. James. I'm not hungry." His stomach made a loud protest.

Annie couldn't help it, she laughed. In a minute Ulysses was laughing, too.

"You know what I think? I think some bully saw you on the way to school with those designer glasses of yours and imagined that you had your pockets full of money. And when he was wrong, he got angry and took your glasses."

His head came up, his eyes big and dark as espresso, and full of knowing.

"They're useless to him, anyhow."

"Did you mention that before or after he hit you?"

His mouth turned up in a slow smile that took over his face. "Bullies don't get irony."

Annie laughed again. At least his sense of humor was intact. "What do you want to do about the lost glasses?"

His grin faded. "Nothing. No money."

"We'll find the money you need."

He shook his head more vigorously. "No. Those glasses cost too much."

Annie started to ask why and stopped. Suddenly she understood the dark glasses. "How nearsighted are you?"

She saw him start to deny it, then stop. "Don't tell anyone."

Annie promised. She would not give away his secret, but she realized she would tell his story. Ulysses's story was just what Louisa's letter needed.

Later, on their way to the mall, Ulysses explained. "Geeks wear glasses, Ms. James. The Bookman is an intellectual. An intellectual wears *shades*." Annie vowed to get him his shades and get him out of a school where bullies ruled, no matter how many committees Josh Huntington wanted her to join.

* * *

On Thursday Annie skipped lunch and left work early, headed for the Century City law offices of Bird, Bartling, and Hines. A sleek L.A. exterior of gray-tinted glass and bands of salmon granite gave way to a Boston interior of print-lined paneled walls, fine moldings, thick carpets, and deep-cushioned leather chairs. Each committee member's place at the long conference table was set with a pristine notepad, a fat, heavy pen bearing the firm's name and logo, a copy of the agenda, and a paper tent proclaiming the participant's name.

There was no sign of Josh, and the only other woman present was arranging fruit, cheese, and bottled waters on a sideboard. The next time Annie looked up, she was gone. The male committee members entered the room, talking, indifferent to who might hear, shedding coats and ties, draping them over the backs of their chairs, staking territory. The younger ones slid their thumbs over their phones, or sent a quick text. Annie took a deep breath. She felt comfortably invisible and realized she'd grown used to invisibility outside of her own close circle of friends and neighbors. She slipped out of her linen jacket and hung it over her chair.

Then the head of the committee arrived. He was the nice man she'd talked to at the Dunes Club, Ned Rothwell, but he looked worried and preoccupied. He told her he hoped he could call on her for fresh thinking about the school. Annie smiled and agreed to do her best.

It would be a matter of days before Ulysses was accepted to Canyon or not. Josh had personally checked the boy's application and taken it to the admissions office. Once Ulysses was in, Annie figured she'd be free to withdraw from the committee. She studied the printed agenda in front of her.

When she looked up, Will Sloan had turned from the windows at the far end of the table. With his dark hair and fierce expression, he looked like a dangerous intruder the fair-haired boys had caught. They were keeping their distance from him. His gaze took in every detail of her appearance as if he'd never seen a silk shirt before. Under his pointed regard she was no longer invisible. What had seemed sensible business attire now felt overly revealing. Her temperature spiked beyond the power of air-conditioning to cool her. She was grateful when Ned Rothwell called the meeting to order and began the usual meeting rituals of self-introductions and opening remarks.

Will studied the documents in front of him as the chair droned on. He had not missed the man's personal welcome of Annie James. The other men glanced at their phones or fiddled with their pens.

Eventually, the chairman wound down, his voice losing energy. He paused, and as the pause lengthened, the fiddling stopped and people looked his way.

"I regret to tell you that what I'm going to say now must remain in this room."

All the thumbs idly stroking phones and all the fingers flipping pens stopped.

Rothwell cleared his throat. "Canyon has defaulted on a loan payment."

He couldn't have stunned them more. The room erupted with questions about the size of the loan, the name of the bondholder, the current revenues of the school.

Annie's reporter instincts immediately kicked in. The chairman was telling them very little. The basics she understood at once. With the financial crisis, the school's endowment fund had lost much of its value at a time when major renovations were underway. So they had borrowed heavily. Meanwhile, tuition revenues had shrunk.

Rothwell wiped his hand over his face. "Canyon is about to celebrate its hundredth anniversary. We can't just let it die."

One of the other committee members pointed out the enrollment figure in the report in front of them. To Annie it seemed that Canyon had the same number of students she remembered from her year there. There was something more to the story. She could see that Will Sloan thought so, too.

Across from Annie Will Sloan's voice was quiet but clear. "So we're being asked to bail dear old Canyon out? To the tune of what?"

Rothwell glared at him and called for a break. "The board has made no decisions, and I don't need to remind you that this matter is strictly confidential. Any leak to the press would be disastrous for Canyon's future."

* * *

When Annie returned to the committee room, Will Sloan stood at her place, looking over the questions she'd noted.

"Excuse me, those are my notes."

"There's a story here, don't you think?"

"I'm sure there is." She turned over the steno pad with her jottings, most of them questions. The chairman's news had shocked her. Canyon had seemed a place far removed from money problems. The South Bay Neighborhood Center felt a perpetual financial pinch, a need to husband its resources to keep the doors open. Canyon was the place of manicured lawns, up-to-date technology, and catered functions.

"What inducements did Josh Huntington have to offer to get you to join this committee?" She looked away. So Huntington *had* offered something. "Did he tell you I would be on it?"

"No, but apparently you knew I would be here."

He nodded.

She looked down. "You don't have any desire to help Canyon, do you?"

"No more than you. What does Canyon mean to you? A place you worked once, ten years ago?"

"I have no interest in the past."

He quirked a brow.

"But unlike you, I would like Canyon to continue in the present."

"Don't worry then." He glanced around. "These guys see the place as a holy shrine."

"Surely some of them also see it as a business."

"I'm the only one who will ask rude questions—like where did the money go? If you really want Canyon to keep going, you'd better be willing to work with me, not Rothwell."

In the end he volunteered them for the last task on the committee's list, looking at enrollment prospects. They had taken no steps to address the loan default issue. Rothwell reminded them that all financial information about Canyon was confidential. Then everyone was up and moving, closing laptops, opening cell phones, making plans.

Will was at Annie's side before Rothwell could get to her. The silk shirt she was wearing offered revealing views of her person and a lacy undergarment with thin straps. He seemed to be in a stuck place in her presence. He had once again devoted a good bit of mental energy to following the dipping scalloped line of her lace and thinking about hooking his fingers into those straps and pushing them down over her shoulders. The movement of putting on her jacket pulled the silk taut across her breasts, and it occurred to him that if he slept with her even once, he could lay all his frustration with Canyon to rest.

He wasn't quite ready for her first question.

"Do you think Josh knows that Canyon is in trouble?"

"You think Canyon's in trouble?"

"There's more to this than one default on a payment."

He nodded. She was right. He would have to look into it. Maybe Canyon was about to go belly-up. It was an astonishing thought. Too-big-to-fail banks had gone down, maybe too-arrogant-to-fail prep schools could fold as well.

When she was safely buttoned into her jacket again, he asked, "When do you want to meet?"

She leaned toward him and whispered. "Never."

"Great! I am very interested in Canyon's future, and I look forward to working closely with you to secure it." He made himself heard by several departing members of the committee.

She glared at him and slipped a small caramel-colored leather purse over her shoulder. "Let me give you my email address. I'm sure we can work most effectively online." She scribbled an address on the edge of her pad and tore off the piece of paper.

Chapter Six

Will waited two days before he called her, rushing through the civilities so she wouldn't hang up on him. He'd managed to find out a lot about her in those two days. "How long have you lived at the beach?" No use hiding the fact that he'd found her.

"A while now." She didn't hang up. That was a plus. He liked the sound of her voice on the phone. "Any objection?"

"I didn't picture you living the beach life. Somehow I thought you'd be married with three kids and living in Glendale."

"Not me. Flavor of the month, that's the way we do things at the beach. Did you want to talk about Canyon?"

"Could we meet some night this week?"

"Not this week."

No hesitation on that one. He was surprised at how keen his disappointment was. "You're all tied up?" Not that he believed her "flavor of the month" comment, but he could imagine her with the man from the Canyon party at the Dunes Club.

"Actually, I volunteer at a local community center."

"Every night? Aren't you curious about what's going on at Canyon?"

There was a long pause. "Did you find something out?"

"What's the name of this center?" He was not going to give away Canyon's dirty little secret over the phone.

"Listen, I'm sure you're not interested. Email me. I promise I'll get right back to you."

"You're sure you don't want to know what the story is about Canyon?"

"I can wait."

But I can't.

* * *

The South Bay Neighborhood Center was a converted retail space, made to look homey with thrift shop furnishings and children's artwork. In the main room kids worked at homework around six long tables. A tall skinny kid with designer dark glasses was the only one who looked up when Will entered.

Annie James, her fiery hair confined in a casual knot, had her head bent over an open book next to a skinny brown Asian kid. Annie kept her finger on the page where the wiggly kid was obviously supposed to be reading.

"This is dumb." He spun his pencil end over end between his forefingers. Will could see a blank sheet of binder paper next to him.

"You can do it."

The kid straightened in his seat, and looked at the book again, his brow furrowed. "This is too hard."

"Not for you."

Annie was the only adult visible, and she had to be concentrating pretty hard on the kid next to her to ignore the rising level of conversation coming from some teenagers in an adjoining room full of computers. The pencil flipped from the kid's fingers and flew across the table.

From the other side of the table his buddies laughed.

Annie shot one of them a glance, and the kid rolled the pencil back across the table. The first kid snatched it up.

"I can't do this."

Annie tapped the page with her finger. "Read that line."

The kid read one word at a time, fidgeting in his chair with the effort.

Annie high-fived him when he came to the end.

Will watched as she coaxed the kid with questions and patient silence until his face cleared. Again Annie put up her hand for a high-five salute, and the kid slapped it hard. Then he bent over his paper and began to write.

"Nice work, Ms. James."

She twisted in her chair to look at him, and he surveyed her openly. He'd never seen her dressed in such vivid color. A snug knit top in lime green hugged her breasts, and a short froth of a leaf-printed skirt showed off her legs. Her toes peeked out of green slides. The kids around her fell silent, not even moving in their chairs.

"Is he your boyfriend?" asked the kid she'd been helping.

"No." Annie rose from her chair.

"Why not?" A dark-eyed girl swept an approving glance over him, and Will worked hard not to grin.

"What are you doing here?" Annie demanded. Her gaze locked with his.

"Nice color." He wondered where the smoke alarms were. It wouldn't do to set them off.

She glanced down at herself. "Not mine. I traded…"

He swallowed. "It looks like you could use some help." He nodded toward the computer room, where the noise indicated that things were getting out of hand. "I'm good with computers."

"Fine. Help." She waved a hand in the general direction of the noise, and he headed for the group of chatting teens.

* * *

Annie noticed the change in the computer room almost at once. The loud, laughter-punctuated flirting had stopped. She could see kids bent over the keyboards, looking at the screens. She relaxed as a tension she hadn't realized she was feeling eased from her shoulders, and she concentrated on the kids at her table.

When Louisa returned from her grant presentation, Annie was supervising the kids' cleanup. "Any luck?"

"Some. The Milagro Foundation is going to help us get five new computers. They won't pay for a program director, but the computers will help." Louisa dumped her bag of papers on her desk and slipped out of Annie's heels. Louisa's fashion sensibility was the opposite of Annie's. While Annie chose neutrals, Louisa chose color, fuchsia, tangerine, or lime, the more the better. Annie loved crisp tailored clothes; Louisa loved everything that draped and flowed. Louisa had explained it to her once. They regularly traded clothes when Louisa had to make presentations to corporations. "I can't believe you wear clothes like this every day."

Annie shrugged. Her red hair always made her feel that she had plenty of color. They traded shoes. "Louisa, that's great news, really. We'll keep working on the rest of it."

"I know. It's just such a drag, always being the one to ask…" Louisa broke off and Annie followed her gaze. Will Sloan was coming straight toward them. Annie hadn't really looked at him yet, but Louisa was giving him a complete once-over. A charcoal gray T-shirt with some tech company's logo in black stretched across his chest and shoulders above khakis and lug-soled shoes.

Louisa glanced at Annie, whose tongue didn't work, and back to Will. "*Who* are you?"

"Will Sloan. I'm on the Canyon New Directions committee with Annie. We've been trying to find a time to meet. Hope you don't mind my stopping by."

Louisa stuck out her hand.

"I'm going to put away the chairs," Annie said.

Louisa looked at her as if she'd lost her mind. She turned to Will. "Want to see the center?"

Annie got the chairs folded and stored and saw the students out the door with their backpacks and the weekly newsletter with its notices about upcoming events. Her autopilot seemed to be working. She could hear Louisa explaining the center to Will and had a cowardly impulse to slip out while they were talking. But she was still in Louisa's clothes.

Ulysses stopped her as he was leaving. "Are you okay, Ms. James?"

Annie nodded.

"This guy won't hurt you?"

Annie shook her head. Will did look dangerous, but he wasn't scaring Louisa, who led him back to the cluttered little office and called to Annie. "Ready to trade clothes?"

In the tiny staff restroom Louisa shed Annie's gray suit in a flash. "Does he want what I think he wants?"

Annie slipped out of Louisa's skirt. Louisa sounded like Tess Biddle. "What?"

"My guess? To rip your clothes off."

"It's not like that exactly. He's pretty hostile where I'm concerned."

"Hostile? That man wants you. Let him drive you home."

"That would be a very bad idea."

* * *

Outside the center the light was fading in the sky, the neon of dozens of signs flaring into their pulsing night brilliance. The Santa Ana winds had died, and cool ocean air flowed up from the beach.

Will had grown up in a neighborhood like this one, just off the coast highway. He was grateful for the familiar noise, neon, and fumes. He needed them to get a grip on himself. Watching her work with that kid brought too much back. He didn't love her. He was over thinking he ever had. She was just some drug he couldn't get out of his system. But her friend Louisa had given him an idea of how he could get what he wanted and be over her for good. It could be a simple bargain, a favor for a favor.

"My truck's just up the block. Can I take you home?"

"Thanks, I've got my own ride." She rummaged in her purse.

"Don't you want to know what I found out about Canyon?" That stopped her. She gave him a wary look.

"Walk me to my truck." He nodded to the right up the hill. She started walking.

"Louisa says the center has major funding problems."

"We do." She kept her gaze on the sidewalk.

"I know someone who could give the center a sizable donation."

She immediately glanced his way. "Don't joke."

"I'm not. I could call this guy tomorrow. The center could have whatever it needs by Monday."

"You would do that? Make that call? Why?"

"I'll make the call, if you'll do something for me. Here's my truck."

She stopped, her puzzled gaze taking in nearly three tons of sleek black metal. She looked more uneasy than impressed, and he suppressed a smile. His mom called it the devil's own truck. He shifted slightly so that he had her between him and the truck.

"Are you sure I can't give you a ride home?" He flicked the key with his thumb, and the door locks shot up. She flinched.

"No thanks. My own truck is just…"

"Fine. Let me walk you."

She hesitated.

"Chicken?"

She shook her head.

He leaned forward, putting his hands against the truck, one on either side of her, backing her up against the black metal. She leaned back, and her breasts arched up to him.

"So tell me, are you sleeping with anybody?"

"You don't get to ask that question."

"You mean there isn't a 'flavor of the month'?"

The trouble with Annie James's eyes was that they were full of expression. Right now in quick succession like the flash of movie trailer images, he saw shock, hurt, and maybe defiance. She turned her head away.

Across the street at the corner, a city bus pulled up, rocked to stop, and let out four people. She seemed transfixed by the scene.

Will watched the passengers hurry off into the night, ordinary people coming to the end of their commute, heading for dinner and family. The bus pulled away before she spoke.

"He's an accountant."

He had expected her to deny that she had a lover. He had to clear a sudden lump in his throat. "So is it a regular thing between you and the accountant, every Saturday night, or Tuesdays, or…"

"No." The word sort of wobbled out of her. Honesty was the woman's great weakness.

He shook his head, dipping closer. "So sleep with me. Tonight."

Her face changed, and she shoved him, her hands on his chest through the thin cotton of his T-shirt. He didn't budge. He wanted more. She hit him, punching his ribs. He only pressed closer, nullifying the force of her blows, filling his head with the scent of her. She dropped her hands and turned her face away from him.

"Let me go."

"Where's that beach attitude?"

She let out a long exhalation. "I don't want to sleep with you."

"Yes, you do. Do you want me to show you how I know?" His gaze dropped to her breasts, and she stiffened, drawing a ragged breath that sent a tremor through him.

"Whatever my misguided hormones are suggesting, my brain still works. I don't want what you want."

"Funding for the center?"

"Revenge." She turned her face back to him, and he shoved back a little, so they were eye to eye.

"Revenge?" He hadn't expected her to see through him.

"That's what you're after. I don't blame you, but I…"

"What? You weren't part of Chambers's little games, were you?"

"I didn't stand up to him."

"Do you think you could have?" He couldn't fault her for not acting. He didn't think any other adults at Canyon had known what

Chambers was up to when he called financial aid students to his office. Maybe the groundskeeper had some idea because he had to supervise their work, but he was almost as powerless as the boys themselves.

"I knew Chambers made you unhappy."

"Why did you leave Canyon?"

"I couldn't work for Chambers any longer."

"Your timing was interesting. You left the day after I asked you to marry me."

"We made a deal."

She said it so quietly he almost missed the words in the roar of the traffic.

"You and Chambers? What kind of a deal?"

Her gaze faltered, and she drew her bag up, hugging it to her chest. "You don't even like me."

He wanted to shake her. *What kind of a deal?* He had believed her to be on his side. If she made a deal with Chambers, he couldn't love her, couldn't like her even.

"Listen. You admit you feel this thing between us. You don't work at Canyon. I'm not a boy. There's no reason for us not to hook up. Consenting adults, the twenty-first century way." He spoke to her left cheek and ear. He pressed her against the truck with his body and brought his face close to hers. He wasn't going to kiss her. He pressed closer, his hips brushing against hers, and once he'd begun, he couldn't stop, he cocked his hips upward. Her breath caught in little exhalations, in rhythm with the strokes of his body, and her eyes went dark with longing. It was crazy, but he couldn't stop. He slid his hands up her sides, cupping her face and turning her mouth to his. He intended the most carnal joining, his mouth open, his tongue intent on entry, but at her first yielding he tasted cinnamon sweetness on her lips.

Something clenched in his chest, and the kiss changed. He was kissing her like he'd always wanted to, like he meant it, like he loved her, which he didn't. He was clear on that.

He broke away. The rasp of their breathing filled his ears. She hadn't touched him except to push him away, and his body was mad for her touch.

She turned to go, her bag still clutched to her chest.

"Wait." He didn't like the neighborhood after all. "Let me see you to your car."

"Thanks. My truck is right there. I'll be okay."

He didn't know whether that shaky *okay* was about the neighborhood or about what had passed between them. He watched her cross the side street and climb into a battered white truck as if it were a place of refuge. It couldn't be the one she'd had ten years earlier, but it looked the same. He meant to move on, to end his stupid attachment to the past. She was not the woman he thought she was. She had made a deal with Chambers. She was sleeping with another man, an accountant, giving him the love she'd denied Will.

He heard the truck engine turn over and watched her drive away. He knew he should shake off the feeling of being let down. She had told him plainly that the past was past. He should meet Beau and his friends at their favorite club, but he stood on the curb staring at the emptiness of the bus stop with its bench and kiosk.

It struck him as odd that she had identified her lover by his profession. Then he understood. On the bench was the face of Harry Ralston, C.P.A. Ralston looked about forty with a TV anchorman's good looks. His ad promised help even if you hadn't paid taxes in years. Staring at Ralston's white-toothed grin, he realized that Annie James had been a little less honest with him than she'd pretended. The bus had pulled away, and she'd been staring at Ralston when she'd announced she had an accountant lover.

Will was on the highway heading south away from Beau's club before he remembered that he had not told her what he'd learned about Canyon's financial troubles.

* * *

Annie found herself in her entry without knowing how she came to be there. He had asked her to marry him in the Hall of Canyon Men. She had been there to set up seating for a pre-graduation event. He'd found her and whirled her around in an exuberant embrace.

The night before they had been in the ER together for hours. A call had come from the hospital that his mother had been taken there after being hit by a car in a crosswalk on the Coast Highway. Annie had found Will unloading rented white folding chairs for the upcoming graduation ceremony. She had driven him to the hospital and stayed with him through the night. In the morning, she had helped him get his mother home to their trailer. She'd never realized before where he lived.

In the Hall he'd released her from his arms and explained that everything was suddenly right. He had received a letter promising him a paid summer internship. He was going to be free of Canyon, free of Chambers. He would have money. He helped her place the reserved seating cards on the chairs, and all that he hoped to do, all that he could see happening in his bright future, spilled out of him. It would start with the summer internship with a Silicon Valley firm. He had no doubt he'd soon be on his way to a brilliant career. He asked her to leave Canyon and marry him.

Annie had declined his mad proposal. She was sure that the unexpected intimacy of the night before had sparked that wild idea. He had almost lost his mother, and Annie had been there. He was full of the exuberance of the moment. His confidence, his certainty of the future seemed reckless to her. She could not believe he could be so sure of his feelings, but he told her his father had married at eighteen. The one thing that kept her strong in the face of his bitter disappointment was her knowledge that young men with bright futures could vanish from life in an eye blink.

When her husband of eight months was killed on a rain-slick northern California freeway, he had been driving her compact. He'd left her his name, a modest life insurance policy, and his truck. Her parents, Doug and Grace Palmer, and her three older sisters, Megan, Meredith, and Melanie, had been prepared to receive the grief-stricken widow back into the bosom of her family. After all no one expected Annie to manage on her own.

But she had. She had loaded all her belongings into her dead husband's truck, collected his life insurance policy, and headed for L.A. She had believed she was doing fine until Will Sloan made his mad proposal.

The following day Will had been accused of burning down the school sign, and Chambers had threatened to take everything from him—his diploma, his college acceptance, his scholarship, and internship. It had been in the power of that controlling old man to take it all away from the boy he had not been able to bend to his will. So Annie had made a deal with Chambers and left.

Apparently Will had not made a perfect recovery from the blow to his pride, but she believed it to be that and no more. He was obviously confident and successful in his work.

He undoubtedly had much more experience with women now, more experience than she had with men. She had not heard from him once since they'd parted.

They were both a little surprised at seeing each other again. No doubt the chemistry was there, but if she held onto her common sense and judgment she could let him go again. Their paths had diverged so much, there was really no way they were going to connect.

Only at the moment things remained a little heated. His kiss was like a small brush fire in the hills that firefighters quickly control but that bears watching lest some hot spot flare up at the first breeze and consume a subdivision. Harry Ralston's face on a bus bench had saved her temporarily, but she'd be in trouble if she had another encounter with Will Sloan soon.

She wandered into the kitchen. The light blinked on her answering machine, and she pushed the message button.

Annie, it's Mom. We haven't heard from you about Luna de Miel. It's what your father wants. Put it on your calendar. And don't worry about a date, dear, the girls can arrange something for you. I think Meredith has someone all lined up.

—Wednesday, 8:17 p.m.

Chapter Seven

"Where were you last night?" Beau leaned against Will's desk.

Will kept his head down. "Sorry I didn't make it to the club. Meet anybody?"

"Yeah. A runner, real pretty."

"Great. Listen. I want to make a donation to this place." He handed Beau the name and address on a piece of paper. "But I want it to look like it comes from Z-Text. Can you write a cover letter? You know, Z-Text Technology Partners prides itself on offering equal opportunities to all the youth of L.A. We're happy to support…whatever?"

Beau studied the paper. "I thought we agreed to talk over any donations you made."

"This isn't exactly a donation. Call it an investment."

Beau looked at the scrap of paper in his hand. "Where is this place? Who are the people? How are you connected here?"

Will grinned. *Thank God for Beau.* They had been together from the first hot days of college football practice. From his New Orleans bred mama Beau inherited his manners, and from his father, the judge in Bakersfield, a first-rate crap-detector. Both had kept Will from the pitfalls of sudden wealth more than once. Among other things Beau had handled Will's "cousins."

There had been a parade of them ever since Will had sold Z-Text, Stetson-wearing sons of Texas, eager to claim their kinship with Will for the first time in his twenty-eight years. At first he'd been flattered. He had taken each cousin to dinner with his mom. Maybe he'd hoped to hear something about the father he'd never known, but the conversation had always turned to money. Did he want to invest in a car dealership or an oil well or a few head of cattle, just to help the family out? It was always a sure-fire deal. *Yer daddy would do it in a lick.* According to his mom, his daddy would have kicked the drawling deadbeats all the way back to Texas.

Annie James was nothing like any of them.

"I want to get laid."

Beau's mouth opened and closed. "I think we could just open the office door here and ask for volunteers."

"I don't want to get involved, just laid." He handed Beau the check he'd written to Z-Text to cover the donation.

Beau glanced at it and whistled. "This is like a prenup figure or a paternity suit settlement."

"I'm good for it."

"So, there's someone particular that you want to get laid by."

Will nodded. *Accept no substitute.* That was one of Beau's lines whether they were looking for clothes or cars, investments or women.

Beau settled in one of the office chairs, apparently at ease, but Will was not fooled. He knew his friend was watching him closely. "Then we really should talk prenup. Who is she?"

"Somebody I used to know."

"Now that you've got the bucks, she shows up again?"

"Actually, she has no idea about Z-Text, and I'd like to keep it that way."

"You don't buy that, do you?"

"Yeah."

"So what's she got that inspires this?" Beau waved the check in the air.

* * *

Fifty people showed up at the center to celebrate Ulysses's admission to Canyon. A banner across the study area proclaimed congratulations in several languages. A radio blasted lively music, and the older kids danced while the younger ones inhaled punch and cookies. Everyone seemed to be laughing.

Ulysses's mom beamed at him and hugged Annie, thanking her for helping him with the application. Ulysses showed her his admission letter with a handwritten note from Josh Huntington saying he would see Ulysses at school. Annie explained that there would be placement tests the next day and then scheduling.

Later, Ulysses's mom expressed a small worry to Louisa. She spread out a map and opened a transit agency pamphlet. With her finger she traced the route. With perfect connections Ulysses would spend two hours going each way. Annie thought of the homework he would have and the time he'd spend away from his friends and family. It seemed too much.

"I'll take him. I go right up the 405 from here, and Canyon's less than a mile west of my exit."

Louisa pulled her aside to thank her, and handed her an open envelope. "Look at this."

Annie glanced at the return address, Z-Text Technology Partners. "Did you make a presentation to this company?"

Louisa shook her head. She was in a long flowing purple skirt and matching T-shirt with purple butterfly clips in her brown curls and purple polish on her nails.

Annie opened the slit made by the letter opener and pulled out the paper inside. Nestled in its folds was a check to the center for two hundred and fifty thousand dollars. Annie gasped. It couldn't be Will Sloan's work.

"Is it real?" Annie held it up to the light.

Louisa just grinned. "Oh, it's real. I Internet searched this Z-Text right away."

"But you didn't make them a grant pitch?"

"Nope. You know what I think?"

Annie shook her head.

"I think your guy, Will Sloan, did this."

"Oh no." Annie looked at the letterhead as if there were some clue there. The name at the bottom of the brief letter was Beau Lassiter, Vice President.

"Remember, Annie, the guy asked me all about our funding. He asked me what we needed. So I just gave him my spiel. And I think he was wearing a T-shirt with this Z-Text logo or something."

"Oh." He had been wearing a charcoal-colored T-shirt with a logo. Annie had hardly paid attention to the lettering.

"So, can you call him? We should thank him."

"Don't we just write this Beau Lassiter person and acknowledge the gift?"

Louisa took the letter from Annie's hand and shook it at her. "Annie, how long have you been here? Has anyone ever given the center a gift like this? We could practically buy the building. We should rename the place the Sloan Center."

"But we don't know that he's behind this generosity." Will Sloan had not been feeling the least bit generous when she'd seen him last.

"So," insisted Louisa, "call him. See what he says. Ask him who we should thank."

"*Whom* we should thank."

* * *

Annie tucked herself in the center's tiny office while the party continued in the main room. Better to call from the center and keep the conversation businesslike, or better yet, leave a message. When she tried his work number and got Z-Text Technology Partners, her stomach took a sudden dip. She asked for him, not sure the person at the other end could even hear her voice. Then he answered. She managed to say her name and exchange greetings.

"The center received a substantial donation yesterday." With her free hand, she brought up a search engine on Louisa's computer, and typed Z-Text into the search box. The spinning rainbow went to work on the old machine.

"That's good news, isn't it?"

"Louisa suspects that you had something to do with the gift."

"Do you think so?"

"Finding you at this number rather confirms it." On the screen in front of her, the search results finally came up. She tapped a likely article on the sale of Z-Text, and scanned the lead paragraph.

"I made a phone call. I told you I would."

"You can't think that because...because of this gift... I..." In front of her on the screen was his name as one of the founding partners of Z-Text and the astonishing sum for which the company had been sold not six months earlier.

"Annie, you there?"

"Hmmm."

"We didn't make that deal, did we? Unless I missed something."

Relief and disappointment coursed through her. "Everyone at the center is astonished at the generosity and very grateful."

"Are you grateful?"

"Not that grateful."

"But grateful enough to meet with me again. I didn't get a chance to tell you what I found out."

And why was that? "You can tell me now if you like."

"We could meet in a public place. Whatever lustful intentions I have, I can't undress you in public."

Annie hung up. The phone rang immediately. She let it ring, until the center's answering machine picked up.

His voice came on after the beep. "Do you really want to record what I might say?"

Annie snatched up the phone. "I don't want to have sex with you."

"Then why did you kiss me back? I've been thinking about that kiss for four days now. There's no accountant lover, is there?"

"You hate me, remember?"

"What about meeting at the library? We can't have sex in a library."

* * *

Josh watched the morning lineup of SUVs and luxury sedans make the loop of Canyon's driveway, parents or drivers dropping off boys too young to drive themselves or too uncool for an upperclassman's carpool. As the cars inched up the drive, he realized Dunsmore was missing an opportunity. A centennial campaign banner should be hanging between the pair of old jacaranda trees at the entrance. Parents would spend the first ten minutes of the day thinking about giving to Canyon.

That was more than he could say for his class. The numbers he'd looked at so far indicated that the class of '05 had pledged a meager five grand to their dear old alma mater. Five grand wasn't going to impress his father or get his trust back. He had already put his condo in Malibu up for rent and made plans to move into one half of his South Bay duplex. The place needed a little work before it was livable.

It wouldn't be so bad if he could get a tenant for the north unit. Then he could pay for fixing up his half. He calculated in his head, at least a sound system, some serious appliances, and new carpets. Then the old bath would have to be gutted and redone. He shoved his hands in his pockets. He'd promised Annie James that he'd meet Ulysses for the boy's first day at Canyon. It was the smart thing to do. He wanted Annie to owe him. She was the only hope he had of talking Sloan into a substantial donation. Alone, Sloan could make their class look good.

It was going to be hot again. The long, fernlike leaves of jacarandas drooped in the warm air. The mist rising from the automatic sprinklers offered only a fleeting sensation of coolness before it dried instantly against his skin. Maybe living in the South Bay wouldn't be so bad.

When the rumble of Annie James's battered white truck interrupted his thoughts, he waved a greeting and ambled down the path to the curb. Now that she was going to drive Ulysses to school, mornings offered Josh the perfect opportunity to keep track of how things were going between her and Sloan.

Her turn came, and she pulled up to the drop-off point. Josh stepped up to the truck and thumped his palms against the open edge of the passenger window. Ulysses scrambled down, dragging a deflated backpack behind him. The kid's hair was geeky, but the dark glasses were indisputably cool.

"Whaddup?" Josh offered the boy the latest Canyon handshake, giving him time to catch on to the moves.

"Good morning, Mr. Huntington."

"Whoa! You wound me, Ulysses. Just Josh."

He shut the truck door and leaned through the open window. "Hi."

"Josh, thanks." Annie James smiled, and suddenly in the warm, stale exhaust-filled air, there was this fresh space. Her smile was sincere. Josh knew. He did not see sincerity often. He did not imagine that she had any illusions about him. He'd make a play for her himself if he didn't need a fat check from Sloan.

He gave Ulysses a quick glance, telling himself to refocus. "How's your Canyon committee going? You're working with Sloan, right?"

Color bloomed in her cheeks, and her gaze evaded his. "We're meeting later this week."

Josh kept Ulysses in his peripheral vision. Everything about the kid checked out. He was legal. He had a Greek surname that came out of the ranks of shipping magnates and international playboys. He was looking around with innate cool, eyes concealed by the dark glasses. He wasn't making any dumb moves. "Listen, Annie, when you see Sloan, could you do me a favor?"

"That depends."

"He's got a great place up in Palos Verdes, and I want him to host a small reunion event for our class. Will you ask him to think about it?"

She gave him a brief incredulous glance, but then she smiled. "Sure."

He thumped the car again and stepped back, taking Ulysses by the shoulders. "Okay. Let me get this guy where he needs to go."

She shifted her truck into gear and waved.

"Later," he called. *Damn.* Sloan had better be making something of this opportunity.

The truck pulled away, and Josh turned Ulysses toward the school. From under the brown arches Chambers stared out his office window at Annie James's truck. *Jeez, not Chambers, too!* Chambers was unmarried, but hardly celibate. The guy was probably doing his new secretary, just like the old one when Josh was at Canyon. Maybe old Chambers still had it in him or maybe he was into recreational Viagra. Chambers caught Josh's gaze, and the blinds flicked closed.

Josh turned to Ulysses. The boy was wiping his glasses on his sleeve, but he hadn't missed a thing. Josh was looking straight into the most knowing eyes he'd ever seen on a kid. Ulysses slipped the glasses back on, and Josh deliberately set an unhurried pace, no need to show Ulysses how to keep it cool. The boy gave him one final assessing glance and fell in with his steps. The kid might make it. He had Sloan's intelligence, but without the anger.

Chapter Eight

Ulysses's green and black backpack hit the floor of Annie's truck with a thunk. The backpack got heavier by the day. He swung himself up into the seat after it. "Hi!"

"Hi yourself. Good day?"

"Yeah." He waved to a blond boy standing on the steps, nothing much, just a lift of his thin brown hand that the other boy acknowledged with an abbreviated nod.

"A friend?"

"Tyler. He's in Dr. Archer's history class."

"How is that class?" Except for his math class, which was some pre-calculus honors group, he was taking the usual ninth grade courses.

Ulysses gingerly jammed the hot metal seat belt fitting into its slot. Annie still hadn't fixed the truck's air-conditioning. "Dr. Archer...speaks...slowly...but...he's...not...boring." Ulysses cracked himself up with the imitation.

Annie negotiated a left turn onto the boulevard. Ulysses's pleasure was palpable. He went on describing his new favorite teacher's style.

"You know how you hold a compass, and the needle sort of quivers before it points north?"

Annie nodded.

"Dr. Archer's questions are like that, like a compass. It's like you're always going somewhere in class, and you can always tell where you are, even if fourteen people have said something."

Annie smiled. She was learning another function of Ulysses's dark glasses, to let him observe people more closely than they thought they were being observed. The new pair they'd bought him out of center funds was working just like the old pair. Ulysses caught on to the character of adults faster than any kid she'd ever met. Except maybe Josh Huntington, who had been born old.

"You always get somewhere in that class. It's like walking up hill. You're watching your feet, not thinking about the top, and suddenly you're there, and there's this view. You see things. It's a good class."

"And Tyler's in this class?"

"Yeah." Annie could feel Ulysses close up, snap shut, cautious about the new friend.

"What else about the day?"

"No girls." He made a face. "Same as yesterday. It's weird. They're useless, but you notice when they're gone."

"Useless! Excuse me, a girl is driving your lucky rear end to and from this exalted institution every day."

He looked at her. "You are a woman, not a girl. It's different."

"Oh. So you will adjust to the no-girls thing?"

"Josh says there's a way to see girls. You just join this singing group, the C-Notes, that goes to other schools. Josh says that seeing girls is one of the 'perks' of joining the group."

Perks, a Josh word if ever there were one. Of course, Josh would weigh the *perks* of an activity, not the activity itself. She tried to think of a way to explain how Ulysses should be cautious around Josh.

While she was thinking, Ulysses began to sing. He sang the refrain from "You've Lost that Lovin' Feeling" in a smooth low tenor that would probably deepen into a sexy baritone as he matured. She realized that he liked to sing. In the truck he generally found a Spanish station and sang along with Alejandro Fernandez or Luis Miguel. He'd be perfect for a boys' a capella group.

"Are you thinking of trying out for this group?"

"Yeah. Josh says he'll get me a tryout next week."

"Great!" Ulysses liked his classes, he was cautiously making a friend; and he wanted to try out for an activity. She inched the truck onto the metered on-ramp of the 405. As her truck's clutch shuddered into gear, she remembered the favor Josh Huntington had asked of her and knew he would ask another. *Perks and favors, the Josh Huntington mode of operation.* She hoped Ulysses would not be learning that.

* * *

Meeting Annie James in her town's public library had a disadvantage Will had not anticipated. For a smart guy, he could be really dumb. The two desk clerks, the white-haired librarian, and three readers lounging on couches in the periodical section greeted her before they headed for a table in the conversation area. He cocked his head toward one of the tables. When she didn't move, he nudged her with a hand at the small of her back.

He sat beside her and leaned close, speaking into her ear and catching her scent. "Does everybody in this place know you?"

"I work the used book sale every month."

"Do you do anything for you?"

"For me?"

"You seem to be volunteer-in-chief around here. I just wonder what you do for yourself." He'd unsettled her just a bit, but she recovered fast.

"I thought we were here to talk about Canyon."

He pulled out his phone and opened his notes. "Should I make a public announcement that I'm not going to undress you here?"

She shivered once, but when she spoke, her voice was steady and cool. "Probably not necessary." She pulled out her own notes in pencil on a spiral steno pad.

Of course, they weren't going to have sex in the library. The goal was to get her somewhere where he could have her to himself and taste her mouth and hear that funny catch in her breathing again and make her admit she wanted him. Then he'd do the walking away.

Her hair was up in her usual style, coiled at her nape, strands of deep red sunset tucked away, except for a few wisps around the edge of her face. She wore jeans and a long-sleeved white T-shirt under a gray fleece vest. The evening fog was in, but he was pretty sure she had dressed to cool the heat between them. Of course, her strategy wasn't working.

She caught him looking and fiddled with her pencil. "Thank you again for getting the center that donation. Louisa wants to rename the place after you."

He shrugged. "I made a phone call."

"It was more than that. I read enough about Z-Text to know your role there. You must have…"

He leaned toward her. "It was nothing, and I did it to get you to sleep with me." It was only fair to be honest with her.

She studied her notepad on the table. Her voice was serious. "You don't want what I want in a relationship. You don't even want sex. You want revenge."

"What makes you so sure you know what I want? Been thinking about me?"

"Look. I know we have this hormonal thing, but we both have other options, other choices. You want to be happy, don't you?"

The question unsettled him. "The way you're happy with your flavor of the month, who happens to be a made-up boyfriend, an accountant from the bus stop?"

She gave him a quick startled glance that confirmed he'd found her out. "Are you going to tell me what you came to tell me about Canyon?"

"Sure, but admit it. You do want sex. With me. And I'm offering. Anytime." He hated her, so why couldn't he keep sex off his brain, or out of his voice, which sounded so rusty with need that she must have heard it. His truck transmission was smoother.

He took a deep breath, got a grip on himself, and held out his phone for her to look at some numbers that had come up on the display.

"What am I looking at?"

"Several things actually. First, there's the drop in the endowment value a few years ago. Two-thirds. There are good governance rules about how much money a school can use from its endowment. With this loss, those rules kick in, and Canyon's hands are tied."

"So?"

"So on to the next figures, the yearly debt service on a modest fifteen million dollar bond. About a mil per year, but Canyon hasn't paid it for three years, not one year."

"That's nuts. Couldn't Canyon have gone to its alumni, its big donors, before it missed a payment? The men on our committee would have helped."

"If they'd known. I don't think they knew about this loan."

"But now they know. At least the members of our committee know. Now the debt could be paid."

"It's close to three mil." Dunsmore had not pulled that figure out of the air when he'd offered Will a spot in the Hall of Canyon Men.

"A large sum to people like me, maybe, but surely the men on our committee have means." He watched her doing mental math. She hadn't put it together. She didn't even guess at his wealth, which meant she still saw him as the penniless boy he had been.

She unzipped her vest and slipped it over the back of her chair. The move exposed the curve of one breast to his gaze and sent a jolt straight to his groin. He started tapping his foot. It took a minute before he registered her next comment.

"A dozen individuals could pay down the debt substantially, and Canyon has hundreds of alumni. I don't see how the board could let the school get behind."

"You're probably right, but here's the thing I found out."

He had her full attention.

"The bond holder *wants* to foreclose. He wants to shut the school down and take the property."

"Why would a bank do that? Wouldn't that mean losing money in the long run?"

Will had wondered that, too. The only reason he could think of was revenge, but his own feelings probably clouded his judgment there. "If the bond holder isn't a bank but a private party, he might be contemplating development, or his motives might not be economic at all. Whoever he is, he hates Canyon, and he's in a position to shut it down."

He thought he was speaking rationally and quietly, but her nearness made him edgy.

She was looking at the figures on his phone, but she reached out unconsciously and pressed her hand lightly against his bouncing knee.

Just like that he went hard. He forgot the room full of people. He just wanted her hand on him. "We should take this outside."

Chapter Nine

The library was one of three sleek curving buildings of dark brown brick that made up the town center and made the place look more like a medieval castle than the municipal center of a southern California beach town. Will led the way along a curling path away from the lighted parking lot until he came to a bench at the end of a shrubbery encircled cul-de-sac. The buildings cast the bench in shadow. The only light came from two high windows of the library behind them. He doubted Annie could read his expression. *Perfect.*

"So what do we do about this bondholder?" She halted a few feet from the bench.

"Find out who he is. Find out what's made him so angry."

"You would do that? You hated Canyon. You told me you wanted to see it fail." She came closer.

"Did you think I was the only one? That there were no other boys who found Canyon…difficult?"

"What puzzles me is how the board could be kept in ignorance of this lack of payment till now. There's a business manager, a finance committee of the board, a yearly audit…" She looked at him. He couldn't see her face, only the puzzled tilt of her head. "Oh, you think Chambers concealed this activity somehow. How?"

"I think Chambers has always been good at managing the school's money in his own way for his own purposes."

"And no one has noticed?" The lights in the windows above them blinked on and off. "The library's closing soon. We should get our things."

He didn't say anything.

"Is something wrong?"

"Just thinking." *Come a little bit closer.*

She did. They were almost face-to-face, and he caught her wrist in one hand. The lights blinked again in the library, and someone passed on the main path.

"Let me get our stuff."

"We aren't through."

He found her other hand and pulled her around the bench, behind the shrubbery, pressing her up against a high wall opposite the library, framing her body with his own.

She went still. He couldn't be sure she was even breathing.

"I have to touch you."

Annie lifted her chin. The only light came from a lamp on the distant path. In the dimness his eyes darkened. His mouth was inches from hers, his lips parted, his breath warm against her. He was going to kiss her as he had outside the center. She tried to think of all the reasons he should not, but her mind was blank.

He leaned into her pressing his full body against her. Her breasts flattened against the hard plane of his chest, and she felt her nipples tighten. He tilted up her chin and took possession of her mouth. His kiss was different from the first time, hungry but shy and waiting for an invitation. She opened to him, and he deepened the kiss, tasting her, causing desire to escalate.

He shoved his hips against hers, and a low hungry sound escaped him. He tugged her T-shirt, freeing it from the waist of her jeans, and slid his warm palm up her ribs to cup one breast, brushing his thumb across the peak so that she arched into him. She twisted in his hold, and his breath hissed, but he held her fixed to the wall.

"Stop." Her protest came out weak and faint, and she summoned the will to try again. "We have to stop. You won't like yourself if you do this. This is all about revenge."

"Does this feel like revenge?" His voice sounded incredulous. He scraped the backs of his nails across the silky surface of her bra, and sensation split open in her.

"Do you know where we are?" She could not keep the amusement out of her voice.

"Not a clue."

"We're leaning up against the police station."

"Damn." His hand stopped its motion.

She pushed him away. With shaking hands she tucked her shirt back into her jeans. She stepped around him and stumbled through the shrubbery onto the faint white ribbon of the path.

"Annie, wait."

"I'm going to get our stuff."

"Wait. Did you walk? I'll take you home," he offered.

When Annie came out of the library, he was waiting. She handed him a folder he'd left behind. He led the way to his truck, conscious of how he'd blown it again. He had planned to be so cool and patient, to draw the conversation out, to let her talk about Canyon until her guard was down. But sitting next to her had not been a patience-inducing strategy.

People around them called good-byes to one another, and engines started up in the parking lot. He managed to get her into his truck, and she gave him a brief set of directions.

"How did you get roped into doing this work for Canyon?"

She glanced at him as she buckled her seat belt. "There's a boy you met at the center, Ulysses. He goes to Canyon now."

"Don't tell me he's on financial aid?" He swore. He remembered the thin shy kid with the dark glasses, his hair neatly combed, his shirt tucked in, his jeans belted at the waist, a kid innocent of style and labels. "Was it your idea to send him there?"

She shook her head. "There's an organization that connects kids like Ulysses with scholarship opportunities. There was an opportunity at Canyon. I might not have picked it, but it beats his local school hands down."

"Does it?" He could not keep the anger out of his voice.

"Yes! His cousin was shot outside the school. Ulysses has already been shaken down and roughed up. He can't get the classes he's ready for. Everything's against him there, and he's a good kid. He deserves better."

"That stuff's normal. It's nothing. It's not personal. You have no idea." He broke off. Could he really claim that Canyon was worse than violence? Could he explain how cell phones and gold chains, the right gym bags, the right sneakers, and bulging wallets meant winning, meant triumphing over some inferior boy, and how a boy like Ulysses would always be the loser in those daily contests? Could he explain how alone Ulysses would be?

She pointed out another turn.

Will had learned quickly at Canyon not to reveal anything about himself to his classmates. *Where do you live?* It was better not to say. Ulysses would not even pass that first test. Where he lived wasn't on his classmates' map. It was somewhere in the vast region of nameless inferior streets outside the accepted and ranked neighborhoods of the Canyon crowd.

Even in the classroom Ulysses wouldn't be safe. Some well-meaning teacher would ask the class to write about their rooms or their neighborhoods, and some other kid would ask, *Do I write about my Beverly Hills house or my Palm Springs house?* And Ulysses would learn never to expose the small, shabby place where he was loved to the contempt of his classmates on the manicured grounds of Canyon.

And the questions game wouldn't stop there. Even though they knew the answers, his classmates would go on asking, reminding Ulysses of everything he lacked. *What cars do your folks drive? What season tickets do you have? Where do you ski?* And when they tired of that game, they would start on the name-calling, and he would bet Ulysses would not be called, "Cowboy" or "Wonderbread," as he had been. And he wouldn't be able to use his fists to earn respect. That lesson had been a hard one for Will to learn.

Annie indicated a brown-shingled house, and he pulled up in front of it and killed the truck engine. "You've got to let me talk to Ulysses. He's got to know what Canyon is really like."

She shook her head. "Will, he's happy. He likes his classes. He has a friend."

"You think so?" She was looking at him like he was some kind of monster who would hurt the kid.

"Josh is looking out for him, showing him the ropes."

"Huntington, that paragon of selflessness? What's in it for him?"

She looked away. So there was something.

"Josh is actually being nice. It may be a new experience for him, but he's there when I take Ulysses to school, and he's helping him to get the feel of the place, to learn to be cool."

Will gripped her arm hard. "You're taking the kid to school everyday? And you're trading favors with Huntington?"

"Trading favors? What on earth are you thinking? You know what Huntington wants me to do? He wants me to meet with you on this committee. He wants me to ask you to host a party for your old classmates. Those are the favors I'm supposed to do. I didn't understand it, but now I think I do. He hopes…"

"What he hopes is that you'll sleep with me, and that I'll be so mindless after sex that I'll write Canyon a giant check."

He let go of her arm and gripped the steering wheel, looking straight ahead. "Where does Ulysses's scholarship come from?"

"A former groundskeeper died without survivors. He specified that his life insurance policy go to support a scholarship student at Canyon."

"Does Ulysses have to go through Chambers to get the money?"

"I don't know." She pushed open the truck door. She could see Irene peeking through the gap in her front curtains.

"If you care about him, find out."

"Are you going to explain?"

"Nope. This isn't going to work after all." He wouldn't even look at her.

She climbed down from the truck.

"Good-bye, Annie James."

The truck engine turned over before she'd even stepped back from the door. She turned and heard it pull away as Irene's curtains twitched closed.

Her answering machine's light blinked at her, and she pushed the button.

Annie, it's Meg. If you want children of your own, not just a bunch of other people's children from that center, you've got to take action. No need to wait for Dad's party. I've got the guy for you. I'll send you his email.

—Friday, 7:30 p.m.

Chapter Ten

Josh pulled into the driveway of his South Bay duplex around nine. He checked his phone, but the glowing line of texts to Sloan remained the same, a one-sided conversation. At least he had a reply from Annie James that she would get back to him. He had no trouble interpreting the data. Sloan and Annie were not clicking, not working together, and not sleeping together. Josh could not ask Sloan for a big check any time soon.

He put away his phone and looked up at the duplex with its "for rent" sign in the window of the north unit. The place was a featureless utilitarian box in sand brown stucco with darker brown trim and the architectural sophistication of a child's drawing. Each wall had exactly one square window, no balcony, but a pair of planter boxes with dead plants. To save a few bucks he had arranged a sublet for the last month of his place in Malibu. Soon he would have to move into the south unit. The thought was depressing as hell.

His phone told him just how far he was from Bar Marmont. It would be packed with women in high heels and designer fashions, ready to mingle and network all night long.

He'd put his pool table up on eBay. If he maxed out his credit cards, he could do the move, and some of the renovations he planned. He'd already had his unit painted and new carpets installed, but he'd held off on further improvements. In the mean time he was economizing, living as austerely as a monk, and the prospect of that austerity lasting for months or years was a bit grim. He had new sympathy for Bernie Madoff's victims.

He leaned his head back against the headrest and closed his eyes. He had no desire to go upstairs to see his new place again. He had to get Sloan and Annie together.

When he opened his eyes, it was almost ten on the dash clock. He realized that he'd dozed off. There was a car parked in the space for the north unit. It had originally been some sort of snappy mustard color, now dulled to ochre, the paint without any shine to it at all. Someone had slapped primer around the wheel walls. He didn't recognize the make, a Porsche knockoff, a bit too long, too flat, too cropped on the rear end.

When he shut the door on the Rover, a head appeared in the driver's seat.

"Hello?"

A teenager with a ponytail, in a white shirt and dark plaid skirt like one of his cousins' school uniforms, emerged from the car and came around it to speak to him. She stuck out her hand.

"Emma Gray." They exchanged a businesslike shake. "We talked on the phone. You were going to show me the place."

He'd forgotten. "Sure." It was late and dark, and he could hardly make out her features or the color of her eyes under the streetlights. Her hair looked…brown. About as exciting a brown as the fading trim on the duplex.

"I'm interested in renting."

Josh was tempted to ask what her parents thought of the idea. "Sure, come on up."

She turned to her rent-a-wreck and glanced around the street.

"It's safe. The fashion police don't ticket eyesores."

She gave one more glance to the car. "I'll follow you."

Josh led the way up the stairs. He hadn't done anything to the north unit except to have it cleaned when he'd had his unit painted. But if her car was any indication, the apartment should suit her taste pretty well.

He opened the door to the central entry and flipped on the lights. One of the bulbs had gone out in the breast of Venus lighting fixture that dominated the shared entry. Its dim light didn't do anything for the ambience. Everything looked as worn and cheerless as Josh remembered.

He stepped aside for her to enter, and as she passed him, he caught a surprising fragrance like vanilla ice cream. "How old are you?"

"I'm twenty-four. I don't smoke, do dope, or party." She went right to the window, opened it, and looked down on her car.

"Listen, I'll just let you look around for a few minutes. I'll wait right here." He sat down on the top step, watching the city glow in the sky above the block of buildings opposite his. Lights were on in several units, doors open, music and TV noise competing with a dull rumble of distant traffic on the coast highway. It was no Malibu view. But in a few more hours it would grow quiet enough to hear the thump of waves crashing on the shore. Maybe his prospective tenant would just go quietly away, and he could get back to solving his main problem.

It was clear to Josh that Sloan and Annie had not slept together. He suspected that it was because Sloan just wouldn't let himself need anyone. But Sloan did need Annie, had needed her from the moment she'd been hired as a temp in the admissions office by Chambers. The girl-less world of Canyon had been harsh, a throwback to the public schools of old novels, but most of the guys in their class had connections through siblings in girls schools and scored invitations to parties and dances. Sloan had not had that. He'd had no softness in his life then, and his personality needed softening, needed about a billion years of a cool stream running over granite to smooth the surface. Annie James was meant to be that cool stream; otherwise the two of them would have each found someone else by now. Josh just had to keep pushing them into each other's way.

His prospective tenant came back with a pencil and one of those little flat black notebooks you could fit in a pocket. "Could you answer a few questions?"

He pulled himself up off the step. "Sure."

He followed her into the north unit. She opened drawers and cabinets, looked into appliances, ran water in every sink, and flicked on all the lights. He doubted the building inspector would ask as many questions, or check on his car as often as she did. "Listen, do you want to talk in the driveway?"

"Great." She took the stairs entirely too fast for their condition and the inadequate lighting, and gave the car another glance. "How much do you want a month?"

It was the easiest of her questions. He gave his price.

There was a long silence. She was clearly calculating whether she could afford the place. He took the time to look at her more closely. Not much there. No noticeable breasts, nothing that really suggested a curve, fine bones, no striking color. Inside he'd noticed that the brown of her hair was not so much like the building's fading trim paint, more like the soft brown of little birds that blended into the scrub brush along the coast. "It's probably too much with your car payments."

"You know, it's not really in very good shape. You haven't made any improvements since the last tenants left. You didn't even replace the entry light bulb. You ought to let me have it for less."

He thought about explaining the workings of a free market economy to her, but she was obviously not well acquainted with money. He settled for saying, "Sorry, that's my best offer."

Just then the car rocked, distracting him. "Your car just jiggled."

She ignored his comment. "You're just being stubborn because you're tired and grumpy. I'm a great tenant. I'll clean and paint and plant things, and the whole place will look so much better, you'll be amazed."

"Do you have a job?" There was probably some form he should have her fill out.

"Yes."

"Where? McDonald's, Burger King, the mall?"

"At Daddy Rock on the Avenue."

"The vinyl store?" He looked at her again. The details didn't add up. She looked seventeen. Daddy Rock employees were usually grizzled music nerds whose legendary knowledge of rock music drew aficionados from all over L.A. They had definitely done dope and partied hard. He suspected that most of them were kidney-transplant recipients.

"If you let me have the place for fifteen hundred a month, I can give you first and last month's rent plus a security deposit tonight."

Ready cash. That was tempting. "So you're the perfect tenant?"

She seemed to know more about rental agreements than he did. He thought her car rocked again, or he was more tired than he realized. When he stared at it, it bounced slightly. "Do you have a dog?"

"No." She pulled an envelope out of her bag. "For my price, you'll get the interior cleaned and painted, window coverings, and new landscaping."

"Landscaping?" The car jiggled again. "There are two planter boxes."

"With a brown building, we should put in lots of reds and golds. Coreopsis and chocolate cosmos to make it look cheery."

She moved right in front of him, as if she could block his view of the car, talking very fast, the envelope extended in her free hand. He sensed her desperation.

The car shimmied, and hatched a small downy head in the backseat.

"You've got a kid."

She didn't even glance behind her. "The apartment's got two bedrooms."

He didn't know how he felt about a kid next door. Might be very inhibiting. "Check it out. The BMW crowd lives here, young professionals, not store clerks with kids."

"Not in your unit." She shook the envelope, as if she were shaking a dog toy and he might take it. "This place is near my work and my son's school. There is a school you know, less than a mile away."

He stuck his hands in his pockets. "The whole town is one square mile."

"Well, renting to us is the generous thing to do. It's heroic." She sounded like Annie James. "Didn't you ever want to be a hero?"

"Never." *I just wanted to sleep with the heroine.*

"Mom?" The voice from the hatchling in the car was small and plaintive. "Are you hungry? I'm hungry."

She didn't answer the boy. All her energy was focused on Josh, as if she could will him to take the envelope. Maybe she could. He pulled his right hand out of his pocket and took the envelope. "Cash?"

"I only use cash."

Jeez, what was he getting into? He thumbed through the contents of the envelope—forty-five hundred dollar bills. "Okay, it's yours."

"Great. You are heroic."

"Don't push your luck."

"Have you got the key?"

"You're moving in tonight?"

She looked away. "Yes."

"Fine."

She opened the car door and scooped up the child inside, hugging him to her. He was more than half her size. She didn't look big enough to carry him. "Who's the other tenant? Who lives in the south half?"

"I do, that is I will."

Her face was ridiculously open. She eyed the envelope in his hand as if she would snatch it back. Then she hugged the child tighter. Josh handed her a key, and she headed up the stairs.

* * *

Will called Huntington early. At sports-radio talk show volume he told Huntington what he thought of using a kid to get Annie to get him to get money for Canyon, for snot-nosed elitists with cell phones and Ferraris. He didn't delete a single expletive.

"Sloan, good you called. Did Annie talk to you about hosting an event at your place?" For a guy with a sleep-thickened voice, Huntington was annoyingly cheerful.

"Huntington, you're effing scum."

There was a pause followed by a patient sigh. "You haven't slept with her yet, have you?"

Will repeated his worst recommendations for Huntington's future.

"Sloan, you only get so many chances at this."

"I don't need you to blackmail her into seeing me."

"Really? You're such a friendly guy, you'll just call her and ask her out? If you can't do that Sloan, you better take my party offer."

* * *

Will did not need to check his messages. He knew what he would find, a dozen texts from Huntington about the party he wanted Will to host and not one from Annie James. The guy did not give up. He answered one text from his mom, who wanted to borrow his truck to pick up trees and plants for her garden.

He glanced around his office. Another day, another week, another zip, nada, zilch. Another set of useless meetings. When he'd sold Z-Text, he had, of course, signed a non-competition clause, and agreed to be available for the new owners to consult. That's why he was in L.A. in the first place and not in Silicon Valley. He was sure when he'd done it that his next big idea was right around the corner. Instead, he seemed to have only one idea in his head, a thoroughly unprofitable idea, a non-innovative idea.

Beau knocked on and opened his door in one swift move. "Ready to call it quits for today?"

"For the year." He tore the top page off his calendar and tossed the crumpled scrap away.

Beau tapped the desk with a wad of rolled up newsprint, some freebie throwaway from the corner stand. "The let's-do-lunch crowd getting you down?"

Will nodded. "Finance guys. Not idea guys."

When he and Beau had their big idea, they'd been working day and night in Beau's dorm room or Will's or in a pizza joint just off campus with free wi-fi. They had not been wearing suits and doing lunch.

He didn't want to do business over lunch with finance guys. He didn't like most restaurants. His companions were either unconscious of the "help" or overly familiar with them. Most flashed big bills, expecting people to jump for the money the way Mae's Dog would jump for a biscuit. He, on the other hand, was too conscious of waiters and waitresses, aware of their stress and fatigue, aware that somewhere in the back dishes were clattering and some sweating boy was scraping greasy plates and hauling out black plastic trash bags full of scraps the overfed didn't touch.

Beau dropped into a chair and pulled it close, leaning his elbows on the desk, serious now. He pointed his newspaper roll at Will.

"Why do I think you're about to say something I don't want to hear?"

Beau grinned. "Because I am. You'll listen because I'm your wise friend who guides you through the dangerous waters of sudden wealth. You'll listen because I'm better than your very own handheld navigational device."

"Better than Siri?"

"Right. L.A.'s a small place businesswise. Up there in Century City, the spreadsheet wizards and hedge fund guys can see each other from their office windows."

"You think Z-Text is out of the loop being down here in the South Bay?"

Beau shook his head. "Doesn't matter. You've got an 'in' with the money folks, and all you've got to do is use it."

Beau let him hang, and Will waited.

"Canyon. You went to effing Canyon. I've been thinking about it since that pinhead Dunsmore showed up. Okay, you don't want to give them money, and you don't want a spot in their hall, but Canyon is bankable in L.A., it's tradable on the market; it's a billion in capitalization, a hot IPO. Use it. Let 'em know you went there."

"Shit!"

Beau blew out a long breath. "Whew! Got that out of the way. Now I know you won't necessarily take my very sage and free advice in this matter, at least not until you've had time to think about it. So let's move right along here, shall we?" He unrolled the newspaper in his hand, spreading it on Will's desk.

"*LA Weekly*?" On the open page he read that a woman could have breast implants for four grand and a modest liposuction for another fifteen hundred bucks.

Beau nodded. "Have you been laid yet?"

"What?"

"For your two hundred and fifty thousand dollars? Did you get laid?"

"Not yet."

"Okay then. On to part two of Professor Beau's seminar on L.A. culture. Complete the following sentence—L.A. is about money and…?" Beau flipped the pages of the freebie paper. "Let's get past all these opportunities for liposuction, breast implants, and vaginal rejuvenation…"

"Sex."

Beau offered him a cocky grin. "I knew you were a bright boy. *Sex* is the correct answer. Let's get you laid." Beau started reading the classifieds.

"And the point is?" Will interrupted.

"You've done something incredibly generous and it didn't work. Right?"

Will nodded.

"Time to change your strategy."

Will tapped a particularly lurid ad in the paper. "You think the HOT OIL RUBDOWN is the way to go?"

Beau looked suddenly serious. "Listen, I know you have weird ideas about women."

Will nodded. It was a fair charge.

"Trust me, the normal dating-meeting-people thing is not that hard. Lots of guys with a tenth of your intelligence manage it very well. I've got five women lined up who would love to meet you. With a little coaching…"

"I'd rather do it myself."

Beau folded the newspaper and stood. Will had the sense that his friend was disappointed in him. "That's your trouble, Sloan. You can't do everything yourself."

Chapter Eleven

In the end Will agreed to follow Beau's lead. If L.A. was about money and sex, the two things he clearly had hang-ups about, no wonder he wasn't doing anything right. But Beau's weekly club crawl only left Will more restless.

Running was a much safer way to take the edge off. So he ended each day with a long run with a good vertical climb at the end.

The house his mother had rejected was an old Spanish-style house on the Palos Verdes hill built in 1929, small by contemporary standards with five thousand square feet, descending through dozens of rooms and lush gardens to a pool-studded lawn. Beau approved of the remodeled kitchen with its eight-burner stove, semitruck sized refrigerator, and miles of Brazilian limestone counters.

Will passed through the right half of a pair of thick, carved double doors that had once graced a convent before the Revolution in Mexico, and punched the code to deactivate the alarm system. The house wasn't Hearst Castle but it would do.

The view from the entry down through the living room with its wall of northwest facing windows got him every time; the whole sweep of the Santa Monica Bay to the glittering rim of the Pacific was his to enjoy. L.A. was better from the hill.

He dropped his keys by the kitchen phone and retrieved a bottle of water from the over-sized refrigerator, uncapping it and returning to the living room. A red and violet sunset filled the windows. He drank it in watching the tip of Malibu where the sun would drop below the horizon in a green flash.

The trouble with sunsets was that they brought his mind right back to Annie James. She was in a category by herself in his thinking about women. He was not the expert that Beau was. In high school he had avoided the girls who sometimes came to Canyon games. Huntington had seemed to know them all, and Will couldn't imagine taking any of them out.

His mom's friends, her fellow waitresses, on the other hand, were the meter maids of male perfidy. A guy opened his mouth, and they had his wheels chalked and his ass ticketed before he even realized his mistake. If Will's eyes even followed a female in the restaurant, one of his mom's friends would smack him and warn, "Don't even think about it."

His mom had more charitable ideas about men, but she laughed along with her friends, and Will never told her about Annie. When Annie refused his marriage proposal, he concentrated on his ambitions. He focused on football and school and his internship. Beau had not only been his teammate, but another intern at the same tech company. Will had been lucky from the first, and before the end of that first season, he and Beau knew they were onto something that would make them successful.

In the dizziness of that success there was a period of partying on campus with jello caps and tequila shots and everyone in boxers and bras. He experienced a rapid learning curve about sex. But the experience left him feeling unhappy with himself. He knew there were girls he had hurt but he couldn't remember their names or their faces. He knew his mom's friends would be shaking their heads over him, and he knew he hadn't been the man his mom expected him to be, or the one that had once loved Annie James.

In the next couple of years whenever he tried to start something with a woman, he found himself stopping before the thing ever got off the ground. Now that he'd seen Annie James again, he figured he was never going to get sex right until he got over her. This time he wanted to do the walking out, and he didn't want to be aching with need when he did it.

He punched Huntington's name on his phone's contact list.

"Sloan, you called. Good man. Still thinking about doing me that favor?"

"Huntington, what are you after?"

"Besides the obvious? Just trying to help an old buddy score."

"I don't need you."

"Oh, I think you do. She's beautiful. She's single. And someone has to make her forget the guy she married when she was what— twenty-one?"

"Apparently no one has made her forget him yet."

"And so far you have blown every chance to be the one. So, here's the last chance I'm offering. Host the next prereunion party for our class up at your place in Palos Verdes."

"And?"

"I'll get her there. If you can't get her from the living room to the bedroom…"

"Why haven't I killed you yet?"

For once Huntington was silent. No glib chatter. Will was tempted to look at his watch to time the pause. When Huntington spoke again, his voice was serious.

"You want to know why? Do you need a history lesson? Because in that cabin at Big Bear when Lynch and Shields and all the rest had stripped you naked and wanted to dump you in her bed, I made them back off. You owe me."

He remembered. What had seemed a joke to all of them, had reduced him to helpless rage on a cold dusty wood floor. Then they'd left him, abruptly. It took him a moment as the details of that night got rearranged in his brain.

"Leave her alone. Leave that kid alone."

"You're in luck, Sloan. I've got to go raise some bucks for Canyon in Chicago and San Francisco. I'll be gone a week. Think about hosting that party. Think about showing her your place."

"I thought the dinner bell stopped them." He still wanted Huntington to back off. One act of self-restraint did not make the guy a hero.

"Sloan, stay focused. I'll handle the caterer, whatever."

"When?"

"Two weeks."

Two weeks. He had two weeks to get her to trust him enough to come to his house. He needed a place to meet her where he couldn't give in to his desire for her.

* * *

Annie looked up from the Strand, the wide sidewalk at the base of the dunes that separated pricey real estate from the public beach. Joggers, cyclists, and in-line skaters veered around her. Behind her waves cracked, broke, and hissed their foaming way up the sand. Above her, the street climbed from the old pier into the busy center of town where she had agreed to meet Will for coffee at an upscale espresso house.

Annie spotted him outside Java Jack's and headed up the hill, adjusting the slim leather bag on her shoulder. He had sounded reasonable on the phone, interested in solving Canyon's unexpected dilemma, but she knew that what he really wanted was answers about their past. She had spent most of the day thinking about what to admit to him. The truth about her deal with Chambers was only likely to increase Will's anger. Whatever Chambers's motives had been, his actions had freed them both to leave Canyon. They just had to hang on to the new lives they'd made. At least this time they were meeting in a crowded, noisy place with no dark paths.

Java Jack's windows were open. A rock sound track blasted the mild September evening and the strolling Friday night crowds on the sidewalk. A poster of a shaggy-haired band in black before a graffiti-marred urban landscape proclaimed their name: Third Eye Blind. The group was unfamiliar to her, and she tried fleetingly to remember a time when she'd known the names of hot rock groups. Then she was caught in Will Sloan's scrutiny. One of the things that set him apart from other men she'd known was his focus. That powerful concentration directed wholly at her reversed the sense of invisibility she usually felt. It made her giddy to be looked at so intently, and she was never giddy.

He wore another charcoal gray T-shirt, no logo this time. He stood aside for her to enter, and slipped his dark glasses into his pocket. Their eyes met briefly, caught, then glanced away.

She made a show of looking for a table though her gaze hardly took in her surroundings.

He leaned over her shoulder as they stood in line, his breath stirring her hair. "I still don't see you living the beach life."

"You thought I was the staid suburban type?"

"If the sweater set fits, wear it." He cocked his head toward a window bench. "There's a table." When she didn't move, he nudged her with a hand at the small of her back. "On the end. Snag it. I'll get us some coffee."

Annie threaded her way through the crowd. So she was unhip in her sweater set and jeans. Better to be safe than chic. She wasn't going to let him see any lace again, that was for sure. The crowd was upscale and trendy, a mix of pretty beach people, indistinguishably blond, tan, and fit, ready to be discovered and cast in a reality TV show. Nearly everyone had a tech toy in hand.

The marble-topped table Will pointed out looked like a postage stamp, and someone had pulled its chair away for another party. She and Will would end up side by side on the cushioned window seat. She slid in, propped her bag next to her, and took out the pad and pencil she'd brought along.

She caught him watching her from the coffee line and bent her head and smoothed her hand over the pad, placing her yellow mechanical pencil just so. On her left a woman with a few years on Annie in a watermelon-pink fringed cami with arms probably defined by hundreds of free-weight reps was describing for her friend the sexual preferences of a new partner with whom she'd begun a relationship. A clear case of oversharing if Annie had ever heard one. It reminded her that eavesdropping was the occupational hazard of the single person.

"Don't you just love the beach life!" the woman's friend commented. Annie tuned them out and checked Will's position in the line. He was paying the cashier.

A couple of minutes later he put a latte and one of Java Jack's coffee smoothies in front of her. "I guessed. Take your pick—hot or cold?"

Annie reached for the latte. He could not possibly remember what she drank all those years ago. Josh Huntington had started the newspaper staff tradition of a coffee run before their regular Thursday meetings. Annie had always asked for a latte. A stray memory surfaced of a warm Thursday morning late in the year when they'd held the staff meeting outside in the quad. Will had stayed in the background, sitting on top of a bench, his upper body in the low branches of a mock orange tree. He spent the meeting tossing the tree's tiny white blossoms at her coffee cup, and missing occasionally, so that the blossoms stuck in her hair.

Sliding onto the bench beside her, he encountered her bag, and with a mocking look, set it on the floor. He rested his elbows on the table and dipped his spoon into the frothy tan goop in the plastic cup. His shirtsleeve bisected the swell of his biceps, and Annie lowered her eyes, but it was no safer to gaze at his sculpted masculine hands. An errant recollection that he was left-handed came to mind.

He looked up from his coffee. "You warm? You want to take off that sweater?"

Heat flared in her. "I'm fine thanks."

He went back to stirring his coffee drink. "Why aren't you married?" His voice was rough with sex, and Annie's stomach dipped like the foam of a spent wave sucked into the curl of the next.

She laughed, trying to make light of it. "Are you kidding? Look around you. We're not living on a marrying planet."

He gave the crowd a slow thorough perusal. "So, why live here? Did you ever even date?"

"Trust me I'm quite the hardened veteran of the local dating scene." It was true. She had tried lots of ways to meet men, mostly at the insistence of Louisa and Tess.

"So you wanted to forget me?" His lashes lifted on an arctic green gaze.

"It was the sensible thing to do." She put as much conviction as she could muster into the claim, but he saw through her anyway.

"Liar."

"You think I didn't want to forget you? That's a man's ego for you."

"I might believe it if you weren't overdressed for our meeting tonight. You look like somebody's Great Aunt Sally from Pasadena chaperoning a cotillion. Do you ever let your hair down?"

She turned on him. "And what about you? You choose to meet…a sweater-set wearing woman, who could be your big sister, on a Friday night during prime…hookup time? From the looks you're getting in this crowd you could have your pick."

"My friend Beau says the same thing. He claims he can get me a new date every night if I want to sample all that L.A. has to offer."

"Sounds like just what you should be doing. Shall we get our business out of the way so you can go meet some…hot…chicks? We were going to talk about Canyon. Did you bring anything to show me?"

"Yeah." He leaned back and dug in his pocket for his phone. Annie took in the long stretch of his body next to hers on the bench and looked away.

He shoved his coffee drink aside, and put his phone on the table, tapping open a file. Annie leaned forward, just enough to see, careful not to brush against his arm. He changed screens. "We probably need a coalition to buy out that bondholder. The question is do you want to keep the place going?"

"Of course, I do." She wanted Ulysses to finish. "Whatever happened to you there, for boys like Ulysses Canyon is the best chance for a good education and a future."

His green glance turned sly. "If you believe in the place so much, why did you leave?"

Annie stiffened. He'd trapped her. He'd led her to make a defense of Canyon, and then he'd sprung his question.

"Did you quit because of me?" His hand brushed back the wisps of hair clinging to the side of her neck.

She tilted her neck away. His gaze didn't waver. She could feel the tension vibrating in his leg through the bench cushion under her. He was looking at her throat.

"Stop it." She pressed her hand lightly against his knee.

He froze instantly, and she felt his whole body tighten under her palm. His left hand came down trapping hers against his thigh.

"Just answer my question." His jaw was tight, his voice strained.

He dragged her palm further up his thigh, the muscle hard under her hand. The driving rock beat seemed to invade her body and magnify the beating of her pulse. He could read her so easily.

"You should be out with friends, club hopping, meeting women."

He leaned close, and Annie resisted the temptation to back away. "You should be married with three kids."

She had tried to forget him. She had tried blind dates, Internet sites, and running groups. She had had a brief relationship with her realtor. After wine and dinner one evening, she had allowed him to take her back to his house, but the plastic covers on the furniture and the vacuum tracks on the carpet had cooled her ardor.

She had even tried the South Bay bar scene until one evening in a beach hot spot a man had broken a woman's jaw. The woman's friends had taken her away, while the man remained to tell the tale to a widening circle of males. In the retelling he kept emphasizing the crack of his fist against the woman's jaw. Annie hadn't waited for the police to come. Somehow after that, she'd stopped trying to meet a man and gone on with her life. She had a life she reminded herself, friends and work and purpose. She lived in a comfortable home in a great town. She could hardly ask for more.

She scooted her tailbone to the back of the bench and tried to think past the heat and weakness in her limbs. Her chest ached with tight pressure. Maybe the age gap meant little out in the world, but in a school it was a line one never crossed. She had been on one side of the line, and he on the other. She had done the right thing. There was no point in undoing what she had done.

His lids were lowered, the dark lashes concealing his expression. His mouth was a bitter curl, and his nose with the finely cut nostrils was haughty as ever.

"I did leave because of you. It was plain that I had to disappear from your life for you to get on with those plans of yours." It was not the whole truth, but close enough, and it had the immediate effect she wanted.

He freed her hand.

Annie grabbed her bag and stood. Her legs were a bit wobbly, but that was only because she didn't do confrontations well. She concentrated on making a swift exit. "Thanks for the coffee. Email me those notes of yours. I'll work them up into some kind of proposal for the committee."

* * *

Damn! He'd blown it, and he was in no state to go after her in a well-lighted public place. It was the same as in the library. He had planned to keep the talk about Canyon until her guard was down. But she had looked so good, and he had felt every shift of her hips on their shared bench cushion. Each move had wafted her warm fragrance to him.

Obviously he was still screwed up in some way from wanting her so much in high school. She had touched him, and once again he'd gone hard. His brain had short-circuited briefly, and he'd forgotten the room full of people. He had just wanted her hand on him. He'd released her, and she'd fled. And he wasn't any closer to figuring out how he felt about her.

She had not answered the most important question of all.

But she had let down her guard a little. Like him, she had failed at forgetting. You were supposed to forget things. He'd read the research. There was even a forgetting curve. Forgetting was a survival skill that allowed you not to get stuck on the first idea you had, or the first person you loved. She could not explain why she had not married. He would bet that Annie James had not forgotten her feelings for him any more than he had forgotten his for her. And he would get her to admit the truth yet. The truth would free them both. He had a party to plan.

Chapter Twelve

Mae stood in the entry of Will's house, dangling his truck keys from one hand, a white plastic drugstore bag in the other. He knew he was in for it. He excused himself from the caterer, who was directing the arrangement of hors d'oeuvres tables.

"Hi, Mom."

"Brought your truck back. Thanks. I got all the trees from the nursery to the house in one trip." She gave him a quick kiss on the cheek and a look that demanded an explanation.

"I'm having a party. For some Canyon people." He held out his hand for the keys.

She lifted one black brow. "And that's why you needed these?" She hefted the plastic bag.

Okay, he'd been excessive with his condom purchases. He didn't know what Annie would like or what he would like or whether he wouldn't just tear a dozen or so in trying to put one on in a lust-crazed moment. And he thought he should have them all around the house in case he didn't make it to the bedroom with her. He reached for the plastic bag, but Mae whipped it behind her back.

"Do you want a few in each bath? I could put out dishes, sort of like potpourri."

"I know it looks like I'm planning an orgy, but…"

"Hugh Hefner, move over."

"There's a woman who might stay after the party."

Mae lifted the bag again, shaking the boxes inside. "For how long?"

Forever. Stupid thought. "A night or two." That should be enough. He would screw his brains out for a couple of days and rid himself of desire for Annie James forever.

Mae handed him the bag and turned for the door. "Honey, I'm impressed."

* * *

A paved courtyard fragrant with jasmine and lighted by tiny lights in the coral trees led to old carved wooden doors thrown wide open. When Annie stepped into the soaring entry beyond them, she found dozens of Canyon men and their women, tanned and coiffured, bejeweled and complacent, filled the place. Everyone seemed to be having a good time, except the host. He looked restless and sexy. He stood looking out at a golden sunset over the bay. That was unfair, to remind her even unintentionally of their shared ritual. One thing she had not really realized before he had come back into her life was how strong a hold on her the past really had. All those safe, sensible dates had been wasted effort.

She had come to tell Will Sloan a few things she now understood more fully. Maybe she had done him wrong once, if it had been wrong to stick to her own principles and refuse an offer of marriage from a man who had not even begun to realize his dreams. But it was pointless for him to indulge his destructive bitterness against her now. No good could come of dwelling on the past. No one knew that better than she did. It was time for him to get a new life, for them both to get a new life. She was going to say what she had to say to their host and leave with Josh. Josh Huntington was her personal "Safe-Rides" program.

Josh handed her a glass of white wine and went off to mingle. Annie headed for Will, her spine straight, her chin up. She had earned her independence, in L.A. of all places. She did not have affairs. She had not given in to men who knew their desires but not their hearts. If she had sometimes been lonely between the vast sprawl of the city and wide expanse of the Pacific, she had toughed it out. She had not retreated to her family.

"Could I have a word with you?"

"Alone?"

"Don't get your hopes up."

"You're giving me that opening? It's not my hopes you have to worry about."

"You know what? It's time to let go of old angers and resentments. Let go of the past."

"Are you my therapist now? You want to stay after the party for a little good-bye-to-hatred ceremony? Huntington has spread yearbooks all over the place, and we could burn them on the terrace."

"Or you could stop glaring at everyone and talk to people. Give them a chance. Try to like them and let them like you."

"Who could I talk to in this crowd?"

"Mike Moreland."

Will glanced over at Moreland, who was in earnest conversation with a brunette in her thirties. She had a point. Moreland was one of the good guys. He looked back at her. "You did a lot for Mike Moreland."

She shook her head. "I was kind to him, that's all."

"No. Let me tell you what you did for Mike Moreland. Everybody called him 'Moron Moreland.' Even the faculty called him 'Moron.' He wasn't a moron, of course, he was just shy, but you got him to speak up in that newspaper group."

"I didn't..."

He stopped her words by pressing his fingers to her lips. "I remember. You were leading a discussion of some issue for the newspaper. I was mentally undoing the buttons of a white cotton blouse you liked to wear on hot days, buttoned up to your goddamned throat. I figured that your bra had to be white or nude because I couldn't see it through the shirt. And Moron jumped in, all excited. You called him *Mike*. Didn't you hear the snickers?"

She shook her head. She was dizzy with heat. Unfair to remind her that he had been undressing her all those years ago.

"You just kept asking him questions and waiting for his answers. I never knew an adult could wait so long for a kid to answer, and finally the guy started to put words together. He made a sentence. No one had ever heard him do that before. You got the shyest guy in our class to say something smart, and he knew it." He looked away from her over at Moreland. "It made me fall in love with you."

She shook her head to deny it.

"You still don't think it was love, do you?"

"I was the only female person in the room, and you were apparently more interested in my underwear than my character."

"I do get distracted by your...lace."

"If you can forget the lace for a moment, there's a roomful of people you could notice. If you would just talk to them, you might like them."

"I don't want to like them."

"Not Mike Moreland?"

His mouth quirked in a small smile of concession. "Maybe Moreland."

"You could be civil. You say they never gave you a chance. Did you give them a chance?"

She didn't know what she was asking, but he wasn't going to let her walk out before he got her alone. "You want civility? Watch me." He lifted the thin gold chain around her neck with its tiny glittering beads, his fingers brushing her skin, waking an answering sensation in her breasts. "But if I talk with them, with Mike and the others, you have to stay."

"I came with Josh."

"So. Don't leave with him." He let go of the chain. It fell warm against her skin.

He walked off, making his way through the crowd straight to Mike Moreland.

* * *

For two hours Annie watched him talk with his guests. Men laughed. Women touched him with casual grazing touches on his arm or his hands. The sunset-stained clouds blazed red and then cooled to lavender and gray as the sky darkened. Whenever she looked up, she caught his intent gaze fixed on her. He moved deliberately from group to group, starting with sweet Mike Moreland and his friend Brian Drosafarian, then moving to Josh Huntington's friends, and finally as the crowd thinned, he was talking to Josh, who was flushed with triumph. He had organized the whole thing. She had no idea what the conversation around her was about. She excused herself and followed a tiled hallway to a bathroom set aside for guests.

* * *

By the time Will had talked to all of his guests, only two couples lingered in the entry with Huntington, who was managing to look about him without offending them.

Will didn't see Annie, but she had to be somewhere. She had been watching him, keeping track of how well he was following through on their bargain. It hadn't been as bad as he'd anticipated. Most of his classmates were engrossed in careers and relationships. One or two had actually started families. No one seemed to think it odd that he was living on the hill and hosting the party. No one seemed to remember that he'd scraped their plates or swept out the classrooms. It was only when he'd talked with Fletcher, Lynch, and Shields that he'd been reminded of the gulf between his past circumstances and his present life.

It was Shields who commented right away on Annie's presence. "I bet she's a lot more interested now that you've got some serious dough."

Will had thought that other women were interested because of his wealth, but not Annie. Tonight he remembered that even Beau had suggested that her return to his life had coincided with his acquisition of great wealth. He dismissed the idea. He didn't think she had any idea of the size of his bank account.

Huntington shook some hands, kissed some cheeks, showed the last guests out, and strolled his way. "Sloan, where is she? You didn't let her leave?"

"We have a deal, which—is none of your business."

"You think she's going to stay. You haven't talked to her for hours."

"I haven't ignored her."

"You could have fooled me."

"Just leave."

"Maybe it's not a good idea to strand her here." Huntington put down his drink and straightened his stance. "It should be her choice."

"Since when have you had a conscience, Huntington?"

"Sloan, she's...good. She deserves..."

"I'll call her a cab if she wants to leave."

Huntington stared at him while a long moment passed. "No you won't." He shrugged and extracted his keys from his pocket. "I wouldn't either. You owe me."

* * *

Annie dampened a paper guest towel, and pressed its coolness to her heated cheeks. He had talked to everyone at the party. He wanted her. She reminded herself that he resented her in equal measure. That's why having sex with him was such a bad idea. But the idea made her pulse race and turned her limbs to guacamole. She could not claim that she would be hurting Ryan. She had mourned Ryan as long as she could. She had tried to remember all the joys and pleasures denied to Ryan that she still enjoyed. Eleven years did not change the injustice of it—that he was dead and she was alive.

And it didn't change the truth of Ryan's love, which was cheerful and affectionate and warm, but not passionate, and the truth that some time between their wedding and Ryan's death, she had realized that her marriage had been a mistake. She just hadn't wanted it to end the way it had.

She had resisted Will the stubborn boy, but Will the determined man desired her in a way that lit her up like the descending sun setting the clouds ablaze. His passion was nothing like the affectionate, fault-finding love of her family. The only problem was that he wanted to be done with her. He wanted a consummation that would squander his desire for her in a single night. If she gave in to him, theirs would be a flaming sunset with a permanent darkness. When he left her, she would be just as cold and gray as those abandoned clouds. But she might be free. They both might be free.

She tossed the soggy guest towel away. Much wiser to stay tough, to find Josh and let him take her home.

When she came back to the living room, everyone was gone. Except her host. The caterer's truck beeped as it backed away. Gravel crunched under its wheels, and the rumble of the engine faded down the driveway. From somewhere on the hill came a forlorn cry. She was alone with Will Sloan.

"Where's Josh?" she asked, her voice unsteady.

"He abandoned you to me."

The strange cry sounded again.

"What's that sound?" She tried to remember where she'd left her purse and wrap. She should call a cab.

"A peacock. They're wild up here." He held out his hand to her, and she took it, and he led her into the living room. "I talked to everyone."

"I noticed."

"I talked to Shields and Lynch."

"Above and beyond the call?"

"In the stratosphere of above and beyond."

"And?"

"They are pretty smart about beer. You'd never know that the two of them together didn't make a passing grade in chem."

"So, it wasn't so bad, was it? Giving your classmates a chance?"

"Lynch is not surprised that you like me now. As he sees it, now that I have all this, I should make up for lost time."

She pulled back against his hold. "You don't think that all this influences how I feel about you, do you?"

"Was I wrong to want you to love me when I had nothing?"

She shook her head. "But it would have been wrong of me to love you before you had a chance to go for your dreams."

"That was then. This is now."

"Yes." She said it, but there was a distinct catch in her voice.

A faint smile lit his face. He let go of her hand and stepped back. Behind him through the open French doors she could see the lights of the city, swirling away below them like some galaxy at the edge of the black expanse of the bay. He looked too sure of himself and her.

"You know I did the right thing. We could not have married then. You would never have had the success you've had. Look at where you are, what you've done."

"So it was all good intentions that made you turn me down, not your lack of faith in me, your fear of starting over." He tugged his sweater free of his slacks.

All her senses went on alert.

He pulled his sweater over his head and dropped it on the sofa.

Annie's stomach plunged, a wild lurching dip. There was nothing of the boy about him. He was a man who had come into the fullness of his power. The green eyes watching her were bold and confident.

"I did make it. You didn't hold me back. What's your excuse now?" His cocky gaze swept from her toes peeking out of the black silk straps of her heels to the place where the black dress skimmed her knees, past the indentation of her waist, to linger briefly on her breasts. Her nipples puckered into tight aching buds against the thin silk of her bodice.

"You don't love me now." She wanted to be clear with him, and maybe with herself, about what was happening between them.

"You loved me once."

It was instinctive to shake her head. "I didn't. I was kind. I was helpful…"

"Like you were to Moreland? Or was it different between us? More like Anne Hathaway and Will Shakespeare?" Will saw the acknowledgment of the truth in those too-honest eyes of hers. "Moreland's a sweet guy, a good man. I'm not a bit like him. So why were you kind to me?"

She let out a quavering breath, half laugh, half sigh. She felt reckless suddenly. "You didn't bend. You didn't crack. You believed in yourself when no one around you believed in you. I wanted to be that tough."

"Was that so hard to admit?"

She nodded.

"Why? Because it makes you defenseless? Because there's no other barrier you can throw up between us?"

He stepped forward, and his arms closed around her, tightening until her breasts flattened against his chest and her heart hammered. He dipped his knees and cocked his hips into her, his expression fierce. He slid his hands down her back, pressing her against him, locking them together. He found the hook at the neck of her dress and the long zipper and peeled the silk off one shoulder and then the other, pushing the dress down her arms.

Will had known she would be perfect for him. Two smooth black cups held her breasts. He ran his thumbs up the faint corrugation of her ribs and brushed them across her nipples, and she arched into this hands. He softened his touch, his thumbs barely grazing her, feeling her tremble.

He lowered his head and kissed the creamy moons of flesh rising above the black silk. Then he reached for the clasp of her bra, freeing the hooks with a twist of his hand. He pulled the garment off her and filled his hands with her breasts. It was his turn to make a choked sound. He tugged her dress down over her hips. It pooled on the floor around her feet, and she stepped out of it, just like that, another small act of participation.

Annie watched his face. She knew he meant to be cold and demanding, but a gentler impulse kept surfacing. He pulled her to him, pressing his chest to hers, skin against skin. The feeling shook her to the core.

Will slid the black slip up her thighs and shoved his leg between hers.

She moaned, and he scooped her up into his arms. "We're going to do this. Now," he told her.

His lips met hers in one hard kiss but her mouth clung to his as if she read the other feelings surging up in him, and he broke the kiss to march her toward his bedroom. He set her down on the edge of the bed, and stepped back, looking down at her, right where he wanted her. But when he moved in on her, she pushed back. He had pushed her to admit she'd once loved him, but he hesitated now, unsure he wanted her full participation. If she gave her love freely, what would happen to his revenge?

Annie held him off with one hand, surprised at her own boldness. "Do I get to look, too?"

She let her gaze climb his body, from his well-made feet, up the long lean legs, to the flag of his desire jutting out against the soft wool of his slacks, then the flat plane of his abdomen, bisected by the line of dark hair. She reached out to skim his ribs with her fingers and drag her palms down his abdomen. She reached for the belt on his slacks, pulling it free. Then she pressed her palms to him, cupping him in her hands. He closed his eyes and drew in a harsh breath. He didn't have all the power here.

He stripped back the covers and boosted her up onto the sheets, turning and fumbling in the drawer of his nightstand for a box of condoms. He ripped it open and spread the string of packets within reach. He touched her hair and released the clip to let it fall down her back and spread it around her shoulders.

He had to look, to worship, and could not disguise the effect she had on him. He shed his slacks and boxers in quick movements, sheathed himself and stretched out full length on her, covering that loveliness with his body, nudging her thighs apart with his own, positioning himself.

Their gazes met. She took his hips in her hands and rocked up to meet him. He kissed her once more with all the heat and longing he had held back for so long, and entered her with a long slow slide.

Chapter Thirteen

When the Power Plant closed, Josh decided to spend the night at the duplex. He let himself in and stripped off his jacket and shirt, kicked his shoes in the general direction of his bedroom, and worked the zipper of his fly. He stripped down to his boxers. He had not fully moved in, but he had a sofa and a sound system.

It was hot again. He cranked open all the windows and reached for his music. His plan had worked. Sloan and Annie James could fuel a heat wave between them that would last for months. He could probably ask Sloan for money by Christmas. He'd win the bet, get his trust back, and be out of this beach backwater.

He wanted something hot and heavy to listen to, something to match the way his blood was pumping. He found it and started the music, tipping his head back, making the first long wail with the lead singer.

He was still singing when the music stopped abruptly. He opened his eyes to find his tenant standing in his living room, glaring at him, her hand on his music player. She was wearing an over-sized white T-shirt, and he was momentarily distracted by a slight quiver of her nonexistent breasts.

"What are you doing here?"

"Turning off the noise. Are you nuts? Or high? Or what? It's after two a.m. You've probably wakened everyone in the neighborhood, including my kid."

The walls of the duplex seemed very close. "I'm used to living where I can play music without disturbing anyone."

She was still staring, scowling actually, and he realized that her gaze was directed at his underwear. *Jeez, she wasn't going to be offended by boxers, was she?* "You made your point. I'll keep the sound down."

"You could use a headset." She turned and headed for the door. "And some curtains," she said over her shoulder.

He sank into the big armchair. Damn, he was going to miss Malibu.

* * *

A cool, gray fog had settled on the hill, and steam from the shower trailed after Will into the bedroom. Every part of him felt extraordinarily alive. His toes felt the thick soft carpet. Smells reached him, clear and sharp as musical notes.

Gooseflesh rose on his arms in response to the cool air. He definitely needed to cool off. He was going to let her go. That was the plan. What he felt this morning was just release and sexual satisfaction, and he would not give in to his body's satisfaction any more than he would give in to the past longings of his heart.

A quick glance told him she had not wakened. He avoided looking longer at her, or her image would get fixed in his mind, and he'd see her over and over in his bed. Not the plan. Turning to his dresser, he cautiously slid open a drawer.

"What time is it?" Her voice sounded faintly chagrined, as if she'd just realized where she'd spent the night.

"About seven." He pulled boxers and a T-shirt out the drawer and turned toward her. She was sitting up with the sheets pulled to her chin, her tumbled curls loose about her face.

"I've got to get home."

"Of course."

"I'll call a cab."

It was impossible to keep his distance. He crossed to the side of the bed. The warm womanly scent of her, of their mingling, stirred him again. "I'll take you home."

She gave a quick shake of her head, looking away. "Not necessary."

A half dozen condoms were still on the night stand, and he glanced from them back to her. "Do you want a shower, some coffee?" His voice sounded raw.

"My neighbors are away. I'm taking care of their dog. I have to go…"

He reached out and brushed her hair back over her right shoulder. "There are towels, shampoo, whatever you need. I'll be in the kitchen."

"Thank you."

He hated that she sounded relieved.

He stood outside the bedroom door until he heard the shower. Then he came back into the room, stuffed the condoms on the nightstand into his pockets and opened the drawer. There were two more packages. He took them both.

* * *

Annie stared at her house, puzzled to be there. She had lost all sense of the time in the fog. The drive had taken minutes or hours. At a long light on the coast highway, he had put her hand on his thigh. In spite of the awkward stretch of her arm across the truck's wide cabin, she had not moved it, feeling the flex of his muscle as he drove, trying to think what she should say at their parting. She wanted to let him go with dignity and courage. She was prepared. This was no unexpected sorrow, no plane crash, flood, or fire. It was merely the completion of an act begun long ago—letting go. They would both start over at last; mourning would be followed by a return to life.

But his thigh under her hand was warm and alive and a link to all they had done the night before. She should be exhausted, but she was bursting with energy. She hoped the letdown wouldn't come until she could curl up alone in her own room.

She hadn't counted on Irene Gale.

Irene was at her front door as they came up the walk. Annie was not going to part from Will Sloan under Irene's curious gaze. It was near nine, and she was in evening clothes, her hair in a loose twist, no makeup. She could see Irene's curiosity, and the tiny streak of defiance in her character, like a minor fault line, shifted and split open. She had broken the biggest rule she'd ever made for herself, and now she had no desire to live by other people's rules.

"Oh Annie, I thought something must have happened to you. Ginger's been whimpering all morning." Her words were for Annie, but her gaze was all for Will Sloan.

"I'm going over to the Biddles' right now, Irene. No need to worry." Annie fumbled her key out of her purse.

"Well, of course. I just couldn't imagine where you were. It's not like you at all to…"

No, it wasn't like her, but Annie was through being the neighborhood saint. She slipped her arm through Will's and leaned her head against his shoulder. It felt right, actually. "Irene, this is Will Sloan, an old friend of mine."

Irene's mouth gaped open just as Annie unlocked her door and stepped into the entry on Will's arm. She swept the door closed on Irene's astonished gaze.

"What are you doing?" Amusement glinted in his green eyes.

"Just letting Irene know that you're the flavor of the month." She dropped her bag on the entry table and set off down the hall. A quick glance over her shoulder told her she'd stunned him. "I need to change. To take care of the dog. Thank you for the ride and…the great sex. You can leave whenever…."

"Whenever," he whispered, and the low sound of his voice momentarily checked her steps.

Annie grabbed jeans, a T-shirt, and sweater, locked herself in the bathroom and tried to concentrate on how hungry Ginger must be. When she emerged to find shoes and socks, he stood at the door of her bedroom looking in.

Everything in her quickened and stirred and fluttered into life.

"Feed the dog," he said.

* * *

Irene's gaze followed Annie across the street and into the Biddles' yard. Great. Because of Irene, she'd let Will Sloan into her house.

Ginger wiggled excitedly and rolled belly up for Annie's attention. She calmed the dog, fed her, and lingered to toss a tennis ball for a few minutes, but she couldn't stay away from home forever.

His truck sat in her driveway, huge, black, gleaming, the devil's own four-wheel drive. Irene's curtains dropped into place as Annie came up the walk. She squared her shoulders and went inside. He wasn't in the living room, kitchen, or family room. He hadn't gone out on the little patio. Annie checked. She took a deep breath and turned down the hall.

He sat in her sagging old wicker reading chair in the corner of her bedroom. "How was the dog?"

"Hungry. Lonely. Wanting someone to play with."

"Who doesn't," he said rising up out of the chair and moving toward her in a purposeful, unhurried way.

She stood docile, as he unbuttoned her sweater. She remembered standing still as a child for her mother's unbuttonings, but his concentration changed everything. Inside she was shaking as if from cold, but she was feverish, overheated, needing to shed her clothes. He pushed the sweater off her shoulders, pulled her arms free of the sleeves, and skimmed her T-shirt over her head.

He stared at her breasts in the black silk bra as if he had not seen them fully the night before, took a deep shuddering breath, then knelt and removed her shoes. She put her hand on his shoulder to balance first on one foot, then the other. She was on fire now. He reached for the fly of her jeans, undoing the button and zipper, stepping forward and slipping his hands inside the denim covering her backside, skimming the jeans over her hips to the floor. He took her hands and helped her step out of the crumpled pants. Then he stepped back and pulled the shirt over his head, shedding his own slacks in a few quick motions. They were both breathing rapidly now. He took her hand and led her to the iron bed with its worn blue quilt.

He pulled the quilt and blankets back, and nudged her up onto the sheets. From his jacket on her chair, he took a chain of condom packets and dropped them on the dresser next to the bed. He climbed in beside her.

This time there were no words just his hands and lips asking. *This? And this? And this?* And her body answering helplessly, opening up to him in an endless *yes.* Afterward she lay warm and limp in his arms, her back pressed to him, while his hands moved deliberately over her, as if memorizing her.

The phone rang, and she stirred, but his arm clamped firmly around her waist, pinning her against him.

After a few rings, the answering machine came on.

Annie, it's Meredith. Mel and Megan are out of control on this party for Daddy. Call them. And for heaven's sake, don't freeze your eggs. I've got the perfect man for you. Barry Edwards. He's free now that he's dumped Stacy. So get a decent two-piece and plan to do the hot tub thing with Barry. Ciao.

It was odd lying in bed, listening to her sister's message while a warm hand grasped her middle and moved lazily up to her breast to play with the peak.

"You have three sisters?"

She nodded.

"Do they usually get you dates?"

"They're not impressed with my dating record."

"Who's Barry Edwards? Should I be worried?"

"No one." The hand at her breast teased the nipple and threads of sensation streaked through her body. "Someone my sisters thought I should try for in high school."

"Did you?" The hand moved down to cover her belly.

"I was never in his league. He was prom king; I was a dork." Her sisters had been the prom queens, cheerleaders, leads in the school plays. She had been editor of the features page of the newspaper and head of the tutoring group. Her sympathies had been for the kids at the bottom of the high school food chain, the brine shrimp, spider mites, and algae of the social world. Maybe that was why she had liked Mike Moreland and sympathized with Will Sloan all those years ago.

His hand brushed the curls at the juncture of her thighs. "Barry Edwards never thought you were a dork."

"You don't know that." She tried to keep the breathlessness from her voice.

"Yes. I do. Barry Edwards thought you were aloof and proud. He was intimidated by your intelligence."

"You're making that up."

"You could tell your sisters you have a date."

"The party's in February." She didn't say that he'd be gone by then, but she didn't need to.

Annie must have dozed. She woke up hungry and heard an answering rumble from his stomach.

"You're hungry." She tried to move, but the arm around her waist held her yet.

"I won't starve."

"We can't stay here all day."

"You're thinking about your neighbor."

"She knows my habits."

"So, it's not your habit to spend all day Sunday in bed with the flavor of the month."

Annie twisted to face him, and the contact, the brush of warm skin against skin, made her gasp, and she saw in his eyes the instant flicker of passion. Face-to-face they breathed roughly.

"I go to the grocery store on Sunday."

"I'll go with you." He rolled away from her, threw back the covers, and stood, leaving her gaping. She hadn't really looked at him, not looked her fill at the long, lean length of him, the turn of his legs, the planes and hollows of his chest and loins, his sex hanging full and heavy against the dark hair.

"You have a choice here. You can look at me like that, or we can go to the supermarket."

"Then I choose—the supermarket."

He laughed, and she felt a sudden ache in her throat. She had not heard him laugh in such an easy, happy way before.

From her driveway, he waved at Irene. In the store he filled a red plastic tote-basket with men's toiletries, a package of boxer shorts, some T-shirts, swim trunks, and steaks. He introduced himself to the staring cashier Annie had known for years.

In the parking lot, Annie found her voice. "You're not moving in with me."

He turned from the bag he had loaded in the truck. "I know."

She tried again. "You wanted revenge, not..."

"What we started isn't finished yet. We couldn't satisfy all that wanting in one..."

"...night."

* * *

The black truck was on the street in front of her house when Annie turned up the lane after work, and two doors down Dan Biddle was watering his driveway in a light rain. Water ran down the shallow gutter at the curb. He dropped the hose and headed her way. He yanked her truck door open before the engine stopped.

"Annie, what's going on here?"

"Hi, Dan. How was your trip? How's Tess?" She climbed down from the truck.

He leaned toward her with a glance at her dining room windows. "Irene Gale says you have a man living with you."

"I have a man staying with me. It's temporary."

"Jeez, Annie. Who is this guy? I mean, a single woman these days. You can't be too careful."

"He's someone I've known for over ten years."

"Oh. So the guy just shows up, moves in? That's crazy. How do you know who he's been—?"

She stepped around Dan and strode to the mailbox. It was empty. "Dan, I'm having a brief affair with this man. It won't interfere with my usual activities at all. I can still watch people's pets, collect their mail, or water their yards."

"Why this guy? Why not me if you want some? I've been here for you, Annie. I'm a friend. I mean, who fixes your truck?"

"Dan, you're married to Tess. Tess is my friend."

"Tess! Tess won't mind. She knows a guy's gotta have a little extra every now and then."

"Thanks for offering yet again, Dan, but I'm not interested." She headed up the driveway, and Irene's curtains twitched.

"You will be, Annie James. You'll get a taste for it. And when you want some, I'll be here for you, like always."

* * *

The house smelled like dinner. Oven warmed air carried the scent of something baking. Habit had governed her actions right to the moment she dropped her keys on the entry table, but she felt disoriented as if she'd opened a familiar door but entered a strange house.

"Hey." His voice came from the living room, and she turned to him where he sat watching a dim sunset through the misting rain.

"You made dinner?"

"One of the useful things my mama taught me."

She stepped down into the living room, moving toward him, drawn by her body's desire as if she had no will. He had set the coffee table for them to eat and watch the sunset, but clouds covered the sky. He reached out and pulled her toward him, pressing her to his length, and kissing her deeply. And what was between them flared up and burned hotly again. His voice rumbled deeply at her ear. She protested briefly about the dinner, and he detoured through the kitchen, turning the oven off, and headed for her bedroom.

In the aftermath she asked him, "What did you do today?"

"I read your newspaper, checked out your bookshelves, scandalized your neighbors—"

"You didn't—"

"—desired you. Same old stuff."

"What about your work?"

"I had a nice talk with Irene when I went out for a run."

"I didn't give you a key."

"There's a backdoor key hanging behind a fern on your patio."

"What did you tell Irene?"

"That I am a dangerous man from your past. By the way, I met your neighbor Dan. What does he do when he's not lusting after you?"

"He's a builder. He does remodels."

"He's not happy about my truck parked in front of your place."

* * *

Will woke in Annie's bed sometime after midnight on Wednesday. She was not beside him. He listened for her in the darkness. Then the smell of onions, butter, and broth came to him. He pulled on a T-shirt with his boxers and followed the smell to the kitchen.

She had something on the stove. The fragrant steam rose from a large pot while she sat at the kitchen table sorting a mound of coins into stacks.

A painful jolt of memory passed through him. His mom counting her tips, saving pennies for a rainy day. "What are you doing?"

She looked up. "Making soup. I always make soup on Sunday, and I forgot." It was an admission of how his being there changed her life.

"And the coins?"

"Oh. I save a few coins every day and roll them up for the church at the end of the year." A blush crept up her cheek.

"You're embarrassed by that?"

"I missed church on Sunday."

"Fallen woman that you are." He pulled out the chair opposite her.

"Yes." She said it too quietly.

He reached out and grabbed her wrist and made her look at him. "I was joking."

She nodded.

He couldn't believe he could look at her like this. She had a way of twisting her hair in a coil, and poking the end through the circle to secure it without clips or ties. He knew now how to release it.

He cupped his hands around a mound of coins and slid them his way. He would keep his hands occupied stacking money.

He knew her body and its secrets, her responses, the stretch and arch of her against him, the clenching of her muscles around him, the sigh that was a near a sob when she felt her climax come upon her.

The pile of coins, hard and cold in his hands, was a reminder of what he did not know about her. He suspected that her neighbors, who watched her so closely, and her family with its daily messages, did not really know her either.

He should have exhausted his desire for her by now through their daily joinings, but something he wanted from her eluded him. If he could figure out what it was, he could be sure that when he left, he would take no more detours into the past.

"What kind of journalist did you want to be?"

She looked up again from the coins. "Where did that question come from?"

"You've quite a collection of books by and for journalists."

"Oh, of course. They're mostly leftover from college." She bent her head again so that the light glinted off her hair.

"So, what kind? Did you imagine yourself with a mike and a crew reporting live from battlefields or disasters?"

She shook her head. "I never thought of TV at all."

"Never wanted to be where the action was happening?"

"No. I think if I had pursued it, I'd be telling the forgotten stories, or if I got lucky, uncovering some injustice that I could bring to light with a story."

"What's stopping you?"

Her hands stilled briefly on the coins. "I think ambition was something I put away for a while. I got out of the habit of…"

"Dreaming?"

"I like my life, you know."

"When did you buy this house?"

It seemed a simple question, but she hesitated just enough to let him know that the truth would be another sign of the way their history was intertwined. Even their separation from each other was marked by awareness of the points in each other's life.

"Six years ago. The market was good, and I had built up a down payment."

He had been graduating from college at the time, imagining her already married to some guy who could buy her things while he and Beau were putting everything they had into Z-Text.

* * *

It rained hard the day his condom supply ran out. He had one left in the pocket of his jacket, which still lay across the reading chair in her room. He'd used half of the toothpaste and shampoo he'd bought, and the T-shirts and boxers had been through her washer. He had lived by a few simple rules in her house. He had used his cell phone to leave messages at work. He hadn't put anything away. He'd appropriated only the towel rack on the far wall of her bathroom and a few tiles in one corner of the counter. Like a careful backpacker, he'd left the ecology of her house undisturbed. No book out of place, nothing in the closet, no shoes under the bed.

A message on her answering machine told him it was time to leave.

Annie, it's Josh. Hey, missed you on campus today. What's going on with our newest Canyon student? Let's talk.

—Monday, 9:00 a.m.

He left a note on her entry table, put his things in the trash cans at the curb, and rolled his truck to the end of the block before he turned the engine on. Irene Gale's curtains never opened.

Chapter Fourteen

Annie drove on autopilot. She would put Will Sloan out of her mind again. She had worked it out. He had wanted to do the walking out on her this time. Well, she knew that in time his effect on her would subside, become a condition she lived with, no known cure, but several helpful treatments. Her sisters were cooking up something. By February she'd probably be ready to meet the men they had in mind for her.

She forgot Ulysses was with her until she flipped on her turn signal as they approached Canyon.

He reached out and tapped her arm urgently. "Don't turn here."

"What?" She realized he'd said nothing for half an hour.

"There's another…entrance. Go there." He waved her forward.

"The service gate?" It was unlike him to be so quiet.

"Yeah."

Annie turned off her blinker and merged back into the flow of traffic passing the main Canyon driveway. "Why do you want the service gate?"

"It's quicker. I've got to get to the library before class today."

She turned into the maintenance yard and pulled up in the gravel area in front of a huge yellow trash compactor. Behind it a path led to the old toolshed with its hidden roof, her old sunset-watching spot. "Listen, Ulysses, I'm sorry I was so inattentive…" He was out of the truck. "Hey?"

He turned back briefly, his dark glasses glinting in the pale morning sun. "You don't have to pick me up today, Ms. James. I'm staying late for a C-Notes rehearsal."

"Okay. We'll talk tomorrow."

"Later." Annie let him go.

But two afternoons later Ulysses did not wave to his blond friend. The boy watched them from the steps, his face pulled in a frown. Ulysses pushed the radio button preset for a Spanish music station and curled away from Annie, resting his head against the door. Before they reached the freeway, he was asleep.

At the apartment complex where he lived, she gave him a gentle nudge to rouse him, and he started, caught his bearings, and slipped out of the truck with a brief thank you.

It was the first time they hadn't talked and laughed about his day. Annie vowed to get ahold of herself. She could not let her sadness over Will Sloan affect anyone else.

* * *

On Friday afternoon when she pulled up at Canyon, Ulysses was nowhere in sight. His blond friend sat hunched at the top of the steps, tracing the lines between the bricks with a stick. Annie was about to leave the truck when Ulysses came dashing across the parking lot. He slipped into his seat, panting, and reached for the radio buttons. "Let's go, huh."

Annie turned the truck engine off.

Ulysses groaned.

The blond boy scrambled down the steps. "Hey, Ulysses."

Ulysses stared straight ahead. Annie smiled at the boy. "I'm Annie James, a friend of Ulysses."

The boy stuck out his hand through the open window. "Hi. I'm Tyler." He looked at Ulysses's unmoving profile. "Just don't quit. I can teach you the songs."

Annie and Tyler waited an excruciatingly long time, and got no answer. She and Tyler exchanged a glance.

"See you tomorrow, man." Tyler stepped back from the truck and shoved his hands in his pockets. Annie turned on the engine and pulled away.

At a signal light with Ulysses's street in sight, Annie broke the silence. "Whatever is wrong, someone can help if you talk about it. Your mom, your uncle, me, Josh, someone."

Ulysses gave one quick shake of his head before he hopped out of the truck. Annie felt she had just remembered a language she'd studied years before. The old idioms of tight shoulders, averted profile, and tense jaw came back to her, the language of a boy whose pride was wounded.

She called Josh, suddenly grateful that she could. The development office said he was out of town. She left a message.

118

It took Josh four days after his return to figure out the change in Annie's routine. He didn't like it. She was a woman of predictable patterns.

On the Friday after his return when she dropped Ulysses in the maintenance yard, Josh stepped from behind the trash compactor, and caught the door of the truck as Ulysses hurried off.

Josh swung up into the truck. "Why the new drop-off point?"

She looked straight ahead, gripping the wheel hard. "Ulysses asked for it. He says he's going to the library before class, and he gets there faster from here."

"You're not buying that, are you? You know this campus."

She shrugged her shoulders.

"You're not avoiding me because you went to bed with Sloan, are you?"

"It's what you wanted, isn't it?"

"And you can get mad about it, if you want to."

"You planned to bring us together from the beginning. From the day I brought Ulysses here, you worked to bring Will and me together—that dinner, the committee, the party, all of it."

He had, and he should be feeling a lot better about it than he was watching her refuse to look at him. Sloan owed him, big, but maybe he hadn't been fair to Annie. Maybe it was a good thing she wouldn't look at him, considering he couldn't tell her the truth, not the whole truth, anyway. "Sloan has wanted you forever. You liked him when no one else did. You stood up for him when everyone else would have let Chambers throw him out and ruin his future. I just wanted to help the two of you get together."

"Like a...pimp."

"Wow! That's good. As nastiness goes, it's fairly minor, but still, pretty mean coming from Annie James."

"Bastard." Her knuckles were white on the steering wheel.

"Better."

Then her shoulders slumped, and she pressed her head against her hands on the steering wheel. "It's not your fault. It was wrong from the beginning. Sometimes, no matter what you feel, you can't make a thing right."

Josh shook his head, though he knew she couldn't see the gesture. The blades of her shoulders sticking up through her sweater made her look fragile. He touched her back, lightly, with his fingertips. He'd pay for it later, for touching her. And he couldn't get off with Chambers's new secretary the way he had with the old one.

"Sloan doesn't hate you, you know." That was a truth, and he felt good about saying it. "You make him need you, and Sloan hates to need anybody."

He flattened his palm so that he could feel the bumps of her spine.

She lifted her head, and he let his hand fall. "I'm going to be late for work."

"You going to be all right?"

"Eventually."

"Hey, listen, I'm a little worried about Ulysses."

"Why?" She was instantly concerned for the boy, her eyes alive with their extraordinary sympathy.

Josh felt a stab of envy for Ulysses. "He's stopped coming to C-Note rehearsals."

"He stays late for them every day."

Josh shook his head. He made himself open the truck door and step down. "Rehearsals are at lunch, and he hasn't made one this month."

"Oh! I'll talk to him."

* * *

Beau Lassiter was pissed. The Crosspoint Venture people had walked. But Will suspected that the real source of Beau's anger was that Will had not consulted him before sleeping with Annie.

"So who is this woman you shacked up with for a week?"

"She's someone I knew a long time ago."

"Define a long time ago. I've known you since you were eighteen."

"I knew this woman then, too."

"Not at school."

"No." No one he had known in college was remotely like Annie James.

"So who is she? Are you going to tell me about her? She must be pretty hot. You're a flaming celibate most of the time."

"I have lapses."

"You're a High Net Worth Individual. You don't want a lapse to bleed you dry."

"Don't worry about it. It's over."

"Don't worry about it. You gave away two hundred and fifty thousand big ones to get her into your bed. You think she's going to let you go?"

"She did the last time I asked her to marry me. This time it was my turn to do the walking out. Come on, Beau, just help me find someone else."

"Like you would ever take one of my picks."

"I might. Give me a chance."

* * *

All the rooms in her house were infected with his absence. He left nothing behind but a note on her entry table.

I've embarrassed you in front of your neighbors long enough.

She refused to cry. She surprised herself by functioning extraordinarily well in the next few weeks.

She enjoyed a Thanksgiving gathering with Louisa's family and the familiar boost in spirits that came with the shift in seasons. Then she burned the cookies for the annual neighborhood holiday exchange and had to dash to a bakery. She was late for the gathering, and Dan Biddle cornered her on the Hansens' porch and pressed her up against the wall and forced his eggnog-thickened tongue between her teeth while he groped her breasts. She stepped hard on his toes and left the party without taking home any cookies.

Coming home from work the next day, forgetting for an instant the pattern of lights at a familiar intersection, she pulled out through an opening in cross traffic. A man in a Jaguar going forty broadsided her from the right. No one was hurt. Her truck was totaled.

Annie's loaner car, a gray compact Louisa had inherited when her mother stopped driving, provoked Ulysses into breaking days of silence.

"What happened to your truck?"

"I made a mistake."

"Are you all right, Ms. James?"

"I'm fine. I'm not so sure about you."

"I didn't wreck my truck."

"Are you wrecking yourself?"

"Just doing what I have to do." The boy's dark glasses flashed, reflecting the morning sun.

"You don't seem to like Canyon as much as you did in the beginning, and you don't see Tyler."

"It's cool, Ms. James. No problem."

But there was a problem. Ulysses's mom was waiting for Annie in Louisa's office with a letter from the school.

Annie saw the familiar arches of the Canyon logo on the letterhead. The dean was writing to say that Ulysses had two D's and an F and that he would have to improve his record significantly by the end of the term in order to keep his scholarship. The school was prepared to offer every assistance. The dean recommended a parent/teacher conference.

Even in her sorrow-induced fog, Annie knew that something had gone wrong. She just had to get Ulysses to admit it. But he slouched sullenly in his chair, hiding behind his dark glasses. He did not want Annie or his mom to go to the school. He insisted he could handle the problem himself. In his posture was the wounded spirit Annie had so often seen in Will Sloan, the dangerous prickly vulnerability, the pride.

She had a sudden clear recollection of Will Sloan telling her to go to the business manager to find out how Ulysses's scholarship was paid. When she called, the business manager assumed a helpful manner, but he insisted that all financial aid was strictly confidential. Annie could not even get him to describe the process by which the family was billed and the aid received. The confidentiality seemed reasonable, but the man's evasive manner left her suspicious. A breezy message on Josh Huntington's phone said he was snowboarding. There was only one person to call.

* * *

Will had been as good as his word to Beau. They'd gone for Irish rock music and soul and old school in Santa Monica, and Latin house, salsa, and hip-hop in Century City. They had mixed with the funk-with-money crowd, Prada-philes, the ultra cool, and the dewy-faced. They'd done a Silicon Beach event that mixed fashion and funding. He hadn't felt at home anywhere except at one Rose Bowl–watching party at the home of a newly-married former teammate.

When he heard Annie's voice on his answering machine, everything he had refused to think about through the holidays came flooding back.

Will, it's Annie James calling about Ulysses. He's not doing well at Canyon, and I can't get any information out of the school. Is there anything you can tell me to help me help Ulysses? You can leave a message. Thank you.

In the end he decided to go by her house on a dry, clear January day. Her neighbor's curtain twitched as he pulled up, and when he rang the bell, Irene appeared in her own doorway to tell him, "Annie's watering on her deck. Keep ringing."

Will nodded and used his cell to call her.

She came to the door in khaki shorts and a white T-shirt, barefoot, her hair in its casual knot, a red watering can in one hand.

"Pretty chicken leaving me a voicemail message."

She didn't speak, just waved him into the house, closing the door on Irene's stare.

He managed to cross the threshold though her breasts outlined by the thin, loose shirt, her legs sweetly curved in all the right places, and her pink toes seemed to have wiped his errand from his mind.

"Your boy's in trouble at Canyon?"

She nodded. "Thank you for coming. Do you want to sit down? Do you want some…water, coffee?"

What he wanted was another chance to walk out on her. The first one hadn't been as satisfying as he'd imagined. From where he stood in the entry, he could see down into her living room on his right and straight ahead the short hall that led to her bedroom.

"Water's good."

She disappeared into the kitchen, and he heard the sounds of her opening a cabinet and then her refrigerator. He took one more look down the hall. Her bedroom door was closed. She could not have known he was coming, but he took it as a sign and turned to the living room. From her front windows she could watch the sunset. It shouldn't matter, shouldn't feel like something he'd lost, but it did. Then her neighbor from across the street with the beach boy tan emerged from his garage. He caught sight of Will through the window and glared. Will gave a nod.

He heard her behind him and turned. She held the glass of water, her arm stretched out to keep him at a distance. He took the water and turned back to the window.

"How's the big guy? Still hitting on you?"

"Dan? What makes you think that?"

"He just sent me his hostile look. I'm betting he'd rather I wasn't in your living room." He turned to look at her. Color rose in her cheeks. So the guy did hit on her.

"What did you mean that you could fix things for Ulysses?" She stepped behind her sofa, hiding her legs from his view.

"Tell me what's going on with him."

He could hear her confusion as she told the tale, only half-listening. He couldn't see her legs, but the shirt was still a distraction, and he was familiar with the story already—Ulysses's fatigue, his sudden embarrassment around his friend Tyler, the lie about having to stay late for rehearsals, his desire to use the school's back entrance. It all meant that Chambers was up to his old tricks.

When she fell silent, he said, "I can fix it."

"I would be grateful."

"More grateful to me than to Huntington?"

She stiffened, and the motion lifted her breasts in the thin T-shirt. "I know you think...I don't know what you think, really, but Josh Huntington has never asked me for sexual favors. He has never even wanted...to have sex with me."

He laughed. She had no idea about Huntington. "But because Huntington helped Ulysses, you agreed to be on that committee, to meet with me, to go to that party." He let it sink in, the choices she'd made.

"I did."

"You must really care about that boy's success."

"I do." Her chin came up a notch.

"You don't have to make deals with me. You could withdraw Ulysses from Canyon. He's bright and capable. That center of yours is a good place. You and Louisa could see to it that he stayed on track to get to college, to get the opportunities he deserves."

"It's true, but Louisa and I hoped his success, his opportunity would open doors for other students at the center."

He turned back to her again, shifting so he could see her legs, keeping his eyes on the pink tips of her toes, so she wouldn't see what he wanted until the trap sprang closed. "So here's the deal."

Her toes curled under his regard.

"I fix it so that Ulysses is the first happy scholarship boy in the history of Canyon, and you spend twenty-four hours with me, a complete day."

She faced him silently, all eyes. "No sex?"

"I'll bring the condoms."

"No sex." She was shaking her head.

"I name the day. Is it a deal?" He put the water glass down on her pine coffee table and moved toward the door. He had to get out of there now.

"Ulysses has to be really happy. He has to be fine. He has to…"

"Is it a deal?"

"Yes."

Chapter Fifteen

A week later Annie knew Ulysses was okay when he and Tyler came down the steps together.

"We're singing at Pac Prep in two weeks, and Tyler's dad says we can earn the money for our C-Note blazers at his office this weekend."

Annie glanced at Tyler, a boy who had never needed to earn anything in his life. He didn't want her to give him away. He'd understood and arranged something for his friend. She gave him big points.

"So, some homework has to get done before the weekend."

Groans.

Ulysses swung his forty pounds of books into the back seat of Louisa's car and climbed in the front. "See ya," he said to his friend.

Tyler was grinning as they pulled away, and Ulysses was full of talk, as if he'd been storing his thoughts for two unhappy months and now had to tell her all.

Somewhere south of Santa Monica he brought up a new subject. "Josh told me he knew you when you used to work at Canyon."

"He did. A long time ago. You were four maybe."

"Did he always do things for people?"

"Like what?"

"Like getting me into Canyon and all."

"He didn't get you into Canyon. He helped with your application, but you got in because you're smart, very smart." Annie spoke quietly, seriously.

"That's the way it's supposed to be, Ms. James, but that's not the way it is at Canyon, not exactly."

She almost pulled over. "Do you want to leave?"

"No. Tyler needs me."

"He does?"

"He's dyslexic, you know. He'd never make it through without me."

"Oh, I didn't know."

"He doesn't want anyone to know. He's sort of like Josh in that way."

She had no idea where the conversation was going. "Josh is dyslexic?"

"No, but he doesn't want people to figure him out."

"What doesn't he want people to know about him?"

"Well, you know how mostly he doesn't do things for people, like getting me into the C-Notes, just because he's a friendly guy."

"I'm glad you know that."

Ulysses shrugged. The dark glasses still hid his eyes. "But that's only part of the truth. Partly he likes people to think he does things to get things, but only partly. Partly, Josh is a good guy. It's interesting to watch him, how he is around you mainly, but around other people, too. Dr. Chambers's secretary would do anything for him."

Oh dear. Annie hoped he didn't mean that the way it sounded. With the dark glasses she couldn't tell. He was fourteen. Surely he couldn't see through Josh that completely.

"So partly he helps me because he wants something from you, doesn't he?"

"He wants me to work on a committee to help Canyon."

"Does he want, you know—sex—from you?"

"No." Annie shook her head vigorously.

Ulysses grinned. "Good. Because I was going to have to *keel* him." His grin was ear to ear, and his accent was the phoniest Mexican accent she had ever heard. He reached down and turned on her radio. In a few minutes he was singing along.

Ulysses was happy. Will Sloan had done something, and she was going to have to pay him back.

* * *

Annie's phone light blinked, and at a press of the button the machine voice told her she had four new messages.

Annie, it's Meg. Can you straighten Mel out about the menu? She's gone Martha Stewart, and you know Daddy's more of a Rachel Ray kind of guy. And get ready to meet Alan. He's got the most amazing voice. You'll be swept away. What can I say?

—Tuesday. 9:45 a.m.

Annie, it's Meredith. Can you believe they've stuck me with the tables? Like Mel is a better cook than I am? She doesn't even pay

*attention to what Daddy likes! Buy yourself a new swimsuit. A
tankini would be cool. Larry is to die for.*

—*Tuesday. 11:12 a.m.*

*Annie, it's Mel. Can you talk to Meg? She thinks she's
producing the Academy Awards. Everyone who ever hammered a
nail for Daddy is going to speak, and she's got her very own Von
Trapp family singing group. We'll be sitting for three hours. The
kids will go nuts. Daddy will go nuts. Call her.*

—*Tuesday. 2:23 p.m.*

*Annie, it's Mel again. I forgot to mention Barry. He is so ready
for you!*

—*Tuesday. 3:10 p.m.*

Her cell phone queue had exactly one text that read *Saturday*.

She called him, got his voice mail, and left a message explaining
that she had a family obligation in Santa Barbara and would be away
Saturday. Would he care to reschedule?

It was civilized, sensible, unafraid.

* * *

He was at her door at six-thirty on Saturday morning, talking to
Irene, his truck angled across the foot of her driveway, blocking her
in. She yanked him into her entry where her overnight bag sat
waiting, and closed the door on Irene's gaze. She glared up at him.
His wet hair showed comb lines, his jaw gleamed, freshly shaven.
The familiar sun-on-pines scent of him in the narrow entry made her
a little dizzy. His eyes were the color of new grass on the hills.

"I left you a message."

"I got it."

"I have a family obligation this weekend."

The green eyes gave no quarter. "The deal is I get to name the
day."

"I'm not weaseling out of our deal. It's just that I have to be
there for my dad."

"I'd like to see you with your family."

She shook her head emphatically. "No you wouldn't. You have
no idea."

He picked up her bag.

"I have things for my dad's party in my car and things to pick up on the way." She caught his arm, warm solid flesh with the muscle flexed to heft her bag. At her touch his expression changed.

"No problem. We'll take my truck."

She pulled back. She'd been careless to touch him.

"When we get there, I'll have to help out."

"I'll hang out with your family."

"Listen, my family is..." She backed into the kitchen, and he put down the bag, following her. She hit the play all button on her answering machine to let him hear her sisters.

He didn't take his eyes off of her. "Apparently, your sisters think you can't get your own...date." The word sent a charge through her. "So show them you can. Take me."

The husky rasp of his voice shut down her thought processes. She didn't know how long they stood there. The first thought that came back to her was a rebellious one—what would Meg, Meredith, and Mel think when they saw him? She had not rebelled in a long time. She had simply stayed away. To bring him into the midst of a Palmer family event, unannounced, unexpected, would be like bringing a panther to a 4-H judging where everyone else's prize pig was on display.

She looked at him. He had no idea. His family was just his mom and him as far as she knew, not a crowd. She had to give him a chance to back out. "It will be a whole day of games, contests, eating, noise, ceremony—family. We won't have any time alone."

He looked at her and then looked down the hall toward her bedroom. "You thought I would just pin you to the nearest mattress for the next twenty-four hours."

Instant heat flared at the suggestion, a match thrown into dry grass.

"You'll have to be nice to me."

"In public."

In the driveway, he stopped her to ask, "Where's your truck?"

"I had an accident. The truck didn't make it."

"When?"

"A few weeks ago."

He let it go, but she couldn't be sure that he hadn't put two and two together.

They transferred the box of Meredith's placeholders from her car to his truck under Irene's interested gaze. Once Annie sat in the black truck behind its tinted windows, she was less sure of her rebellion. Poor kidnapped Persephone had probably felt safer looking across the chariot at Hades.

"Nice cup holders." She waved to Dan Biddle in his boxers, newspaper in hand.

"The coffee's for you."

"Thanks." She cradled the warm paper cup in her hands.

"Tell me about your family."

"You don't really want to give me that kind of opening."

"But you want to keep my mind occupied."

"Right. Well then. My family collects trophies. They win things—tennis tournaments, triathalons, 4-H contests, spelling bees, choral competitions, and building awards. My sisters even won the cake baking contest at the end of seventh grade home economics class."

"Which sister?"

"All of them. One after another."

"And you?"

"I don't compete much." She fell silent until she caught his gaze, then she didn't let herself run out of things to say until they crossed the L.A. County line and were winding their way along an undeveloped stretch of coast between the waves and tall sand dunes at the foot of dry, chaparral-and-cactus-covered hills.

But she couldn't ignore what was between them forever. "I can't talk for twenty-four hours." She looked over at him. He seemed to have all his concentration on the road.

"You think talking keeps me from wanting you?"

"You said…"

He slanted her a glance. "You've always been wrong about that."

"Oh."

He reached for her hand and pulled it, a gentle relentless tug toward him, so that she had to scoot sideways up on the edge of her seat. He pressed the flat of her palm against his groin.

She felt her whole body flush with awareness and longing. She should pull her hand away immediately, but couldn't do it. Under the thick outer layer of his fly, she could feel the long, firm shape of him. He was telling her that his desire for her had not changed.

Will wanted to close his eyes and give in to the feeling of her hand on him, but he happened to be driving along a curving two-lane road at a dangerous speed. He hit the right turn signal and the brake and maneuvered them off the highway, slowing the truck to a stop at the edge of the road, gravel crunching under the tires.

Traffic roared by. It was hard to remember what the plan for the day was. He was supposed to make her want him this time, not expose his own raging desire.

"We could climb into the back." He knew the timbre of his voice gave him away. He glanced at the narrow bench-style seat behind them. "Tinted windows. Plenty private." He stopped himself from begging. "Or we can make it to your father's party."

The open window let in the tang of ocean air. He let his head fall back against the headrest, his eyes closed. For the longest time her hand didn't move though he willed it to.

Finally, he heard her take a deep, shuddering inhale. Her hand slid away back to her lap. "To the party."

He opened his eyes. She didn't look at him, but he could see the flush of her skin, the tautness of her breasts.

"Give me a minute?"

She nodded, and he opened the door and jumped down from the truck to the let the sun and breeze clear his head.

Chapter Sixteen

The parking lot of Rancho Luna de Miel was crowded with SUVs
and vans, nothing smaller than a mini tour bus, and most of them
plastered with the college decals of his old rivals. Will was definitely
in enemy territory. Six children, flushed from heat and play, in
matching dark-blue T-shirts surrounded the truck as soon as he
pulled into a spot. The shirts read "Doug Palmer Retirement
Celebration" in white lettering above a child's drawing of a house
and the date. The kids' took a menacing stance and regarded him
with suspicion. The look they gave Annie said, "You're in trouble
now!" No one said a word.

Annie climbed out of the truck and came around to his side.
"Don't say I didn't warn you."

"You're not their favorite aunt apparently."

She laughed. "Hardly."

He lifted their things out of the truck, thinking back to her
sisters' phone messages and the things she'd said on the road.

"Where's your truck, Aunt Annie?" asked the littlest girl.

"My truck had an accident, so I came with my friend Will Sloan.
He's my guest, so be nice to him."

A tall blond kid, about twelve, with a mop of lemon yellow hair
and a sneer leaned toward the kid next to him, almost his clone, and
said in a voice with no volume control, "Boy is Mom going to be
mad."

The clone nodded somberly. Then the corners of his mouth
quirked up in a wicked little grin. "Yeah!"

"Do you play football?" asked the tall one.

"Some."

"Flag football's our first game," the kid said. "I dibs you for our
side."

Will glanced at Annie. She nodded. "Sure."

"You're the last ones here," announced the littlest girl.

"We're supposed to show you to your cottage," the clone added.

"Does he come, too, Aunt Annie?"

Annie lifted her chin, in a familiar gesture he was glad to see.
"Yes, he does."

The troop of Palmer cousins led them to their cottage along a winding path between beds of pink and white geraniums and tufts of something purple that looked like tiny bursts of fireworks. Annie gave her bag to one of her sturdier nephews and her purse to a small niece. The rest raced ahead.

At the cottage door they debated who'd won. They didn't stop to accept Annie's thank you. The tallest boy handed Annie one of the blue T-shirts and a printed schedule of events. Football was at the top. The kid pointed up the hill.

As they turned away, Will heard the clone ask the tall one, "What do you think Mom's going to do?"

"I don't know. I just know she's going to be steamed."

The stucco cottage had a red tile roof and a terra-cotta porch made cool and dim by thick vines of bougainvillea and jasmine. Inside was a living area with a plaid sofa facing a rustic stone fireplace at one end and a kitchen/dining area at the other, and off of the main room, a short hall opened on one side to a bedroom and on the other to a bath. No way would Annie James escape him tonight.

He carried their bags into the bedroom and dropped them in front of the closet. In the living room she was studying the printed schedule. He took it from her and grabbed her around the waist from behind, nuzzling her neck, whirling her off her feet, and using his body to walk her into the bedroom.

He held her facing the bed. "Looks like a nice bed, wide, comfortable, sturdy." He hadn't really been joking about pinning her to the mattress.

A shudder went through her. He breathed in her scent, trying to judge her reaction. In the truck she had hesitated, letting her hand linger a long time on his erection.

"How are we going to explain how we know each other?"

"I'll just tell your dad that I've been lusting after you for ten years and that I'm looking forward to the opportunity to sleep with you tonight."

She twisted to look at him, obviously alarmed. "You wouldn't."

He sobered at once. "It would be the truth, and it would put everyone's mind at rest."

She shook her head, clearly panicked at the idea.

"Do you want me to leave?"

"No, but…"

"Don't you want to shock your sisters?"

"A little, but it is my dad's retirement party."

"How about this, my company gave the center a donation. You called to acknowledge the gift and got me on the phone."

"That'll work. Thanks."

He held her a moment longer. "Before the night is over I'm going to show you that we're not who we were ten years ago."

* * *

They changed for the games on the program and followed a well-worn dirt path uphill through a narrow stand of eucalyptus to the main ranch house and three levels of pool and lawn. They carried the boxes of party supplies Annie had picked up for her sisters. Squeals came from two little girls splashing in the shallow end of the pool. On the next level Annie's brother-in-law, Jake, was handing out flags to potential football players in the middle of a wide lawn. Matt, Meredith's oldest boy, the one who had greeted them in the parking lot, spotted Will and waved him over to join the men. He put his boxes down on a picnic table and stunned Annie with a quick kiss full on her mouth before he jogged off to join the men.

At the other end of the patio her uncles were tending a large open barbeque. Her dad was surrounded by friends, all the men with whom he had built houses—carpenters, plumbers, electricians, architects, roofers, tile guys, and his indispensable bookkeeper.

She didn't see her mother, but her sisters had gathered to present a united, disapproving front—Meg, crisp and neat in her khaki shorts and blue polo shirt; Meredith in a lime green tube top and cropped white pants, a lean, mean, running machine; and Mel, in soft flowing peach linen shorts and shirt. The steep rocky outcrop above the ranch looked more hospitable.

Megan led off. "Annie, why didn't you tell us you were bringing someone?"

"You knew we'd been planning this for weeks." Meredith went straight for the box of placeholders. "Do you know how awkward this is? I mean Larry's dying to meet you!"

"Who is this…person? What were you thinking?" Melanie had her hands on her hips.

Her sisters' eyes were on Will as he crossed the field to meet the other guys. Will was shaking hands with her brothers-in-law, then all heads on the field turned toward Annie. *Oh what had he said? Date? Or friend? Or worse?*

There was a coin toss, and all the guys on Will's team removed their shirts. They were going to be the "skins."

Will shirtless gave a whole new meaning to the "skins" concept. From his wide sloping shoulders, his flat muscled chest tapered to the band of his dark green shorts. Her brothers-in-law were fit, good-looking men, and Barry Edwards, whom she recognized at once, was aging in a Richard Gere sort of way, but Annie could feel the collective brain of her sisters sizzling as they took in Will's proportions.

"What does he do?" asked Meg. "Construction?"

"Fireman?"

"Lifeguard?"

Annie found her voice. "He works for a tech company." As soon as she said it she realized she didn't really know what he did, or how he'd become so successful. She had not even questioned that amazing house on the hill.

Meg turned to her. "Well, Alan is an established dentist. He's got a great practice. The kids love to go to him. And he's in the men's chorus here in Santa Barbara."

Meredith turned on Meg. "As if Larry didn't have his own business. Dad has relied on Larry for every house he's done for three years, and not just for linoleum, but for marble, or tile, or wood. He can do it all. He is such a craftsman."

Mel spoke last. "I won't even get into it about Barry. You know Barry. He's gone through so much with his divorce. Stacy just flipped out. She brought the kids over one afternoon like they were going to play and went off to Las Vegas."

"How are his kids?" Annie asked.

"They are so little."

There was silence as they watched the game begin. The two teams lined up, facing each other in the middle of the grassy field. Each side had a boy quarterback, and a line of men. At the snap, there was a brief chaotic ballet of male bodies, then a halt. Will surrendered the flag he'd pulled from Barry Edwards's shorts. They lined up again.

"How old is this guy?"

"Twenty-eight."

"That makes you some kind of cougar, doesn't it?"

"You definitely need someone older. Twenty-eight. He won't be ready to make babies forever. Face it, at your age you just haven't got time for a fling with this guy."

"At least Barry's got maturity.

There was another scramble on the field, and Will held up another flag.

"He's been to college I hope."

"I haven't married him."

There was a tense silence, and Annie had a mad impulse to giggle as she realized that her sisters were imagining what she had done with him.

Meg recovered first. "How did you meet him?"

Annie stalled. The teams were lining up again. The ball had changed hands. John, Melanie's husband, was saying something to Will. They came out of their brief huddle. When the snap came, the ball went up in a wobbly pass from Matt. Barry Edwards batted it away from John, and it landed in Will's hands. He made two quick moves, little shifts of his hips, and then they were all staring at him in the makeshift end zone. His teammates high-fived each other.

Annie turned to her sisters. "His company made a donation to the center. That's how I met him. Excuse me. I've got to find Mom."

* * *

Her mother was in the big ranch kitchen surrounded by stacks of plates and lunch fixings.

"Oh Annie, you made it. Did you bring the placeholders?" Grace Palmer's blue eyes snapped with focused energy.

A dozen heads of local varieties of lettuce sat in leafy greenness on a large butcher-block island.

"Can you help, dear? We've got caterers for the dinner, but Melanie's planned a light lunch, too. She's thought of everything."

Annie found an apron and washed her hands.

"The girls have done such a good job. The tables are lovely! Meredith is so creative!"

Annie nodded, looking for some clue as to what her mother wanted her to do. She settled on the lettuce.

"And you'll love Mel's menu. She's absolutely outdone herself." Her mother began to spread walnut halves in a shallow baking dish. "Of course Megan put together the program, and it's so nice of people to come. Really. Doug is just tickled."

Her mother didn't seem to need a reply so Annie took a head of lettuce to break up and rinse in a sink built into the center of the island.

Her mother nodded. "Oh thanks, yes, that's just what's needed. The girls are so excited. They've been working to get these three young men here for you."

"I gathered."

Her mother paused and looked at her directly. "Now you may like one better than the others, but I want you to be fair and take time for each one."

"Mom, I brought a date."

Her mother's mouth fell open. Her perfect auburn bob framed her ridiculously disappointed face.

"Mom." Melanie's voice came from the patio door. "You have to see this. The twins are swimming."

Her mother looked from Annie to Melanie. "Of course, dear." And back to Annie. "Annie, the girls…"

"Mom, come on," Melanie called.

"I'm coming."

Annie turned back to the lettuce. The untouched heads regarded her with leafy indifference. Her mother's tray of walnut halves lay abandoned on the main counter. Washed pears lay draining in a colander, and when she checked the refrigerator, she found wedges of blue cheese, uncrumbled. Time to help out.

When Annie emerged from the kitchen, the football players milled about on the patio, Will in the midst of her brothers-in-law and her sisters' three candidates for date-of-the-day.

She looked them over from the kitchen doorway. There was a boyish-looking blond with striking blue eyes who looked a lot like her neighbor Dan; a brunet with a longish spiky crew cut, multiple piercings, and very nice arms; and Barry, tall, lean, and graying.

"I thought I recognized you," her brother-in-law Jake was saying to Will as they grabbed waters buried in big buckets of ice. "You played what—wide receiver?"

Will nodded and tipped back a bottled water. Annie watched his throat work.

"Those were some good years for the Cardinal. You didn't think about turning pro?"

"No. I had a business opportunity. It seemed like the time to focus on that." He cast Annie a quick glance. Someone had given him one of the blue, Palmer-family T-shirts, so it was easier to look at him.

"Hey, Annie." Her brothers-in-law lined up to hug her.

"Still in L.A.?" Jake always asked the question as if he expected her to move home next month.

"I hope you know what you're doing," whispered John.

Her dad kept her in a tight hug for a moment, and she wanted to stay there. Then he pulled back to give her a look that said she'd set the cat among the pigeons, but his smile warmed her.

She turned and faced the others for the inevitable introductions.

"Annie, have you met—" Jake began.

Will stepped to her side and draped a warm arm over her shoulder, offering her a sip of his water. She took the plastic bottle and tipped it up to her lips, conscious of the staged intimacy, of the public claim he was making.

"—Alan Overbeck," Jake finished.

Annie shifted the water bottle to her other hand, and dutifully shook hands with Alan, the boyish blond, and Larry, the spiky brunet, and said hello to Barry, all with Will Sloan's arm around her shoulder. Apparently the panther had no intention of sharing his kill with any other cat.

In the buffet line later, Meg deftly slipped her candidate between Annie and Will. Annie smiled at Alan. They settled at one of the checkered cloth covered picnic tables. At the center of each table was a replica of one of her father's projects, set in a miniature landscape of cut flowers. Each place was marked with a bright miniature mailbox with a place card in the box. Her sisters really had outdone themselves.

Her mom's advice to be fair came to mind as she turned to Alan. She could do that. She could give him a chance. And she did. She found Alan admirably passionate about his work. He was enthusiastic about the effects of pit and fissure sealants for kids and thoroughly approved Annie's type of toothbrush. When he understood her coffee drinking habits, particularly her preference for European roasts, he was even more impressed with the results she got out of her brush.

* * *

Will watched Annie handle her would-be dates. She had warned him about her juggernaut of a family, but the real thing made him rethink some of her choices. The sisters en masse reminded him of those retired military vehicles donated to local police forces around the country. Annie with her quiet kindness seemed likely to be run over and flattened by them, but she seemed to be handling Alan.

He realized he could read Annie better now without hearing a word she said. She was being polite or kind or *civil*—the word came to him, her word. It was a mix of the two really—kindness and openness to the other person. The dentist did not impress her. Will relaxed and ate his burger and listened to the talk at his own table for a while. One thing was clear. Annie James didn't visit her family often.

Will had more trouble watching her with the cocky linoleum layer, who sat down on her left, cutting the dentist out and making her laugh, genuinely laugh. He said something funny every other minute it seemed. Will wanted to think the guy didn't listen to Annie or have any real interest in what she might say, but he had to admit that he hadn't made her laugh like that, and the desire to make her laugh, a thing he hadn't known he wanted, became a pressing need. Today he wanted to make her laugh. Here where she was outnumbered and outgunned by her sisters, he wanted to make her laugh.

At his decidedly male table he held up his end of the conversation without too much effort. They talked college sports, debated with mock heat whether the American League could really be considered baseball, and became mildly serious over what the economy needed most.

Barry Edwards, the third would-be date, stuck with Will at the non-Annie table, watched him carefully. "Apparently you know Annie."

"My…the company I work for made a donation to the center where she volunteers. She called to thank us and got me."

"When was that?"

"September."

"So this is a long-term relationship already?" Jake suggested.

"Doug, that's your cue," said John. "You should ask Sloan what his intentions are toward your daughter." That got a laugh from everyone at the table except Barry.

Doug grinned. "I'd rather ask him what this company is."

"Z-Text. We find the pattern in the data that you didn't know was there."

"So how's the company doing?"

"We haven't tanked."

"What do you do for them?"

"Consulting, mainly."

"You're not very forthcoming." Barry wouldn't let it alone, and the sound of cutlery and dishes became awkwardly loud. Just then two boys came up to drag Jake off to a chart at the other end of the patio. Will picked up his plate and followed. A large sheet of butcher paper taped to the wall was marked off in rows and columns in bright marking pen colors. Will could see categories of competition across the top and teams descending along the left side. A side column listed ways to score points for participation and victory.

"What's the competition for?"

"Family tradition. We always have games when we get together. Each family is a team."

"So Annie's a team all by herself?" Her name appeared alone at the bottom of the chart.

The boys were already filling in points for their victory in the football game. One of them looked up at him. "Aunt Annie's not much of a competitor."

Will grinned. "But I'm on her team, right?"

Doug Palmer came up behind him. "Yes, you're on Annie's team." He clapped Will on the shoulder.

Will took a marker from one of the boys and added his name under Annie's and put a win in their row for the football game.

Another realization hit him hard as he did it—he wanted her to win, to win big. "What's next?"

"Tennis!" The boys spoke as one.

Will nodded. He caught Annie's gaze from across the patio and headed her way. "Time to play tennis, babe." He left her would-be dates and her sisters staring, borrowed some equipment, and planted Annie at the net of one of the courts. He ran around behind her, smashing balls at their opponents. At first she just stood stunned, but when one of Meg's balls came right at her, she seemed to wake up and get tenacious. It wasn't pretty, but they did win.

Tennis was followed by horseshoes, at which Annie proved she was pretty adept. By the final event, a water balloon toss, she was flushed and laughing. He picked a yellow, grapefruit-sized water balloon from the bucket of filled balloons, hefted it, and checked the knot at the top. She picked a smaller orange balloon, breast-sized.

The yellow balloon was cool and heavy and alive in his hands, and just like that he wanted to fill his hands with flesh. He swallowed carefully. "What you want is a balloon with a little give, but a good firm skin."

She laughed. What a sweet, sweet sound. He had not heard it often. "What you want is not to drop it."

"That too." She caught his gaze and put her balloon back into the bucket.

He turned her around, nestling her into the curve of his body, warmth to warmth. His arms around her, her hands in his, he demonstrated the catching technique he learned years ago. "Never let the balloon hit your hands. Your hands move with the balloon's flight."

Her bottom pressed against his groin, and he froze. He could feel a tremor run through her. He stepped back, and they took their spots in two ragged lines of competitors facing each other across the grass. The odds were not in their favor. Each of her sisters' teams had two or more pairs in the line up. It didn't help that he wanted to throw his balloon straight at her and have it break over her and plaster her wet T-shirt to her body.

He reminded himself that he wanted her to win and sent her an easy lob without too much arc.

She caught it, exaggerating his instructions to follow the balloon's flight. The lines stepped apart. He kept his concentration through more tosses, more distance between the lines, and lots of yelling from the onlookers. The first balloon to break broke over Jake, Meredith's husband.

"Sloan, you have an unfair advantage—all those years catching footballs."

"Hey, we're just a two-person team," he shouted back, his eyes on Annie. "We'll take all the advantages we can get."

In the next round one of the boys sent his balloon skyward, and it broke over his partner. They started shouting recriminations at each other. The lines were dwindling.

Annie's face was flushed pink; strands of her red hair had escaped the casual knot at her nape, loose around her face and ears. And he wanted her, *wanted her*. He didn't trust himself not to tumble her to the grass with her whole family looking on.

The stretch of grass between them widened, littered with bright red, orange, and yellow bits of balloon. The balloon in his hands felt fragile, but she caught it gently while around them balloons broke and water flew. When there were two couples left, Annie and Will and one of Annie's uncles and his wife, Will grinned at her. They'd already won in a way. None of her sisters or their kids were left. One more easy lob, and they had it all. She held the balloon. He offered her an encouraging smile.

She smiled back a slow smile that showed him just a second too late her intent. Her arm swung up for an overhead, and she sent a low hard pass to his chest. He tried to spin away, but the thing caught him, and exploded, soaking him from chest to knees.

He took one look at her face and set off after her. "You're going to pay for that, Annie James."

Behind them people shouted and laughed, but she kept going. He chased her back to their cottage and caught up with her at the door. He flipped her around, her back against the wood, and pressed his wet body against hers, panting, gulping for air, alive, happy. His mouth came down on hers, and she opened to him, and he was lost.

When he could think at all, he said, "If you wanted to see me naked, you could just ask."

Her eyes got big. "I didn't."

"Oh yeah? What was this for?" He held his wet shirt away from his body. "And guess what, you get your wish."

She shook her head, fumbling for the doorknob behind her and stumbling backward into the cottage.

He followed, stripping off his shirt, kicking out of his shoes, and flicking open the fly of his shorts. She put out a shaking hand to stop him or to draw him near.

"Annie, it's time to admit it."

Her gaze rose to meet his. "It's hard to let go of the past, you know."

"No one knows better. We've missed out on ten years."

Her eyes flashed with some pain, but she straightened her shoulders and he grasped them lightly in his hands. "What is it? What did I say?"

"It's ten years that…"

There was a gasp behind him, and he turned to find Meg staring at them. She looked right at Annie. "You were with this guy before Ryan was even cold in his grave, weren't you?" The pitch of her voice rose an octave in one sentence, and then she was gone.

He went cold instantly, his skin puckered with it, as if he'd been doused with ice water.

Her eyes were as sad as he'd ever seen them. "Meg's right. I forgot Ryan. He died, and I forgot him. He didn't deserve to be forgotten, but I forgot him."

She dropped her gaze, looking at the floor. A long shuddering sigh escaped her. He braced himself for more of her confession. "I even wrecked his truck. I kept it going for all this time, and now I wrecked it. I wrecked it because…"

He reached out a hand, slowly, carefully, not letting himself move or come closer though he wanted to hold her as tight as he could for as long as he could.

She took a step back, shaking her head, refusing comfort. "I wrecked it because I was thinking about you. I could forget him, but I couldn't forget you. I was a terrible wife to Ryan."

Chapter Seventeen

In the end she did not see him naked. They showered separately, and he waited for her out on the little porch. Her sisters also waited for her. When they went up the hill, nothing was said at first as they got drinks and mingled with still more guests who had arrived for the dinner. It was only when her mother asked Annie to help with one elderly guest that her sisters struck.

"Meg says you've been involved with this man for ten years."

"I did meet him ten years ago."

It took Meredith all of a second to do the math. "Then he was eighteen. Eighteen!"

"What were you thinking?"

"Were you that desperate? You could have come home. Santa Maria men might not be as sophisticated as L.A. types, but they are solid, decent adults."

"Where did you meet him really?"

"Does it matter? And, we haven't seen each other for ten years. We just met again by accident this fall, that's all."

"You're having sex with him, that's obvious, but did you have to bring it here? We're all here. The kids are here. This is a family event."

"Everybody here knew Ryan. We all loved him. He was part of our family." Melanie's words stopped them all.

Annie felt herself falter. That was their big weapon. But she felt strangely indifferent to their attack. Her confession to Will had had some effect, some release. She had told the truth to another person.

"You have to ask him to leave," Meredith announced.

"Or we will," Meg added.

Annie shook her head. "I will not ask him to leave."

"You did this just to show us up because we planned Daddy's party and found you some decent men to consider when you couldn't find anybody on your own."

"I did find someone. I will not let you embarrass him in any way. He's my guest, and he stays. And what we do or do not do in our cottage is entirely our business."

* * *

Will watched Annie disappear and reemerge from the kitchen followed by her sisters. She looked calm. They looked high on outrage.

"What are your sisters up to now?"

She didn't look at him. "They are regrouping for another attack."

His hand squeezed hers under the table. He wanted to know what they'd said, but he knew he needed to wait to get her alone. "Remember, I'm on your team."

She turned to him then and smiled. "Thank you. I know that now."

And he knew he was through with revenge and punishing her and himself for the past. They had both had their demons ten years earlier, and because his were in front of him every day, and hers were distant, he had blamed her for not being strong. Now he knew she was much stronger than he'd ever imagined.

The evening dragged on through speeches, stories, and jokes honoring her father. There was a video tribute, and her sisters honored him with a plaque, which Melanie read. Meg's children sang a medley of his favorite Beatle songs, and the audience joined in.

At midnight Doug Palmer thanked them all for everything, acknowledged their support, and called for his wife and daughters to join him for a moment on the little dais they'd set up. Annie stood at the edge of the family, a little apart, not in anyone's embrace. Will doubted that anyone noticed. Then Doug Palmer looked around for her and pulled her into the center of the photo. Phone cameras flashed briefly, and the party started to break up.

He grabbed her as soon as he could and pulled her into the shadows beyond the patio. Her skin was cool in the night air, and he tucked her into his arm and held her through the farewells as the party broke up. As the dinner guests left, and Annie's sisters herded their cranky offspring to bed, Will drew her away from the crowd.

They were silent on the path to the cottage. Stars filled the night sky, more numerous and more brilliant than any they could see from L.A. He led her into their cottage and cradled her in his arms on the couch in the dark. Outside the crickets made their noise.

Her back rested against his chest. He could rub the top of her head with his jaw and smell the freshness of her hair. He had come with her to take from her yet again, to demand that she yield up her person to him for all the times he'd wanted her and been denied, for wanting her still against all reason, for knowing she had wanted him and denied them both. Now he didn't know what the plan was, but she had shared a truth with him that had turned him upside down.

"You shouldn't care what they say."

"They're my family."

He couldn't argue with that. "Do you want my opinion of your sisters?"

He could feel her smile. "Is it unfavorable?"

"Unprintable even."

He succeeded in making her laugh, not the full, happy laughter they had shared in the afternoon, but a more rueful laugh, an admission that her sisters were ridiculous and hurtful. It was a start.

And with that shared laugh, the awareness between them bloomed full and ripe. He held himself very still, conscious of his erection pressing against her. She couldn't miss it, but he meant to offer only comfort and understanding.

"Thank you for being on my team today. I know it wasn't your plan."

She twisted in his arms, and her breasts pressed against his chest, her body nestled between his spread legs. His heart beat frantically. He pushed his hands up into her hair, held her face, and brought her lips to meet his.

He felt her pull back at the same moment he heard footsteps and fierce whispering on the porch.

"Hey Annie, Sloan?" It was her brother-in-law Jake.

Annie pushed away from Will, and he helped her off his lap into a sitting position. He pulled his shirt out of his slacks, and reached for the lamp on the end table. They looked at each other, mussed, obvious, and regretful.

Don't panic, he mouthed. She grinned back at him. He flipped on the TV on mute, and she slipped off the couch and into the bathroom.

When he opened the door, he was staring at the three sisters, the three suitors, and three very sheepish brothers-in-law.

"Time for a little friendly competition," Jake announced. He held out a scratched blue box of Trivial Pursuit that Will suspected was older than he was.

* * *

They left their cottage around seven. Technically, their deal was over. Twenty-four hours had passed, the last six of them in a raucous game of Trivial Pursuit that Annie's sister Meredith and her husband Jake had won. On the way back to L.A. Annie dozed at Will's side. He could look at her, and touch her as much as he wanted, but she wasn't his. He had tried to make her his with bargains and blackmail and sex. He had thought the sex would be enough for him. He would sleep with her, and everything would be settled. But he wanted something more from her that still eluded him.

He left her in her entry with a kiss that Irene could not observe through the closed front door.

He didn't say good-bye.

* * *

After he dropped her off, he stopped by his mom's place. He couldn't say why. He just felt as if his mom's wisdom might rub off on him.

The day was cooling, but the Southern California sun still burned hot in the sky. When Mae's door opened, Dog jumped wildly in greeting, until Mae made the beast sit. Will stepped inside, studying her, thinking something had changed, her hair, her make-up. Her toenails, painted deep pink, peeked from a pair of animal print stiletto mules. She wore linen slacks and a gauzy pink tunic.

"Going somewhere, Mom?"

"I have company." She grinned at him.

He halted. "I'll catch you later then."

"No. Come and meet Frank." She led him out through the small living area to a backyard he hardly recognized. The cement had been replaced with irregular brown flagstones bordered by a low gray-green ground cover. The ivy was gone. In its place were olive and lemon trees and clumps of purple flowers and gray grasses arranged in a gentle slope around rocks and paths of gravel like dry streams.

The cinder block wall had disappeared behind a screen of climbing jasmine.

Sitting under a tan canvas umbrella at the patio table, utterly relaxed, was a tall fit man who looked to be in his fifties in a subtle leaf-print Hawaiian shirt and khaki slacks. He looked like a happy man with a beer in his hand, and a basket of chips and bowl of salsa in front of him. The man looked up and then stood as they emerged from the house.

"Will, this is Frank Stewart, he created this landscape design for me. Frank, my son Will."

They shook hands, taking each other's measure. Will could see that Mae was not wasting any more time. He accepted a beer and a seat under the umbrella. Mae's salsa was as hot as he remembered it, and Frank clearly relished the stuff, a good sign.

Mae let her guests talk about the new landscape and Frank's business and Will's for several minutes before she stopped them and told Will it was time to come to the point.

"What's this visit about?"

"Nothing. I just wanted to see how you were doing. The garden looks great, and I see that you're still adding to the shoe collection."

She looked unconvinced, but she laughed. "I am."

He stood up to leave, and accepted a fierce maternal hug that sent Dog into a spinning, barking frenzy. Frank casually quelled the dog, another point for Frank. Mae pulled away, and gave Will a searching look that said he didn't fool her in the least. She walked him to his truck.

"So, should I ask whether Frank is an honorable man?"

"Oh, he's a good one, but we'll take it slow. You, on the other hand, seem to have a heartache as big as Texas. Are you going to tell me what's going on?"

He shook his head. "It's something I have to work on."

"At least tell me her name?"

He laughed. His mom was going to see through him no matter how old he got. "Annie James, Mom. You met her ten years ago when you had your accident. She was with us in the hospital that night."

He watched as understanding dawned in her eyes. "And you've seen her again? At that Canyon dinner, and since then? Oh, you were so angry. Is that it?"

"It hasn't been my finest hour."

He accepted another hug and went home thinking about his mom's shoes. He had used his money to buy things, too, but he wasn't sure that any of his purchases had given him the happiness his mom got from her shoes.

With Beau's help, he had found most of his purchases satisfying. He liked having nice things. He'd made a mistake thinking the house on the hill would please his Mom, but he'd been able to correct that mistake. He had ended up liking the house for himself, and he liked his truck.

But when he thought about it, his money had been most satisfying when he'd used it to get to Annie James, when he'd been able to write that check for the center and when he'd made a private arrangement with Canyon's business manager to pay Ulysses's bills.

Another brilliant Southern California sunset blazed in the sky above his house on the hill. He had told himself that wanting Annie James was all about the sex, that once he had slept with her, he would be done wanting her. The sunset made a liar out of him. He wanted something else entirely, something warm and generous and sweet, like laughter and victory and forgiveness all at once. He just had to figure out how to get it without utterly humiliating himself.

Chapter Eighteen

On Monday as they reached the Canyon gates, Ulysses asked Annie, "When are you going to get a new car, Ms. James?"

"I hadn't thought about it. Any recommendations?"

"Something with some, you know, cool, like my shades." He pulled them down to give her a look over the rims and wiggled his brows at her.

"May I point out that once again you are knocking your ride to school."

"Hey, Ms. James. The Bookman has his standards." He grinned at her. "And besides, this car is so not you."

"Why not?"

Ulysses shrugged. "It's the color of cement for one thing."

She left him at the drop-off point where his friend, Tyler, was waiting. Ulysses was happy and thriving. Whatever Will Sloan had done had ended the misery of the past few weeks. She didn't know what he'd done, but she assumed he'd made a phone call to the dean or the admissions director, and that as a man, or an alum, or a potential donor, or however the school saw him now, he'd had an impact, where she had failed.

And then he'd been on her doorstep to claim his bargain, and they'd been off to Luna de Miel. Once her thoughts reached that point, she realized she had some serious thinking to do to understand what had happened between them.

She had expected sex. He seemed to enjoy the pure revenge of making her helpless with desire and then walking out on her. That had been his plan from the moment they'd met at the Dunes Club. But at Luna de Miel he had become her friend, her ally, her protector. He had been possessive of her, staking some kind of claim, but not insisting on sex, not even on the road when she had been so tempted. He had learned things about her that she never meant to share. She had unlocked the box of the past and let her worst secrets escape. She had admitted what she did not think she could ever admit. She had forgotten Ryan because of Will.

They were at last, even in some sense, all wrongs exposed and forgiven. That made them free to go on. Will's parting kiss had been gentle and undemanding, a sign of forgiveness. If he could forgive her, then she could forgive herself, too. It would not be easy, but she had gone on without Ryan and she had gone on without Will once before. She could do it again. The point was to go on, not to get stuck in some hamster-wheel loop of regret. She would take baby steps.

The first step she could take was clear to her when she pulled into her usual spot in the employees' lot. When she got out and looked at Louisa's car, she knew Ulysses was right. A gray compact indistinguishable from concrete was not her. She needed to go car shopping.

And, come to think of it, her job wasn't really a good fit either. She would talk with her boss, Rob Parker, about stories she could and should be writing, stories about resilience and impossible comebacks.

When she got home, her mailbox had the usual catalogues and flyers, an odd manila envelope, and an invite to the Canyon gala with a handwritten note from Josh scrawled across the fold—"Just say yes."

She waved to Irene and ducked inside before Dan could catch her. Her answering machine light blinked, and she braced herself for her sisters' messages.

Annie, it's mom, I'm worried about you. Don't blame the girls, okay?

—Monday, 9:24 a.m.

Annie, it's Meg, Meredith is not even going to call you. What kind of sister are you? You and your eye candy friend really upset the game standings.

—Monday, 12:00 p.m.

Annie, it's Mel, once you come to your senses, I really think you should give Barry another chance. A little maturity is very attractive in a man.

—Monday, 3:12, p.m.

Annie, it's Dad. Thanks for coming. Whatever anyone else says, I think that young man is a keeper.

—Monday, 5:30 p.m.

Her cell rang, and she dug it out of her bag. It was Josh.

"Hey, did you get your gala invite?"

"I just did."

"Open it?"

"I just got home."

"Well, don't wait."

"Okay." She nudged the front door with her hip and put the phone down to open the heavy envelope with its elegant card of invitation. "It looks great, Josh. You do good work."

"So, are you and Sloan an item at the moment?"

"No."

"Then be my date for the gala."

"Your date?"

"My guest, then, if you are uncomfortable with the date thing. You'll see Ulysses sing with the C-Notes."

"I'd like that, Josh, and I'm grateful for all your kindness to him and to me."

"Hey, you know me, this job has got to have some perks, right?" He rang off without waiting for a reply.

Annie stood in the entry, trying to understand what Josh was up to now and thinking of Ulysses's observation about Josh's character. As she pondered whether Josh was acting strategically or generously, Tess pushed through the open door. Her glance went right to the invitation in Annie's hand.

"It's from that hottie, isn't it?" Tess grinned. "I recognized that palm tree thing."

Annie nodded. "Tess what brings you over here?"

"Just wanted to bring you this." Tess offered a bottle of Zinfandel. "To thank you for watching Ginger." Her gaze was still fixed on the card in Annie's hand.

"Thanks." Annie took the wine and handed the invitation to Tess.

"Wow, Annie, this is great, a gala. Things are finally happening for you. You've got to let me take you shopping. You can't wear a gray suit to an event like this. You've got to wear something that'll rock every man in the place."

"Just one man will do." Annie thought she understood Josh, after all. With him kindness was just a strategy. He'd had one goal from the beginning.

She had a goal now, too. She would take Tess up on her offer. It was time to ditch her old car, her old job, her old look. She had been holding onto mourning, wearing it in her heart. Time to let it go.

Chapter Nineteen

Quite a different notice came from Canyon in the wake of the gala invitation. It came by mail to Ulysses's mother, who understood little of the formal letter, just enough to be alarmed. She had called Louisa, who understood it completely. Louisa called Annie with the news just as she was ready to leave for work.

Dr. Chambers had suspended Ulysses from Canyon.

Louisa's message stopped Annie cold. She stood in her entry, her keys and bag in hand, while a wave of feeling took her back to the moment she'd been sitting at her desk in the reception area at Canyon when Dr. Chambers, in his academic robes, had summoned her to take notes on the proceedings to expel Will. At the time she had been frightened and mystified. In the meeting she had only spoken out because she had known the truth that Will was not guilty of vandalizing the sign. At the time she hadn't really blamed Dr. Chambers. She had thought him mistaken, but she had not believed that he would deliberately ruin a boy's life. Now she knew better.

* * *

Annie saw that nothing had changed in Dr. Chambers's office since her last confrontation with the man, not the book-lined walls, the rich carpet, or the giant oak desk. The room had the feel of a London gentlemen's club, and Dr. Chambers had used its academic trappings to brand the Canyon School as the last bastion of male education in L.A. Once, long ago, Annie had been impressed.

What had changed, she realized, was her. Repeated contact with Will Sloan had stirred a dormant rebelliousness in her nature. This morning she felt as if a half dozen sleepy earthquake faults had slipped a little, releasing pent up energy she hadn't known she possessed. She was not going to let Chambers crush one more boy.

"Ms. James."

"Dr. Chambers." She forced herself to greet him civilly. "Do you have a few minutes to talk about Ulysses?"

Chambers removed his glasses and gave them a careful wipe with a soft white cloth. He did not rise. He did not offer her a seat.

He appeared to be a busy man, annoyed by a tedious interruption. "I am afraid, Ms. James, you are interfering where you have no right to concern yourself."

Annie crossed the room and slapped his letter down on his desk. "I represent the boy's mother, who does not speak English."

"Ah." He put his glasses back on, but did not look at the letter.

"His mother would like a complete explanation and investigation into the matter of Ulysses's suspension."

"Ms. James, you of all people should remember that some boys on financial aid cannot handle themselves in this environment. The wealth of others proves to be too much temptation for them, and any violation of the school's honor code is a grave offense."

"However, Ulysses has not come before the honor council. According to Tyler Dalton, Ulysses was programming Tyler's phone at his request."

"Perfectly natural for one boy to want to cover for another."

Annie did her best to keep her temper. "A two-minute investigation of this matter clears Ulysses's name, but you haven't investigated."

"Ms. James, do not forget that as head of school, I have ultimate authority here. You are not the boy's parent or relation, and in fact, you have no legal ground to be involved in this matter. You don't do the boy any favors by behaving in this confrontational way."

"I know that Ulysses looks rather alone and defenseless, but I assure you he is not. He will have a lawyer if he needs one. Is it still Canyon policy to require a vote of the senior faculty to expel a boy?"

"I advise you to tread very carefully, Ms. James. You would not wish to come under scrutiny yourself in this matter."

"Me? I think you must explain yourself, Dr. Chambers. Driving a carpool is hardly an offense."

"Nevertheless, Ms. James, your conduct will not bear scrutiny. Years ago as an employee of Canyon you aroused the lascivious desires of our students by your manner and your dress. You would find an investigation of your past, or even your present relations with former Canyon students, very damaging to your career. Indeed, I have documents that might lead to criminal prosecution in your case."

Annie stared at him. Was he mad? "Documents? What are you talking about?"

"A letter from Will Sloan to you. Believe me, Ms. James, the terms in which Mr. Sloan expresses himself, suggest an entirely inappropriate degree of intimacy between an adult employee of the school and one of its students."

Will had written her a letter? And it had ended up in Chambers's hands? And he'd read it?

Her stomach knotted with a sickening wrench, and her fists clenched at her sides. She felt violated. She wanted to smash something, to pull down the façade of scholarly concern with which Chambers surrounded himself and dash his books to the floor. She took a breath, staring at the carpet, controlling her anger, and realized that both Will and Ulysses had stood where she stood now in front of Chambers's desk. If he was capable of such intimidation tactics against her, what had he done to them? It was time for her to get reinforcements.

"Dr. Chambers, you may believe that you can stop my inquiry into your treatment of Ulysses, but the boy has friends who will not permit him to be unfairly deprived of his place in this school."

"Ms. James, if you value your career, you will cease to meddle in this situation at once."

"Perhaps you need my employer's phone number, Dr. Chambers?"

She stepped forward and seized a heavy pen from his desk, and scrawled her editor's phone number across the cover of the *Independent School Journal* lying on his desk.

She left Chambers's office nearly bursting with rage. Will had been right about him all along. She had not seen it. She had merely seen a self-important man with a pompous manner. She had missed how cruel and manipulative he was.

Coming out of the reception area she crashed directly into Josh Huntington. It was a jarring collision. She hadn't been looking where she was going. He caught her by the shoulders to steady her on her feet.

She looked up then. "Oh Josh, I'm sorry."

"Whoa, what's going on?" He released her shoulders and glanced around. It was too early for most of the staff, and way too early for any students to be on campus. He tried a joke. "Hey our date's not for two weeks."

"Chambers has suspended Ulysses."

"Why?"

"For stealing Tyler's cell phone, which, of course, he didn't do. Chambers is a sly, cruel, manipulative, heartless bastard."

Again Josh glanced around. "Come down to my office. Let's talk about it there." He put an arm around her shoulder and steered her past reception.

He settled her in a brown leather wing chair. "Can I get you a coffee or something?"

She shook her head. "That man makes me so angry. I don't even know why. I should pity him, I suppose, but I don't think he has an honest bone in his body. He just wants to hurt kids like Ulysses, and it's my fault."

Josh pulled up another chair. "It's not your fault that Chambers hates financial aid students. He always has. He's got sort of an Ebenezer Scrooge thing going." Josh gave an imitation of Chambers's voice that made her smile, "Canyon can't afford to give *idle* boys an education."

"You may be right, but I didn't handle this morning's confrontation well, and now…" She couldn't sit. She stood and began to pace his office.

"Now what?"

"He threatened me."

"Okay, I'm not following you here. He threatened you?"

"I thought I could appeal to his sense of fairness and justice. I tried to explain that Tyler and Ulysses are friends. Ulysses is good at programming Tyler's phone and helps Tyler use it to keep on track with homework and tutoring sessions. I asked Chambers to investigate further. If he let Tyler explain how the boys work together, he would see the truth. He refused. I reminded him that it takes a vote of the senior faculty to expel a student. You told me that."

Josh nodded. "Chambers did not like that little reminder of school policy, did he?"

She laughed. "Not at all. He told me he has evidence in his files that would make me liable to criminal charges for my relationship with Will ten years ago." She shuddered again at the thought. "As if that had anything to do with Ulysses now."

"What does he mean 'evidence' in his files?"

"Apparently he has some letter Will wrote to me. I never received a letter from him. It shouldn't matter, but I can't press him about Ulysses while I...after I..."

Josh held his breath. "Did you two work it out?"

She shook her head. She couldn't look at him. She would have to get someone unimpeachable to support Ulysses, maybe Tyler's father or Ned Rothwell from the New Directions committee.

"You'll let me know if you two get together, won't you?"

"What?" Josh was watching her closely. "So you can ask him for money?"

He flushed. "Lots of money. Don't sell yourself short. If Sloan gets you out of this thing, he owes me, big time."

"I'll be sure to tell you if we work it out, but Josh, right now Ulysses is what matters, and Chambers thinks he has all the power."

"Maybe it would be best if I handled this one."

"Would you?" She wanted to trust him, but there was something hesitant in his manner that made her doubt him.

"Sure. Let me see what I can do, but let's get you out of here before Chambers figures out we're conspiring against him."

At the door she turned to give him a quick hug. "Thanks."

* * *

By Friday evening Will was impatient for everyone to clear out at Z-Text. He had an idea, and he needed quiet to work on it. He turned down a chance to go clubbing with Beau on Pico. It was a source of tension between them that Will had stopped calling the women Beau had picked out for him. He couldn't explain it to Beau until his own head was clear. He hadn't seen Annie James in days. He hadn't made love to her in months. He hadn't thought about her for nearly three minutes. He didn't sleep in his bedroom anymore. Working on the idea that had come to him after their Luna de Miel weekend was the one thing that kept him going.

When he finally closed his computer, he felt he had the outline of a concept that even Beau would like. He shut everything down and stepped from his office to the mezzanine. Below him the deserted Z-Text atrium looked dead, and for a moment he wondered if he'd imagined the whole thing, working with Beau and realizing they had a big idea, the warehouse where they'd started, the team they'd built, their first client, and then the take off, with clients seeking them and everyone on the team working around the clock and on weekends. It had been quite a rush while it lasted, but the only smart thing to do had been go public or sell it. He had realized that idea development was the work that appealed to him, not running a business. And he'd believed he would have other ideas, new beginnings. And then he'd come to L.A. and the well of ideas had gone dry. Nothing had come to him. It had been a complete brain freeze. For months he'd been a bench sitter on the team, but now at last he felt he had something to offer.

He pushed away from the mezzanine railing and started down the stairs. He'd head home and go for a run. As he reached the landing and turned toward the front of the office, two shadows darkened the tinted glass of the entry doors. His gaze followed the flickering shadows, and in a minute he heard pounding on the glass. At the bottom of the stairs he could see through the doors and recognized Annie's protégé, the boy called Ulysses, with his inevitable dark glasses. Beside him was another boy, a blond. Will's mind went immediately to the thought that Annie might be near.

He let the boys in. Ulysses spoke first, reminding Will that they'd met and introducing his friend, Tyler. Tyler Dalton was as Canyon as a kid could be with a mop of golden hair. He wore an untucked blue Oxford cloth shirt with the sleeves rolled up, sagging khakis, and reef sandals.

He offered his hand, and Will shook it. "What's going on?"

The boys exchanged glances, apparently deciding who would speak, then spoke together. "We need someone we can trust."

"Why me?"

Another quick wordless consultation passed between the two boys. "Ms. James trusts you," Ulysses announced.

Does she? That was news to him. Will stared at the unreadable, unyielding young face behind the dark glasses.

"Chambers suspended Ulysses and wants to expel him," Tyler blurted out.

Will stayed focused on Ulysses. "Apparently you're getting to know Headmaster Chambers pretty well. Sounds as if you've been freed."

Again the boys exchanged a look. "Will you help us?"

Their friendship stuck out clearly. They were in this together, and it rocked Will. "You want to stay at Canyon?"

They both nodded. In looks they could be Huntington and himself when they'd first met almost fifteen years earlier, the fair-haired rich man's son and the dark-haired scholarship boy in the wrong jeans and sneakers. How could they be friends? A friendship between them went against everything Will knew about Canyon. How could Tyler Dalton, living in some palace in the hills, be friends with Ulysses Aristedes, whose mother rolled out her bed on the living room floor of a crowded apartment every night?

Both boys watched him. He could not say no to their friendship. "What do you want from me?"

"We need to move some stuff from school to a safe place."

"Stuff?"

"Evidence that might hurt Chambers." They were scared and giddy and keeping up their courage by sticking together.

"What evidence?"

"Files." Ulysses said it solemnly.

"Tonight?"

Two heads nodded.

"Where do you want to take this 'stuff'?"

Ulysses looked around. "Here, if you'll let us."

Why not? Ten years after he'd been accused of burning down the sign, he'd actually be guilty of a crime against Canyon. "On one condition. If there is any chance of being caught, you guys get lost. Do you understand me?"

Both boys nodded.

"So tell me what's going on."

The story came out in a jumble of intertwining accounts, the boys finishing each other's sentences about the cell phone and Chambers's accusations. In the end they revealed that Annie had intervened, and Chambers had threatened her.

"What do you mean he threatened her?"

The boys did not know, but they knew that after his meeting with Annie, Chambers had sent his secretary to the basement for some old files. Huntington had helped the secretary retrieve them, and later when Chambers sent the files to the dumpster, Huntington had called Tyler to intercept them before they got lost. The boys had retrieved the files from one of the grounds keeper's electric cars and moved them to a secret hiding place.

"Chambers is hiding something, isn't he? Something that could mean trouble for him?" Ulysses suggested.

"Paper files from the basement? Sounds like old news to me." Will didn't doubt that Chambers had secrets. He just doubted that Chambers's old secrets could save Ulysses. On the other hand, Chambers's desire to destroy those files now was suspicious.

Ulysses nodded. "Could it be stuff from when Ms. James worked at Canyon?"

Will hadn't thought of that. Of course, she had been an employee of the school, but he doubted there would be anything harmful to her in some old files. What he needed to do was to keep the two budding Edward Snowdens in front of him from getting themselves into real trouble. "Tell me where this stuff is, and I'll get it and bring it here."

Two stubborn, closed faces looked at him. Clearly they had no intention of relinquishing their adventure.

"We have a plan." Ulysses looked to Tyler for confirmation. Tyler nodded. "There's a play on campus tonight. With so many cars, no one will notice us parking in the back."

"What about your parents? Won't they wonder where you are?"

"I told my mom I was with Tyler."

"My dad thinks I'm with Ulysses. If he calls, he'll call on my cell."

"Great, I'm aiding and abetting the oldest form of parental deception on the planet."

He got them to agree to call Huntington and Annie. Over burritos in a mall food court he had a chance to observe them further. They trusted each other, relied on each other, and abused each other—the way he and Beau did, the way male friends did. Simultaneously, they broke into song with a piped in oldie on the mall sound system, some guy singing about going down on his knees and begging his girl please to come home. Ulysses and Tyler, who knew nothing about begging, harmonized gleefully with the music.

"We're supposed to sing at the gala with the C-Notes," Tyler announced. "So we have to get Ulysses back into school."

Will was stunned. *Ulysses in the C-Notes!* When Will was at Canyon, the C-Notes had belonged strictly to Huntington and his friends. No one on financial aid would have been considered for the group.

* * *

Floodlights lit the bronze and stone Canyon sign, a replacement for the wooden one that had burned two nights before their graduation. Security waved them into the parking lot with a line of playgoers, and Ulysses directed Will to a parking space at the far end of the lot. If he had to return to the place, it was definitely better to come in the dark. He took a flashlight from his glove compartment and followed the boys through a line of tall shrubs separating the parking lot from the maintenance yard.

The boys led the way quickly and confidently, gravel crunching under their feet. He could smell cut grass and decaying trash. In the distance he could hear the ticking and spray of the automatic sprinklers on the playing fields. Then he smelled jasmine and stopped cold.

"You're going to the toolshed." His voice had a rusty sound to it.

"Yeah. The roof's kind of a secret spot. No one can see you there."

He knew that. Anyone who'd ever done grounds work at Canyon knew that. He knew just how the slope of the roof nearly met the hillside above and you could step out onto the roof surrounded by mounds of bougainvillea and star jasmine that overgrew the place. And from the roof you could watch the sunset. And, if you were lucky, the woman you loved would watch the sunset there, and you could leave her things—an apple, a bottle of water, a message. And she might tell you not to, but she couldn't stop you or catch you at it.

If Ulysses knew the roof spot, then he'd done grounds work, too, which meant Chambers was still Chambers. Will allowed himself to hope that the boys had actually found some damning piece of evidence against the old tyrant.

The boys led the way around the shed up the hill and over to the roof, following a path he himself had made. Ulysses pulled a tarp off the old truck seat that still sat there, and the flashlight revealed three good-sized cardboard file boxes, bulging with manila folders.

"So what is this stuff?"

"Files from your class."

"My class? And these are going to help Ulysses how?"

"We're going to ask Josh. There has to be a reason that Chambers wanted them destroyed."

Will wondered whether Huntington really thought the files incriminated Chambers or whether the master manipulator simply wanted another chance to throw Annie James in Will's path.

No one noticed them putting the files in Will's truck. At Z-Text he turned on the lights in one of the downstairs meeting rooms off the atrium, and they set the boxes on a long conference table.

Tyler wanted to know if they could call out for pizza. Will showed him Z-Text's kitchen instead. The boys were microwaving popcorn when Huntington arrived. He exchanged the Canyon handshake with both boys and congratulated them on saving the files from the dumpster.

"Will helped us take them from Canyon," Tyler offered.

"Really." Huntington turned to him. "You don't know what a nice guy that makes him." He looked around. "So this is Z-Text. Now that it belongs to someone else, what do you do here, Sloan?"

"Where's Annie? I thought you'd be serving her up on a platter about now."

Huntington looked at his phone. "She just texted me. She's on her way."

"Does she know what you want from me?"

"Actually, she does, and you know what, Sloan, she still likes me. She's my date for the gala. So, do you want help the kid, or not?"

Date. He tried not to react to the word, but it seemed to reverberate in him. Images assaulted him, of Huntington touching her on the small of her back or putting an arm around her shoulders or leaning in close to her ear. "What are these files anyhow, Huntington?"

"Our class files. Canyon keeps everything in the basement. It's like a Pentagon vault down there, and Chambers's secretary has the key. I helped her move them upstairs to his office this morning. The old man was desperate to find something in here today. He pawed through the boxes himself. Then he wanted to get rid of them. Suspicious, wouldn't you say?"

Huntington turned his glance from the boys in the kitchen to Will. "They look like us, don't they? I mean us when we were fourteen."

"Except they're friends."

"We could have been friends."

Will started to shake his head.

"Yeah, we could have, Sloan. I offered that first day in Mr. Keane's advisor group. You rejected me pretty quick, pretty hard. You're a prideful guy, Sloan."

Huntington strolled into the kitchen and directed the boys to move their popcorn and sodas away from the files on the table.

Will watched the boys nudge and jostle each other, and a sudden sharp memory came to him of standing in the sunny quad at Canyon surrounded by guys who all dressed alike and called each other by name. One blond kid had strolled over to him and smiled, but Will had been conscious only of what an outsider he was and how he had paint on his hands that matched the color of the benches around them. He had shoved his hands in his pockets and cut the kid off. *What if he had smiled at that kid and stuck out his hand?*

He was reeling from that thought when Annie James arrived.

She gave Huntington a quick friendly hug and the boys a serious look. "I should take you both home. I know I started this thing by asking Josh for help, but you two should not be part of it. It's too risky."

Ulysses and Tyler tried to look sheepish and failed.

"Let them stay. We can protect them," Will offered.

Annie looked at him in surprise.

"Now that we have the files what do we do with them?" Ulysses asked.

Will knew the answer to that one. The files were data, data that made Chambers uneasy, so that meant the data would reveal something if they found its patterns. "Put them in order, the same documents arranged the same way. Then we see what patterns emerge."

The boys dug in with Huntington's help, pulling files out of dusty boxes.

Will kept his gaze on Annie. He took her arm and pulled her aside to one of the couches on the far side of atrium. Once again she was in jeans with a white T-shirt under a gray fleece vest. It reminded him of meeting her in the Library. When she sat, he settled next to her. She shifted, putting a small space between them, and pulled a heavy manila envelope out of her bag, laying it across her knees.

"So Chambers threatened you?" He kept his voice low, for her alone.

Her breathing caught and then resumed. "The boys told you? He says he has a letter from you to me that he claims is evidence of an inappropriate relationship. He suggested that I would face criminal charges if I crossed him over Ulysses."

"Did you believe him?"

"I never received a letter from you. Did you send one? When?"

"I did send a letter, later that summer. Apparently you had already left Canyon. I didn't know. Canyon was the only address I had for you, so I sent my letter there."

Next to him she drew circles around little strings of letters in her neat handwriting on the outside of the plain envelope. "I never expected to hear from you again."

"Isn't it time to tell me why you left Canyon?" His voice roughened.

"I should, shouldn't I?" She looked at him then. "We don't need secrets anymore. Will you tell me what you did for Ulysses?"

"You first."

She folded her hands over the manila envelope on her lap. "On graduation morning Chambers named you as the one who burned down the sign. He called a quick meeting of the senior faculty. He claimed he had proof of your guilt and recommended your immediate expulsion. No graduation, no diploma even. He proposed taking everything away from you, but school policy required a vote of the senior faculty. Josh told me that. I was only admitted to the meeting to take notes, but I couldn't let him do it. After all, I knew where you'd been the night of the fire. So I spoke up. I told them about your mother's accident and that I had been with you in the ER that night."

Will swore.

"When the vote came, the faculty wouldn't let him expel you. I was proud of them, but I knew that what I'd done was unforgiveable in his eyes."

"And?"

"And he took me aside afterward. He told me he would not tolerate public defiance. I could resign immediately or never work again, anywhere."

"And?"

"I told him I would hand in my resignation as soon as you had your diploma. It was the last bit of bargaining power I had."

It was hard to look at her. Her head was still bent over the envelope clenched in her hands. He'd misjudged her badly for a long time, thinking her weak when she'd been stronger than he'd ever imagined. It was several minutes before he could see again the little codes she had circled on the back of the envelope. There was something familiar about them.

"What are these?"

She opened the envelope and drew out a sheaf of papers. "These files showed up in my mailbox at home. There's no return address. I suspect the business manager sent them. I didn't understand them at the time, but I went back to them this week after Chambers suspended Ulysses. They look like statements, but I can't figure out why Ulysses has such a complex sequence of expenses and credits in his account. I think there has to be some financial impropriety here."

He looked at the document. Its familiar pattern sent a molten spurt of anger coursing through him. He had known what Chambers was doing to Ulysses. He had even taken steps to stop it by speaking to the business manager directly, and clearly, the man suspected something. If Chambers knew that his underling suspected him, it would explain why Chambers wanted to discredit Ulysses and get him out of Canyon.

Will brushed the papers aside and came to his feet. "It's time for Ulysses to tell you what it's like to be one of Chambers's financial aid boys."

He stuck his head into the kitchen where the boys had arranged the files in long rows.

"Hey, we found something," Tyler announced.

Ulysses looked up and sobered at once when he saw Will's face.

"Thanks, Tyler. We'll get to what you found in a moment, but it's time for Ulysses to talk about what really happens at Canyon." He gathered them together in the atrium, and made Ulysses sit next to Annie. He knew the boy would need support.

He fixed his gaze on the boy and made his own confession first. "I was a financial aid student at Canyon. It was back when Ms. James and Josh were there. Most boys at Canyon don't know about the secret place on top of the toolshed, but you and I both know that place is there. How do financial aid students discover that spot, Ulysses?"

The boy looked at him from behind the dark glasses, and for a moment Will thought the kid wouldn't crack, but Annie touched the boy's shoulder, and he began to speak.

"We know it's there because financial aid students do grounds work, and cafeteria work, and clean up. We paint, and mow, and weed, and scrape plates. Lots of stuff." The boy paused, and in a different voice, he said, "You see it costs more than just tuition to go to Canyon, and every boy has to do his part."

"That's what Chambers says, isn't it?" Will asked.

Ulysses nodded.

"When you have these conversations with Chambers, how much are you usually short?"

The boy looked at his hands and took a deep breath before he looked up. "The first time it was one thousand. That didn't seem so bad, and I worked really hard to make it up, but the next time it was two thousand, and I knew I couldn't earn that much in the time I had. I would have to cut classes and miss things."

"Like C-Notes rehearsals?" Annie asked.

Ulysses nodded.

Will was on his feet. He had to move. He made a quick circuit of the atrium, conscious of the angry sound of his footsteps on the granite floor.

When Annie James's stricken gaze met his, he stopped. "I didn't know. I never knew. That's what your meetings with Chambers were about?"

Will turned to Huntington. "Why does he do it? What's the big temptation? The financial aid fund is small. The total school budget can't be more than twenty million."

"Twenty-two actually." Huntington shrugged. "Chambers likes to control the money himself, to dispense it as he sees fit. And he likes to treat himself well."

Will swore. "He gets plenty of perks—a house, a car, a six-figure salary, benefits. So I don't get it."

Huntington actually looked thoughtful. "Try to think like Chambers for a minute. It's a privilege to attend Canyon. Nobody gets a free ride. Chambers likes his financial aid students humble and grateful, not cocky and confident. That's your flaw in Chambers's eyes, Sloan. You were never humble. Or grateful, for that matter."

"Still, why embezzle from the smallest fund at the school?"

"Sloan, Sloan, Sloan. The close proximity of billionaires never brings out the best in little men. Chambers wants to meet money with money. He wants to golf at the Riviera Club or Pebble Beach or St. Andrews, even. He's pretty good, you know. He wants dinners at Reign and Flints, the right car, Zegna suits, and a Rolex the size of a cinnamon bun. That stuff adds up. And then there are his vacations and his projects, like that paneled room off of his office with his private bath. I don't think the budget paid for that."

"He only does it to fatherless boys, doesn't he?" Annie's voice was very clear. "That's part of the pattern, too."

"Those moms probably think the guy is Santa Claus." Will was thinking. He hadn't bothered to figure it out when he'd been the one in Ulysses's position, but now he realized that Chambers had to be keeping two sets of records. That's what the documents in Annie's mystery package revealed. One set of records laid out Chambers's manipulation of various funds, and one set was for public scrutiny. So, there must be something on Chambers's hard drive that would reveal the fraud.

"Huntington, how friendly are you with Chambers's current secretary?"

"Hey, not that friendly."

"But you could get the password for his laptop, couldn't you?"

"I could."

"Good. Email it to me."

Ulysses spoke up then. "So what we found in the files doesn't matter?"

Annie turned to him. "What did you find?"

The boy shrugged. "Something weird with the grades."

They all moved to the kitchen where Ulysses put two transcripts side by side on the big table. "Each file begins with the final transcript."

"The one the school sends to colleges," Huntington explained.

"Then," said Tyler, "you have these other grade reports, the ones that go home each term."

"See," Ulysses pointed to a pair of papers, "they don't match. Here, Mr. Keane gave this kid a B, but on the final transcript it's an A-."

Huntington whistled. "Grade tampering. No kidding. No wonder Chambers fired our college counselor." He looked at Will. "Remember? He had his secretary do our transcripts, a very sympathetic woman."

Annie looked at the boys. "How many of these did you find?"

"Eight so far," Ulysses said. "Should we look for more?"

Annie nodded. For the next hour they catalogued data. Ulysses found Josh's file and read the grades and teachers' comments, until Josh retaliated by reading Will's file.

Tyler stopped the battle by holding up a different file. "Look at this kid. A's on everything. No need to change his grades."

Huntington flicked the manila folder to read the label. "Jack Joyce, smartest guy in our class. He's the only one I couldn't find for the gala."

Will remembered him, a short, intense kid, pale, with glasses and inky black hair. "The Invisible Man they called him."

"He was only sixteen at graduation," Huntington pointed out.

"Where did he go? Harvard?"

"Nope. He went to Berkeley, but he grew at least a foot and dropped out to become a mercenary in Africa. He's probably still there, if he's alive."

Will shook himself. It was strange to be talking to Huntington, just talking, remembering stuff, finding out that Huntington remembered it, too. In fact, Huntington seemed to remember everyone from their class.

Huntington was looking at him with an odd half smile. "You know what's funny?"

"What?"

"Jack Joyce burned down the Canyon sign."

"He what?"

"You know he hated Chambers, thought the guy was a fraud. Remember Chambers's monthly talks on manhood and morals?"

"He still makes them," Ulysses said. "In the Hall of Canyon Men."

Will turned to the kid. "No kidding. Does he still take a letter from 'school' and make it the theme of his speech? S was—"

"—Study, Strive, Stick to it, and Suc-ceed." Ulysses and Tyler spoke in unison.

Huntington grinned. "What I remember is Sloan's version of that speech."

Both boys turned to Will, looking at him with undisguised admiration. "You mean you're the Sloan of Sloan's Law? '*Slack, Slide, Suck up, and Score*'?"

"You should see your face, Sloan. You look like somebody hit you. You're part of Canyon history, a legend."

Will laughed. The laugh came from some unexpected place, and once he started, he couldn't really stop. The others joined in, and Annie James smiled at him, and he thought, *I love her. I never stopped loving her. No, that isn't quite right. I've fallen in love with her again in a new way.* There was clarity for you, a fog-lifting, driving-straight-into-bright-sun blinding realization. He loved her, and she was going to the gala with Huntington. The pattern of his life hadn't changed after all.

Around two a.m. the boys needed food again, and then they started to nod off in their seats. The three adults moved into the shadowy atrium.

"We don't really have anything that helps Ulysses, do we?" Annie sounded discouraged.

"The only way to help him is to oust Chambers." Will was clear.

"Hey, I thought you were going to let me handle Chambers." Huntington put his arm around Annie and gave her shoulders a squeeze.

"You'll never oust Chambers, Sloan." Huntington shook his head. "The guy's untouchable. He has parents and board members eating out of his hand. Everyone's convinced that he 'made' Canyon what it is today."

"Apparently he did it by tampering with the grades." Will thought grade tampering was the least of it, and dipping into the financial aid fund was like filling your plate with hors d'oeuvres when there was a big buffet on the table. Chambers had to have done more.

Will exchanged a look with Annie. He could see that she understood him. Plainly, Huntington did not know about the unpaid bond debt. Three million dollars was a sum that must have tempted Chambers, but they needed evidence to expose him.

Huntington looked at the two of them. "What? You know something that I don't?"

Will nodded. "Surprised? You put us on that New Directions committee. Just know that if Chambers has been doing what I think he has, it's too late to save Canyon."

Again Huntington looked at the two of them, his expression sober. Will thought he looked like a guy facing disaster. Then the old Huntington was back. He stood and dug a car key out of his pocket.

"Forget about Chambers for now. If any of this stuff gets out, it will hurt Canyon. No use blowing the place up before next Saturday. Let me keep working on the guy from the inside. You want Ulysses to sing at the gala, right, Annie?"

Annie nodded.

Will looked at her. He could not believe she wanted Ulysses at the school for another minute with all she now knew about Chambers. Even if she decided she did not love Will, she cared about the boy.

"Right, I'll keep working on Ulysses's singing at the gala." Huntington headed for the door. "Remember, Annie. We have a date."

Will shook his head. "Just get me that password, Huntington."

The door closed behind him, and Will turned to Annie.

They were alone in the deserted room except for the sleeping boys. Will didn't trust himself to speak. He knew he might do something stupid like beg. He helped her rouse the boys enough to get them into her car and buckled up.

At the last moment, she rolled down her car window to thank him, and he heard himself say, "You're going to the gala with him?"

She looked straight ahead over the steering wheel. "He's working to get Ulysses back in school."

"I doubt it. He's just conning everyone. He's working the system for his benefit and not for kids like Ulysses. He's conning you."

"I think maybe he's only conning himself." She shivered in the night air, and he backed away from the car. "Will *you* come to the gala?"

"Me? Come to a Canyon party at Canyon? You've got to be kidding."

Chapter Twenty

When Josh pulled through the Canyon gates on Monday, a student protest worthy of Berkeley greeted him. The gala banner had been covered with a sign that read "Save the Bookman," and boys in their C-Notes khakis and blazers stopped each in-coming car to offer the driver a flyer. He rolled down his window, and the senior head of the C-Notes handed him the piece of paper. The document read like a mini-Declaration of Independence with Chambers in the role of King George. At least the kids had been paying attention in their history class or watching the Twitter feed from Tahrir Square. It ended with a list of demands to oust Chambers over his treatment of financial aid students and his mismanagement of the reputation of the school. Josh had to admit that it was a pretty thorough road map for an investigation. He had no doubt that the same info was all over the social media. He wondered briefly how long it would take his father to hear the story. By the end of the day every Canyon family would be taking a side for or against Chambers. Not a comfortable spot for the old man to be in. Not good for Canyon if the real story got out.

He pulled into his parking place. Chambers was going to be pissed and out for blood. Dunsmore would be wringing his hands and whining. The blinds in the headmaster's office twitched. Josh killed his car engine. One thing at a time. He would have to keep his cool if he wanted to keep his job. Whatever Sloan knew and wasn't telling, Josh still needed Sloan to give big by the gala, and he needed to keep Annie on his side until then. He had to hang on for one week.

He didn't get halfway across the reception area before Chambers's secretary snagged him.

"He wants to see you now," she said, her face blank, not at all friendly.

"Got it."

Chambers didn't wait for Josh to close the office door. "Huntington, this is your fault!"

"What is, sir?" Josh took a position mid-carpet facing Chambers's *Titanic* of a desk.

"This absurd protest." Chambers waved an arm at the window behind him.

"My fault, sir?"

"You sponsored that boy Ulysses."

"I did, sir, thought he was a good fit for the school. How did he end up suspended? The C-Notes are really behind him."

"You expect me to believe that students organized this ridiculous display?" He waved a crumpled flyer in one fist.

Chambers was so pissed that Josh could see his options disappearing. Appeasing the old guy seemed the best course of action.

"Sir, you know I wouldn't do a thing to disrupt the gala or our fundraising efforts. Remember, we've still got a chance to get three million out of a single donor."

Josh took in Chambers's flushed face. More likely the piles of pledges would be unfulfilled, and the gala invitations discarded. If the gala happened at all, it might be more like the gathering of an angry mob outside the castle walls, pitchforks in hand.

"That James woman is behind this. She thinks Canyon owes an education to misfits and mongrels of every stripe. Well, she's crossed me one time too many, and she'll pay for it." Chambers stretched across the enormous desk reaching for his phone.

"Sir, I wouldn't..."

"Huntington, you've got until the end of the day to nip this thing in the bud, clean it up, turn it around."

"Easiest thing in the world, sir. You can end the protest yourself."

Chambers's hand stopped in mid-reach.

"Reinstate Ulysses. You can have the kid back in class by noon, and the whole thing's over."

Josh could see from Chambers's expression that he'd just made a big mistake.

Chambers picked up his phone and punched in a number. "Never mind, Huntington. Just clear out of your office. A letter of resignation on my desk by end of day will do."

Josh stopped at the door, and looked back. "Sir, have you read that flyer? You might want to contact your lawyer."

"OUT!"

Whoever was on the other end of the line had his ears blasted. Josh closed the door and started a slow stroll toward his office. He realized with a brief pang that he would miss Canyon. It had been his home more than any of the places his family inhabited. He had less than a paycheck in his bank account. His tenant's rent wasn't due for two weeks. Everything he'd worked for, and he had worked for it, seemed to have slipped through his fingers. He knew he was in for a big letdown, but in spite of it all, he couldn't help grinning. Chambers was going down. Josh would be willing to place a bet on it.

He had not reached his office before he got his first text from one of the guys. It was Lynch. "*Wtf is going on at Canyon?*" He had packed up his desk when he heard Dunsmore storming around in the office next to his. No doubt, Chambers had fired him, too. Josh made a call to the movers who had settled him in his South Bay apartment to come get his things from the office. At least he had another chance to impress his surly tenant. From the Rover, he sent a quick text to Sloan with Chambers's password. "Your turn to be the hero."

A local TV truck had pulled up outside the school by the time Josh reached the end of the long drive. A male reporter in a sports coat and tie stood with the Canyon sign behind him speaking into his mic, cameras rolling. Josh would hear from his father soon.

* * *

Annie got a call from her boss, Rob Parker, as soon as she came in. Rob rarely looked up from his computer screen in the course of a work day. He didn't this time either.

"Annie, do you know some crackpot school principal named Chambers? Malcolm Chambers? The fellow called me this morning. He seemed to think I should pay attention to his ravings."

"He's the head of Canyon School." It was clear that Chambers had made good on his threat. She squared her shoulders.

"The Canyon School in the news today?"

"In the news? Really?"

"Some protest going on there. Exclusive boys school caught fudging the grades to give the privileged even more of an edge." He turned his laptop toward her so that she could see the images on the screen.

"Hmmm." She saw Tyler Dalton, in his C-Note blazer and khakis, looking like the quintessential prep school boy, handing a flyer to the driver of a large black luxury SUV. "Probably not the whole story. What did Chambers want?"

"He wants me to fire you. He sent me a fax. It's here somewhere." Rob glanced briefly at the jumble of papers on the table beside him. "Seems to be a love letter from some besotted youth. Chambers apparently thinks I care who falls in love with my writers." Rob actually looked up from his computer. "As if I could let you go, Annie. You know those stories you wanted to write?"

"About resilience and comebacks?"

"About the underdog, anyway." He waved a hand in her direction. "Why don't you look into this Canyon thing, see if there's an underdog story in it? If there is, I wouldn't mind publishing it." Rob's gaze returned to his computer screen.

"Oh, and you can have that fax from your admirer if you want it."

Annie slipped around Rob and picked up the paper he indicated from the pile and held it in her hand on her way back to her own cubicle.

Dear Annie,

You have been Annie in my mind for a long time, though I have not had the right to call you by that name. It has been two months since our last conversation, and I can't stop thinking of you. I have tried to replace thoughts of you with new impressions—people, work, long hours of practice with my new teammates. I am rarely alone with my thoughts, and still nothing dulls the ache of your refusal. You may say that it's too soon to overcome such a disappointment. I say it doesn't matter how much time passes.

You must admit it was my first attempt at a marriage proposal. That it was spontaneous and unpolished argues for my sincerity. I realize now that I caught you unprepared. But I ask you to think of everything you know about me and not to think my love for you a slight or passing thing.

I can wait a long time for you. Uncertainty is what I suffer from now. A word from you makes the waiting bearable. Please let me know that we can meet and talk, away from Canyon.

He had signed it with a scrawling signature. She had not guessed that he had been capable of such generous feelings toward her. She had imagined all along that he had resented and hated her from the moment of her refusal. Her cubicle, which had seemed a safe place in which to retreat from the world, now seemed unbearably small. She wanted vast skies and endless stretches of beach where she could shout and dance and live out loud.

Later, when she could think again, she found the video of the protest at Canyon on her computer news feed. The story emphasized the school's high tuition fees and its exclusiveness and suggested that such a place was a lumbering dinosaur in the 21st century, part of a toxic old boys pipeline to the Ivy Leagues. The story wasn't real journalism. The report raised no questions. No investigation was ongoing. It was all about gates and luxury cars, a story that confirmed what people already thought they knew about Canyon. No one watching the clip would suspect that something unusual was happening.

What Annie saw was Tyler Dalton trying to save his friend. And that was the story she needed to tell, or rather it was story that Ulysses and Tyler should tell, the story about the unlikely friendship between two young men who had learned to navigate the vast gulf in their circumstances to find out they could be friends. To tell it she had to bring Ulysses and Tyler together and introduce them to the world.

* * *

Will was puzzling over Huntington's text when Beau breezed into his office around noon. "Got something you'll want to see." He handed Will his phone, and Will clicked on the loaded video. It was small, but he could see the familiar Canyon sign behind a TV reporter with a mic. He punched up the volume as the shot widened out to show a group of boys in blazers handing flyers to drivers as cars entered the campus. One boy held up a sign that read: "The Bookman in. Chambers out."

Beau nudged him. "Keep watching. You won't believe what the camera catches next."

In the next seconds Will spotted Elliot Dunsmore at the edge of the frame as he pulled out of the gate and drove away. The camera went back to the reporter.

"Sweet, huh, to watch that guy slink away, like a rat from a sinking ship."

Will played the clip again a second and third time. Each time he got a little more of the picture. The boys protesting were the C-Notes, and one of them was Tyler Dalton, Ulysses's friend. That Ulysses's Canyon classmates would rally to support him overturned everything Will knew about Canyon. What Annie James had said to him more than ten years earlier, that it was his choice to deal with his circumstances with anger or with openness, came back to him. He realized he still had that choice. And he had something he had not had as a boy—he had the power to make a difference at Canyon, at a place that was ready for a change.

Beau had likened Canyon to a sinking ship, and maybe it was. Will knew that information about the bond payments would not long remain private under the media's scrutiny. If anyone wanted to save Canyon, that person would have to act immediately. How odd that Will Sloan should be the one who could.

He found Jack Joyce's file in the boxes the boys had left at Z-Text and tossed it on Beau's desk. "Beau, can you do me a favor? Find this guy. He's holding a bond that I want to buy."

"Buy? How much?"

"We'll start with three mil."

Beau was looking at the file. The thing had the Canyon name all over it. "Wait, three mil, as in the money Canyon wanted from you in the beginning?"

"That's the figure. Turns out, you're right. Canyon is a sinking ship, unless somebody buys that bond from this guy."

"And why would you do that?"

"Same reason as before. There's a woman I want to…please."

"You know what I want to know?"

"What?"

"When do I get to meet her?"

"As soon as I get her to say, 'yes!'"

Chapter Twenty-one

Will reached Canyon in twenty minutes even in midday L.A. traffic. The protesters were gone; the parking lot was empty. Chambers's administrative assistant, Danielle, told him that the old man had called a headmaster's holiday and sent the students and faculty home. The woman did her best to stop Will from entering Chambers's office, but in the end, she backed down. He asked her to be available to prepare a letter.

The room had all the stern authority Will remembered. It was easily twice the size of his mother's trailer. The high ceiling and wall of windows gave the heavy furniture room to breathe. The books, the framed diplomas and awards, the black chairs with their gold leaf college insignia were subtle, old, masculine, and meant to intimidate. The vast oak desk was as threatening as a tank. The sofa with its arched back was like a throne framed by heavy blue velvet curtains on either side of the expanse of glass. The view looked out from under the arched veranda down the long, palm-lined drive.

As a kid he had felt a stomach-churning awkwardness on entering the room. His worn shoes had held him rooted to a spot on the carpet a respectful distance from Chambers's desk, a line not to be crossed. Will had always been eager for each session to end and conscious that Chambers could prolong or shorten his humiliation on a whim. That carpet, however, had helped him stay in control. Each time he unlocked more of its intricate pattern as Chambers worked to goad him into an outburst.

In spite of the hot L.A. sun outside, the room was cool. Chambers sat at the over-sized desk with a drink in hand staring with an unseeing gaze at his laptop screen. He had removed his horn-rimmed glasses and loosened his dark blue and yellow striped Canyon tie, but he still wore his blazer and crisp white shirt.

When he looked up, he seemed more weary than surprised, but Will did not miss the quick furtive way he closed down his laptop and pushed it away. A small thing, those few strokes of the keypad, meant to look as if Chambers were merely making a polite shift of attention from screen to visitor. Chambers would not back down willingly. He had the meanness of a cornered snake.

Will took a moment to glance at the book-lined walls. He picked a slim volume off the shelf, *The Aims of Education,* and let it fall open in his palm. The spine did not crack. The unmarked pages had the stiffness of a book that had never been read. It shouldn't surprise him. He had always known that Chambers, the scholarly school head, was a sham. The room reminded him that both he and Chambers had made the same mistake of thinking a person's surroundings defined him. Will had not recognized the mistake until now.

Now he realized that Chambers was the little man behind the curtain who had found a way to feel powerful in the strange moneyed world of L.A. Chambers had never once quoted a book or pulled one from the shelf to share. All their conversations had been about money. As Will was not a paying customer, he needed to earn his keep, so he would not be a drain on Canyon.

He found the spot on the carpet where he used to stand and endure that brand of humiliation and glanced down briefly. The carpet had not changed; his shoes had. He tried to summon his old feeling of helpless rage, but the past had no power over him. He thought instead of Ulysses standing there and Annie at work somewhere in her cubicle, both of them confined and constrained by Chambers's threats.

"We've had a lot of conversations in this room. This one will be different."

"I suppose you've come to enjoy Canyon's embarrassment."

"I've come for your signed letter of resignation."

Chambers head jerked back in a sharp snort of laughter.

"In triplicate. One for the board, one for the school community, and one for me."

"You've got an inflated sense of your influence at Canyon, Mr. Sloan, if you think you can impose such terms, indeed, any terms, on me. You may have made a fortune, but you were never a part of Canyon. You were an intruder then and you still are. You will never belong here."

Will pulled one of the black chairs up to the desk, and took a seat. "It's not so much my circumstances that matter today, but yours. I'm offering you the only terms you'll get, a chance to go quietly, before the press gets hold of the details of your situation. No board involvement, and no scrutiny of your mismanagement of school funds."

"You have no proof of anything."

"I have boxes of files that reveal a pattern of grade tampering."

Chambers waved the idea away. "I fired the fellow involved in that little scheme years ago. He'll bear the blame."

Will wondered briefly whether Chambers believed his own bull. It didn't matter. He pulled a small black zip drive from his coat pocket, and held it up between his thumb and forefinger. "You know what this is, Chambers? It's a zip drive. It's smaller than some bullets, but just as lethal. Z-Text puts its software on these drives. A drive like this can suck all the data from your device in minutes."

He leaned across Chambers's desk, reaching for the laptop. Chambers grabbed for it and missed and fell back in his chair. He straightened at once, trying to look unconcerned. With unhurried movements, Will disengaged the power cord and flipped the laptop open. He rebooted, entered the password, and inserted the zip drive into a port. Instantly, lights blinked on the drive as it engaged, starting the data transfer.

"You won't find anything." Chambers voice was smug.

"Oh, I will. Did I mention that Z-Text has software that penetrates encryption? The CIA covets our design."

He glanced up to see the change in Chambers's face.

"Finding patterns is what I'm good at. I can tell you about the pattern of this rug, you know, about how often the pattern repeats in each of the border bands, and where the anomalies are. I can find data you think you've erased. What I do with that data depends on you."

"I think you forget what you owe to Canyon."

Will nodded. "I do owe Canyon a great deal. This is my chance to repay that debt, to rid the school of its biggest liability."

"Now look here, Sloan. I made this school. When I took over, Canyon was a boys' club for a few wealthy adolescents slouching their pimply way to third-rate colleges if their fathers could donate enough money. I brought rigor to the program and national recognition to our college matriculation. Don't think you did not benefit from Canyon's reputation, or that you can injure it now and escape the consequences."

"Was it the grade tampering that put Canyon on the map, do you think?"

"You've stolen school property."

"Recycled it. A few boxes of files from the dumpster, not three million dollars."

Chambers blanched. "Where did you get the absurd idea that I stole anything from the school?"

"The financial aid fund was just too small."

Chambers pushed back in his chair and stood. "You think you have it all figured out, but you don't. You might be able to get rid of me, but you can't save the school."

"Because there's a bondholder who wants to foreclose?" He got Chambers's full attention then. "I know about your bond problem."

Chambers took a swig of his drink and put down the glass. "Well then, you know Canyon is doomed."

Will shook his head. "I doubt it. You see, I know who holds that bond, and your letter of resignation might just persuade him to change his mind about foreclosing."

Chambers made a choked sound. "Who put you up to this? That woman?"

"You mean Annie James. It's a good thing you didn't speak her name. You hurt her, Chambers, when she was young and vulnerable and grieving. You did it for spite, out of everything that's mean and small in you. You hurt Ulysses and who knows how many other boys who were made to stand on this carpet and suffer because they lacked the financial resources to buy your favor."

"She can still be prosecuted for her relationship with you."

Will shook his head. "She'll never be prosecuted for anything. She's going to be my wife."

The zip drive finished its work. Will disengaged it from Chambers's machine and set the laptop back on the edge of the desk. He held up the drive for Chambers to see. "Shall I call your administrative assistant in to take a dictation?"

* * *

Will returned to Z-Text by three. Beau had found Jack Joyce, and Will went to work on the guy immediately. He plugged the zip drive into his own laptop and started the process of decoding its data. The proof of Chambers's frauds would be there. He asked Beau to hang on until he'd finished his conversation with Jack.

It was a measure of how strained their friendship had been in the last few months that it took a lot of convincing to get Beau to stay, but he did. The others had left for the day when Beau sank into a chair opposite Will's desk. He kept his arms folded across his chest, and his face wore its most skeptical mask.

"So did you give away more of your money?"

"I did."

"How much?"

"You don't want to know."

Beau came out of the chair and stomped around the office swearing in a way unlike his usual cheerful manner as the vice president of ambience and irreverence.

Will deserved it. He said nothing until his friend calmed down a bit.

"Is it about that woman again?" Beau asked when he finally stopped ranting.

"It is, and I can explain, but first, just look at this." He opened the file of his new project and turned his laptop Beau's way.

When Beau finally lifted his head, his familiar grin was back in place. "You're back, really back. I thought we'd lost you, buddy."

"Almost. I took an off-ramp into the past there for a few months. I needed to figure some things out."

"So when do we start on this thing?" Beau indicated the image on Will's screen.

Will held up the tear-off calendar. He had about a month to go before the non-competition clause released him. "Soon. But first I want you to help me buy a diamond."

"Whoa! Time out!" Beau made the classic T sign with his hands. "Who? You haven't even seen anyone twice. Oooh, the woman from the center?"

"Her name is Annie James. I've seen her quite a bit actually, but not nearly enough. Maybe a lifetime will do."

Beau just looked at him. "You are way ahead of yourself, aren't you? Sleeping with her is one thing. Marriage is something else."

"You'll meet her first. I'm going to ask my mom to host a party for us."

Beau pointed a finger at Will's computer screen. "Okay, I get it. You're happy. It's a new thing. It's good for business, but are you sure about this woman?"

"I'm sure."

"I don't know." He studied Will's face. "This change in your personality may take some getting used to."

"You'll get used to it. You've never steered me wrong, so I need you for the diamond thing."

"You're on."

Chapter Twenty-two

At seven a.m. on Saturday, Josh's tenant knocked on his door. Out of deference for her sensibilities, Josh pulled on a pair of board shorts before answering her knock. She was gone when he got there. Stuck to the doorjamb was a sticky note that simply read "SINK." He knocked on her door, and she showed him the clogged sink filled with brown greasy dishwater. He assured her he'd get right on it. He opened the cabinet doors under the sink and looked at the plumbing, just a pipe, curved like a "J" meeting another pipe at a right angle. He wasn't doing anything. How hard could it be to take the pipes apart and remove the clog?

He returned to his unit. He needed coffee. One good thing about being fired—he now had the espresso machine from his office in his apartment.

As a tenant, Emma Gray had been as good as her word. She never seemed to slow down. She had painted her unit and filled the two planter boxes below the windows with red and gold flowers. It wasn't a *Sunset* magazine spread, but even he had to admit, the color livened up the place.

This morning she was down in the driveway with the hood of her sad mustard-colored car open, doing something apparently competent with an oilcan, some rags, and a set of small wrenches. Her boy—the kid was named Max—was playing beside her, sending a pair of bright blue and red toy cars down the slight slope of the driveway, and launching them into the air off a makeshift ramp. Every once in awhile the boy peered under the hood at what she was doing, and she stopped to show him and let him help.

Josh liked the way she paid attention to her kid, and he liked the curve of her bottom in shorts as she bent over the engine of the car. He was surprised by the womanliness of that curve. She claimed to be twenty-four, but looked more like seventeen with her brown hair in a ponytail. Still the curve was real and feminine.

There was no way he was going to attempt to fix a sink under her critical gaze. His phone's ring tone went off persistently in his pocket, but he ignored it.

At two he was eating a sandwich when she knocked to announce that she was walking into town. "Sink?"

"Hey, leave your door open, and I'll get to it while you're out."

The look she gave him was unflatteringly doubtful. "Whatever."

As soon as she and Max disappeared around the corner, he gathered his toolbox and a bucket from the garage and spread some newspaper on her clean kitchen floor. He could do this. She had no reason to doubt his competence. He emptied the sink of as much of the sour brown water as he could. It was dark and cool under the sink, so he retrieved a flashlight from the Rover and angled it to shed some light on the pipes, pipes that hadn't been touched in twenty years it looked like. He was lying on his back applying WD-40 to the pipe joints when he heard them return.

With a side glance he could see a pair of sweet curving legs disappearing into khaki shorts, and he could smell sunscreen and woman. Abruptly he went hard.

"Need any help?" she asked.

"No, thanks. I've got it." He was just fine. He was lying on his back on a cold floor in a pair of trunks that felt like they had Everest in them.

"Okay. I'll let you get on with it."

He heard her moving around the small kitchen. Her leg brushed his when she opened the refrigerator. "Sorry," she murmured.

He was sweating and trying to think about pipes and wrenches, and none of it was helping. Her footsteps went away, and he took a deep breath.

Then Max was squatting next to him, peering under the sink.

"You're fixing our sink." He sounded much more confident than his mother.

"Yeah."

Max asked him about the wrench, the WD-40, the pipes, and the water supply system of the greater Los Angeles metropolitan area. He didn't have a clue, but he kept trying to answer the kid's questions honestly. It seemed important not to mislead the boy. A shift in topic caught him unprepared.

"Is that your winkie?"

"My what?"

"Mom and I call it a winkie." Max lowered his voice. "What do you call it?"

"A penis." He managed to open the wrench wide enough to grip the pipe fitting.

"Yeah, Mom told me that one, too." Max settled on the floor next to his hip.

Where is your mother? He didn't hear her, but unless she was in her bedroom, she could hear their conversation. He pulled on the wrench. The pipe didn't move.

"Your winkie's sort of poking up."

"Sometimes it does that. It's normal." Josh tried to keep his tone even. The kid didn't have a dad to talk to about these things. He gave the wrench a harder twist.

"Yeah, mom said so. Is it big because you're big?"

"It's a grown-up size like you have a boy size." Josh put more pressure on the wrench.

"Do you ever touch it?"

Two things happened simultaneously. Emma shouted for Max, and the pipe fitting loosened and six inches of slime and muck hit Josh's chest before he could scramble out of the way. He pushed out from under the sink and rolled to his side, brushing most of the gunk off his chest. He got to his feet and made himself meet his tenant's eye.

Cold slime was trickling down his belly toward his still too-obvious erection. Dignity was not an option. He was a slime-covered, lust-crazed incompetent.

"Call a plumber." He dropped the wrench in his toolbox.

"It's Saturday. It will cost a fortune."

"I'll pay for it. I'm going to go clean this muck off."

* * *

Josh took a long cold shower. He soaped away the muck, but still he stayed under the spray, waiting for the water to wash away the hot residue of embarrassment.

Sexual humiliations were for adolescents, but he didn't remember having any. He'd always had control. He could coax a necessary erection out of a wisp of stimulation or hold an inconvenient one back. Girls and women, his piano teacher, his mother's friends, and later Chambers's secretary, had been willing to teach him their secrets, and he hadn't had any trouble catching on.

He'd always been able to find what he was looking for, and he'd been light years ahead of his classmates in understanding what to do with it.

So what had happened to him under that sink? Some stealth erection? A tractor beam from Death Star Emma Gray pulling him in? He did not understand the attraction at all. One moment the woman looked like a scrubbed teenager, and at other times when she headed for work at Daddy Rock, she looked as pierced and inked as a death metal band. Neither look appealed to Josh, and he put the attraction down to stress and deprivation.

He'd lost his job. His vision of putting on a great gala and getting his classmates to break the record for class giving at their ten-year reunion had vanished. He didn't know what he was going to do with himself. He had avoided the Power Plant so far, knowing he'd be in for merciless ribbing from the guys and the demand that he pay up on his bet with money he didn't have. But he couldn't keep hanging out in his apartment lusting after his tenant. The Power Plant was his best option.

* * *

Huntington wasn't answering his texts, but Will figured the Canyon crowd in the Power Plant microbrewery could point him to the guy's lair. Beau had located Jack Joyce, and Will had faxed Joyce that third copy of Chambers's resignation. Their negotiations were off to a good start.

He had also talked to Rothwell to let him know what the situation was. Rothwell was just the sort of alum who would have credibility with the board when the news of Chambers's wrongdoings emerged, and the guy would handle it with discretion.

Lynch's Cheeto-orange hair led Will to the Canyon table in the crowded brewery. Shields spotted him first. "Hey, Sloan, come to gloat? Huntington's taken a bath, lost it all—job, bet, and trust."

Shields made an "L" with his fingers indicating Huntington.

So Huntington's friends saw him as a loser. Will wondered what the bet was and how Huntington was managing without his trust.

"Not my year." Huntington raised his glass in a weak salute to misfortune as he slid over to make room for Will in the booth.

"It must be great to have friends you can count on, Huntington."

"Discretion is not big with this crowd."

A blonde waitress asked him if he wanted a drink and he ordered. "You ignored my texts."

Huntington laughed. "Seems a fair return. How many of mine did you ignore?"

"So what brings you here, Sloan?" Lynch asked.

"Money. I understand you'll match me in any donation I make to Canyon." The waitress brought his beer.

The trio turned on Huntington, instantly aggrieved. "Hey, that wasn't the deal."

"What was it then?" Will enjoyed their discomfort.

After a pause, Shields admitted, "We said we'd do ten percent."

"Ten percent might help." He let them wait.

Finally, Shields asked how much Will planned to give.

"I believe the figure needed is three million." Actually, he was letting them off easy. His deal with Jack Joyce, if it went through, would be for a good bit more than that.

Lynch spewed a mouthful of pretzels, then coughed and choked and reached for his beer while Shields thumped him on the back.

"But if you all can't manage that, you could help to get everyone to the gala."

"The gala?" They turned on Huntington. Shields said, "I thought you said the gala was not happening?"

Will looked at Huntington. "You sent the invitations, didn't you?"

"The school did, but that was before all this stuff…"

Will shrugged. "So we have some calls to make this week."

"Calls?"

"We're going to call everyone on Huntington's guest list and personally urge those people to come."

"So you're saying we don't have to give money, if we make these calls?" His old classmates regarded him warily while their waitress wiped up Lynch's spewed pretzels with a dishcloth.

"Works for me." Will thought Annie would be proud of him for letting them off so easy. He took a few minutes to clarify how they would do the calls. Josh had access to the list of invited guests on his computer, so Will invited them to Z-Text to use the phones there. They set a time and the others drifted off leaving Will with Huntington.

"I have something that will interest you." Will took Chambers letter from his pocket.

Huntington read it and whistled softly. "How did you get him to do this?"

"Just pointed him in the direction of his own self-interest."

"But it won't save the school, will it? Chambers needed that three mil from you in August to do what?" He handed Will the letter.

"Pay a bondholder, but the letter has saved the school. I faxed it to Jack Joyce this afternoon."

"Jack Joyce is the bondholder? The Invisible Man?"

Will stood up to go. "You know one thing I like about you, Huntington?"

"Enlighten me, Sloan. I thought there was no end to your contempt for guys like me."

"I like your intelligence." He stuck out his hand, a thing he could never have done at Canyon. Huntington shook it. It made him like the guy more, but it didn't make him crazy. "One more thing, Huntington. She may be going to the gala with you, but she's going home with me."

Chapter Twenty-Three

In the end Josh's father did not summon him to the family mansion, he merely had the law firm that administered the trust send a letter. It arrived on the morning of the gala and explained in legalese that because Josh had not fulfilled the terms of their agreement, he would not receive any monies from his trust until further notice. Josh tossed it on the pile with his other bills and notices.

He'd had some time to figure things out in the week since he'd been fired, and Sloan had come to the rescue. Even if you only counted Sloan's three mil to pay the current debt on Jack Joyce's bond, that made their class, the class of '05, the biggest ten-year reunion donors ever. He suspected that Sloan had bought the bond outright, but Sloan wasn't saying. Josh would announce their triumph at the gala. By the end of the evening, he would meet two of his father's three conditions. Maybe the old man would relent.

Josh didn't bother with shorts. He took his espresso to the window and checked out the view. It was still no Malibu, but maybe when his father gave in, Josh would move away from his tenant. He could definitely use an upgrade from his current situation. Meanwhile, tonight the guys had a limo. Josh and Annie would be in it. With Chambers and Dunsmore gone, Sloan had put some friend of his on the details of the gala. Sloan's friend reported that the arrangements Josh had made were still good. The caterer, florist, valet service, band—all the vendors planned to fulfill their contracts regardless of Canyon's public woes. The story had continued to get local coverage with lots of shots of the Canyon gates and interviews with celebrities—Hollywood producers, actors' kids, and politicians' sons—who'd once attended the school. The board chair appeared before the cameras making repeated assurances that the school was sound. Video of the protest had had lots of hits on the Internet, especially after news of Chambers's resignation hit the media, but Annie's newspaper had run a series of articles on its webpage presenting a different view of Canyon, and a rival video of Tyler and Ulysses talking and singing and telling their story had drawn almost as many viewers as the original protest.

Tonight he'd know whether the school had a prayer of surviving.

* * *

Annie's neighbors all contrived, in one way or another, to see her off in the limo in a cobalt blue dress that Tess had encouraged her to buy. Its sheer sleeves sparkled with tiny rhinestones like a night sky. Irene, of course, had her watering to do. Dan was washing Tess's car. Tess simply came over to zip Annie into the dress and prompt her not to settle for less than the hottest man with the biggest bank account. She didn't tell Tess it wouldn't matter if such a man took any notice of her. Her only concern was with the one man who had laughed at her suggestion that he come.

In the limo there was no privacy for a talk with Josh, neither to thank him, nor to ask what he would be doing next. His friends ribbed him about being a big loser, but their jibes did not seem to affect him in any way.

At Canyon a few TV news people had stationed themselves outside the school gates, but inside, the mood was celebratory. Annie entered the courtyard on Josh's arm and saw at once that the gala was a smashing success. She turned to him with a smile. He did have a talent for throwing a party. The strings of glittering white lights that wrapped the trunks of the palm trees could hardly compete with the glittering crowd. The packed courtyard rang with talk and laughter. A dozen people came up to Josh at once to shake his hand or offer an air-kiss. Annie slipped from his hold as the Canyon crowd claimed him. For a moment her unanswered question consumed her. She looked blindly about. It was impossible that Will would come. She suspected that he misunderstand her relationship with Josh. Josh was like a younger, ne'er-do-well brother she'd never had. Josh seemed to be a classic case of failure-to-launch while Will, she now knew, had been a man almost too early in life.

Then she spotted Will at the upper end of the courtyard, looking down on the scene. He started toward her, moving easily through the crowd, as aloof and self-sufficient as ever, in black evening wear with an open-collared white shirt. The capacity for command that he had not been able to exercise as a younger man was in his step and in the way crowd parted for him.

A man with a clipboard, perhaps the caterer, stopped him for a brief word. Will's gaze never left her, but he answered the man, who bustled off.

She could not look away. Her heart repeated a simple refrain that he'd come for her. *For her.*

He stopped in front of her, and the rest of the party faded away. "I didn't think you'd come."

He gave her a scorching look. "You didn't think I'd leave you to Huntington, did you?" He took her hands in his. "We have to stop meeting in places where I can't make love to you."

The words warmed her instantly.

"Enjoy the party. Be good to Josh, but I'm coming for you later," he promised and kissed her once lightly.

* * *

Josh nursed a series of drinks and managed a number of conversations. By his count most of the big fish had come, as well as the loyal masses. When the party reached critical mass, it would be time for him to do his host bit. Without Chambers or Dunsmore, it was up to Josh to welcome everyone. He might not be the assistant development director any longer, but he was the class of '05's rep.

He kept an eye out for Sloan and saw the guy zero in on Annie. Sloan did not have an ounce of humility, but apparently he wasn't going to monopolize Annie all night. Josh watched her find Ulysses's mother and take her to meet the Daltons. Not much else seemed to be happening.

At last the moment seemed right. He stepped up to the makeshift podium, quieted the band, and took the mic.

He thanked everyone for coming and for supporting Canyon so generously. He got them all on their feet and cheering by saying, "Canyon's had a great first hundred years, and we're looking forward to the next hundred."

Once the applause died, he launched into a little speech. "You may have heard that we've had a change of leadership at Canyon this week. The sudden departure of our long-time head of school comes as a surprise, but not a catastrophe. Although many of us will remember Headmaster Chambers's shaping role in our lives, the New Directions for Canyon groups have been working hard to shape Canyon in her next century. They're here tonight. Please thank them for their work."

He waited for another round of enthusiastic applause to die down.

"Again your generosity makes Canyon's future possible. We offer a special congratulations to the class of two thousand and five, who, thanks to the generous contribution of a single anonymous donor, has set a new ten-year reunion giving record of over three million dollars."

That news created a buzz.

"If any of other classes want to step forward, consider the development office open. Now, let's get back to the party. Please welcome the C-Notes, Canyon's a cappella group, one of its oldest traditions."

* * *

Annie was standing with Ulysses's mom and the Daltons when the C-Notes bounded up to the podium and started an upbeat version of "Happy Birthday," encouraging the crowd to join in. She understood better now how Tyler had come to be such a staunch friend to Ulysses. His parents were good people.

With each song, the line of blazer-clad boys shifted, until Ulysses and Tyler were front and center, laughing and hamming it up. They crooned a love song to melt the hearts of every female in the crowd. Annie couldn't help smiling. She felt Will come up behind her. She half-turned to him, and he leaned to whisper in her ear. "After the singing, you're coming with me." She caught his hand in hers, and hands linked, they listened to the singers until, as the last note quivered away, Will pulled Annie with him through the crowd.

* * *

Josh watched Sloan pull Annie away from the crowd. *You owe me, buddy.* Sloan with Annie—that was the real triumph of Josh's night, his biggest success and one no one would ever see. He was musing that maybe his next career would be matchmaker when a tap on his shoulder made him turn.

"Mother." He always had the feeling he was looking in a mirror when he faced his mother, and if he'd learned anything in high school bio, it was not to be vain about his own looks. He had pretty much inherited the package from her. Tonight she was in a classic champagne-colored Dior with pearls the size of martini olives.

"You made a mess of things, haven't you, darling? Do we have to do an intervention?"

"I thought Dad had intervened." Josh was used to operating in the world without any particular notice from either parent, so his father's ultimatums had been a bit of a shock.

His mother smiled her brittle smile that barely creased the edges of her mouth. "Unfortunately, your father has no idea how to manage you. He thinks money moves you."

She took a sip of golden wine, almost the color of her pale hair, making him wait for whatever cutting thing she would say. But after a pause she only patted his cheek lightly with her free hand. "Don't worry, darling. I'll find a woman who can manage you."

* * *

Will led Annie around the glittering courtyard to the old hall. With a key he'd obtained earlier, he opened one of the tall wooden doors. It helped to own that bond. A patch of light from the courtyard spilled in a long shaft across the polished wood making a path for them. The old floor creaked under them as they entered, and the mingled smells of old things—wood and banners and metal shields and trophies—greeted them. He found the lights and let the door close behind them, cutting off the noise of the party.

The lights made a hum and offered a faint illumination.

He turned her in his arms and kissed her at once because he could, and because he needed to after all the obstacles, uncertainties, and delays that had held him back for so long. He was as thirsty as the earth after a long drought.

When he could check himself, he held her close, pressing her head to his shoulder. "You know why we're here, don't you?"

Annie felt Will's voice rumble against her ear. "I hope so."

He pulled back and tucked her arm in his, setting them on a circuit round the hall. "Last fall Dunsmore and Chambers offered me a place in the hall. I turned it down. Rudely. My mama would have been ashamed of my language, but I couldn't think of this room without remembering that you turned me down here."

They stopped under the portrait of a very young man in the uniform of the American Expeditionary Forces, the first Canyon alum ever to die in war. He had been nineteen.

They were both looking at the young soldier, talking in low voices.

"Can you forgive me? I believed I was right in acting for you, for your future. I had just met your mother. I knew her hopes for you. It would have been unforgivably selfish of me to stand in your way."

She felt him shake his head. "You've got it backwards. You were right to turn me down."

"Was I? I believed I was."

"I need you to forgive me for that first proposal."

"I thought you hated me."

"If I did, it was because I was the selfish one. I wanted you then, but I wasn't thinking of what you wanted." He looked at her. "Did I even say I loved you that day? I was so full of my own plans, so sure my great success was just around the corner. I didn't have a vision for our life together."

Will started them walking again, under the fixed gazes of more young men in uniform.

"I was afraid. I didn't think I deserved happiness. I was sure that if I said yes to you, a terrible tragedy would follow."

"My fault. I should have picked a better spot for my proposal, but on that day it was here or the top of the tool shed."

She could see that he had laughter in his eyes. "You brought me back here."

"You made me realize that I already have a spot in this hall." He pointed to one of the banners that hung above the portraits, a football championship banner. "I love you, Annie James. You make me want to kneel." He released her and dropped slowly to one knee, taking her hand. "Will you marry me?"

Annie put her free hand on his shoulder and knelt down, matching him in humility. "I love you, Will Sloan, and I will marry you."

From his coat pocket he produced a red ring box. He took her hands again, placed the box in them, and waited for her to open it.

In a black velvet bed a single significant gem sparkled brightly. Annie leaned forward and kissed him softly, holding him to her with the lightest touch of her lips.

He slid the ring on her finger. "You know this means you've got to go home with me tonight."

"And ditch Josh?" She smiled at him.

"I told him it was going to be that way." He rose and lifted her up with him.

"Did you? You were that sure of yourself."

"Sure of you."

* * *

Will angled his truck across the foot of Annie's driveway, blocking in the small gray compact she'd been driving. Annie understood that he would always be that man who boldly claimed her. He helped her down from the truck, and they stumbled slightly on the uneven bricks of the path to her door. He took her key and turned out the porch light as soon as they stepped inside.

She dropped her bag and stepped out of her heels. In the entry they kissed and peeled away each other's garments, breathless and laughing.

He broke their embrace, and they clung together catching their breaths, until he steadied himself and took her hand. "Bed. Now."

He led the way to her room. She found the light, and they made a brief ceremony of shedding the last of their clothes. She climbed first into the bed and looked back at him, standing beautiful and naked, his hand on the lamp switch. She read his hesitation. He'd come to her tonight with a whole heart and with nothing else beyond himself and his ring. It flashed on her finger as she reached out to pull him toward her.

"No more barriers between us." He flicked off the light and joined her in the bed.

Chapter Twenty-Four

Annie opened her eyes to sunlight streaming through the high windows above her bed and a warm arm flung across her ribs. She smiled at Will's need to lay claim to her even in his sleep. As if he felt her shift from dreams to consciousness, he pulled her closer against him. His first waking inhalation stirred against her hair, and Annie snuggled deeper against him, intrigued by the way his body responded to her slightest move.

"Good morning, my love." His hand found her breasts and drifted back and forth across them lightly. "I can hear you thinking."

"Guilty."

"You are mentally composing a to-do list."

"Habit." She turned to face him. "But I am open to joint decision making."

"Fair enough. What's on your agenda?"

She hesitated. There were so many things. She should be thinking only of him, but there was still a world beyond her bedroom with her family and his mother.

At her hesitation he took over. "First things first, then. When should we marry?"

"Soon."

"Right answer. June?"

"We'll never get Luna de Miel in June."

"Ah. Another right answer to an unasked question. But you forget you're marrying a High Net Worth Individual." He flipped her around to face him, and her breath caught at the more intimate contact with his body. "We can have Luna de Miel all to ourselves if we want it."

Some time later, as their sated bodies cooled, Will asked, "So who makes the coffee in our household?"

* * *

In the end it was after ten on a bright beach day before Annie again thought about her to-do list. She stood in her living room, looking out at the black truck at the foot of her driveway. A belated thought occurred to her. "Oh dear. All my neighbors watched me leave with Josh last night."

Will came up behind her, coffee in hand. "Where's that flavor of the month spirit?"

"You do know that I am more of a same flavor every time kind of girl." She looked over her shoulder at his laughing green eyes and dark, dark hair. "Kind of a pistachio-with-chocolate-sauce sort of woman."

"I know." His expression sobered briefly, and then the laugh lights returned to his eyes. "But we've got to face your neighbors some time, and besides we're going car shopping this morning."

"Car shopping? What happened to joint decision making?"

He pointed to her driveway. "That loaner you're driving is not you."

"Hmmm. Someone else mentioned that. Why do you think it's not me?"

"That car's so polite, it's invisible. It's an apology of a car, waiting for someone to run right over it. You need something with some attitude."

"Your truck has enough attitude for the whole block."

"Well then, something with audacity and a cool factor. I was thinking of a soft top convertible with some serious European engineering, something with zip but not flash."

"You've been thinking about this."

"About you. Always." He put his arm around her, just as Dan Biddle, picking up his newspaper across the street, saw the truck. Dan glanced up, and Annie waved. The man behind her whispered, "And think how a sporty convertible will look parked next to those monsters your sisters drive."

"Oooh, you're wicked, you know."

He kissed her shoulder. "We can stay here and torment your neighbor, or go car shopping."

Annie laughed. "Car shopping."

Will took a last swig of coffee and grabbed his key. He was shirtless and in his dress slacks. She raised one brow.

"We'll stop by my house first, and if you don't mind, we'll go by my mom's later."

Annie just watched him. She had not realized how happiness would suit him, how it would alter the lines in his face and deepen the green of his eyes. "Give me a minute, will you? I want to leave my family a message."

He flashed her a grin and stepped out the door, and she heard him greet Irene.

Annie picked up the phone. Her busy sisters would be out tracking down bargains and taking kids to lessons or competitions.

Hi Meg, it's Annie. I am returning Mel's pamphlet. No need to freeze my eggs after all. Save the first weekend in June. Talk to you soon.

Hi, Meredith, it's Annie. Will and I want to thank you for introducing us to Luna de Miel. Save the first weekend in June for us.

Hi Mel, it's Annie. I'm sorry Barry's not for me, but I know you can help him find someone. Will and I hope you'll save the first weekend in June.

Hi Mom, hi Dad, it's Annie. Will and I would like you to save the first weekend in June for our wedding. We'll come up to visit soon. Love you.

WANT MORE OF KATE MOORE'S

CANYON CLUB?

IN EARLY 2015 WATCH FOR:

Golden Boy

Josh Huntington opened his door. Seven years earlier, with money from his now vanished trust, he had purchased a brown stucco duplex four blocks from the beach in a little town south of the L.A. airport. When he bought the place, he never expected to live there or to be landlord to the particular tenant whose urgent knock had roused him at noon from a dreamless sleep.

Emma Gray looked like a landlord's worst nightmare with her leather-gloved fist stopped midway in its path to his door. Rouged lips, nose piercings, and smoky, kohl-lined eyes intensified the glare she gave him. Purple streaks in her hair hung long and straight over her ears. Her black, skull-and-crossbones tank top bared trails of lurid floral tattoos running across her collarbone and down her upper arms. A wide, metal-studded black leather belt cinched her waist above an incongruous schoolgirl plaid pleated skirt. Her slim legs, encased in fishnet hose, disappeared into unlaced industrial strength black boots.

She looked seriously aggrieved that he'd opened his door wearing only a pair of black silk boxers.

"Don't you ever wear clothes?"

"Not in bed." Her gaze dropped. He might have made her blush. Hard to tell under that Swedish Death Metal band look. At least she lowered her fist. "What's the problem—Sink? Refrigerator? Shower?"

Her gaze dropped again. It was a mistake to think *shower.* The very word triggered images his brain ought not to entertain about his tenant, his prickly, independent, don't-touch-me-ever, single-mom tenant, whose rent he needed. He might be at low tide, but not that low.

They stood looking at each other in the common second floor entry under the breast of Venus overhead lamp fixture while he waited for whatever she intended to say. He had time to imagine several intriguing possibilities before she finally got the words out.

"I need your help."

He did not move. He did not betray by so much as a flicker of a glance the satisfaction it gave him to hear those four words from the girl who did everything herself. "Do you?"

She glanced back over her shoulder at her unit. That meant she was thinking of her son Max, a towheaded six-year-old. "Yes."

"What can I do for you?"

"My babysitter didn't show and hasn't called, and I'm due at work in fifteen."

He noted what she could and could not say. "You want me to watch Max?"

"He can take care of himself, really. He has toys and snacks. He'll just play while you…whatever. You just have to check on him once in awhile and call me if there's blood, vomiting, unconsciousness, or visible bones."

"Define 'once in awhile'. Like every five minutes, or every half hour?" He should not have her on, but the temptation was too strong.

She blew out a short, sharp breath. "If it gets too quiet, you know, you should check."

"So you want me to keep the music down and keep my door open."

"Can you do it?"

It was instinctive for her to doubt his capabilities. To ask for his help she had to be desperate. He straightened and stopped his teasing. "Listen, let Max know the plan. I'll put on some clothes and take him to the park, or something. How long will you be gone?"

"Six." She turned away. "Thank you."

He left the door open and drifted back into his bedroom to find some shorts and flip flops and contemplate how to take advantage of his minor victory….

AUTHOR'S NOTE

Schools and scandal seem to go together and grab headlines when they do. Headmistresses shoot their lovers or tamper with grades and scores. Students invent yet new high-tech ways to cheat. Teachers and students seduce each other in cloakrooms and closets. Team pranks and parties go awry. I did not have to go far in my research to find dozens of tabloid-worthy school scandals, and I owe a great deal to those reporters who probed for underlying details of human character. Without ignoring the real damage a scandal can do to a school, my focus was on a romance with a happy ending. Any similarity between the characters in this book and real people is entirely accidental. Any similarity between these characters and the characters in Austen's *Persuasion* is by design.

ABOUT THE AUTHOR

Kate Moore's first romances were "True Romance" comics read at a cabin in the woods by Lake Tahoe. She rediscovered her love of Romance while teaching at a boys prep school in L.A. and quickly moved from reading Austen and Heyer to penning her own stories set in Regency England and contemporary California. Her heroes are honorable loners, and her heroines are warm-hearted practical princesses with long to-do lists. Now a multi-published author, three-time RITA finalist, and Golden Crown winner, Kate lives north of San Francisco with her surfing husband and her children's dogs. She loves to hear from readers.

Did you enjoy this book? Drop us a line and say so! We love to hear from readers, and so do our authors. To connect, visit www.boroughspublishinggroup.com online, send comments directly to info@boroughspublishinggroup.com, or friend us on Facebook and Twitter. And be sure to check back regularly for contests and new releases in your favorite subgenres of romance!

Are you an aspiring writer? Check out www.boroughspublishinggroup.com/submit and see if we can help you make your dreams come true.

www.ingramcontent.com/pod-product-compliance
Lightning Source LLC
Chambersburg PA
CBHW060810120626
46557CB00001B/161